Neil Flambé

— and the —
MARCO POLO MURDERS

Also by Kevin Sylvester

Neil Flambé

and the
MARCO POLO MURDERS

KEVIN SYLVESTER

SIMON & SCHUSTER BOOKS FOR YOUNG READERS
New York London Toronto Sydney New Delhi

SIMON & SCHUSTER BOOKS FOR YOUNG READERS
An imprint of Simon & Schuster Children's Publishing Division
1230 Avenue of the Americas, New York, New York 10020
This book is a work of fiction. Any references to historical events, real people,
or real places are used fictitiously. Other names, characters, places, and events are
products of the author's imagination, and any resemblance to actual events
or places or persons, living or dead, is entirely coincidental.
Text and interior illustrations copyright © 2010 by Kevin Sylvester
Cover illustrations copyright © 2014 by Kevin Sylvester
Originally published in Canada in 2010 by Key Porter Books Limited
All rights reserved, including the right of reproduction in whole or in part in any form.
SIMON & SCHUSTER BOOKS FOR YOUNG READERS is a trademark of Simon & Schuster, Inc.
For information about special discounts for bulk purchases, please contact Simon &
Schuster Special Sales at 1-866-506-1949 or business@simonandschuster.com.
The Simon & Schuster Speakers Bureau can bring authors to your live event. For more
information or to book an event, contact the Simon & Schuster Speakers Bureau
at 1-866-248-3049 or visit our website at www.simonspeakers.com.
Also available in a Simon & Schuster Books for Young Readers hardcover edition
Cover design by Laurent Linn
Interior design by Laurent Linn and Tom Daly
The text for this book is set in Goudy Old Style.
The illustrations for this book are rendered in pen and ink.
Manufactured in the United States of America
0914 OFF
First Simon & Schuster Books for Young Readers paperback edition October 2014
2 4 6 8 10 9 7 5 3 1
CIP data for this book is available from the Library of Congress.
ISBN 978-1-4424-4604-5 (hc)
ISBN 978-1-4424-4605-2 (pbk)
ISBN 978-1-4424-4606-9 (eBook)

To Mom and Dad, who taught me how to cook (among a few other valuable things), and who made sure I absorbed as much as possible from Julia Child and the Galloping Gourmet.

And to food banks everywhere for all the great work they do. Please donate today!

PROLOGUE

VENICE, 1324

Marco Polo lay on his deathbed, smiling weakly at the loved ones who had gathered by his side. He tried to open his mouth to speak, but even that simple effort exhausted him. He lay still, wishing he had the energy to tell them that he was ready to go. He had lived a good life, a long life, a wealthy life.

Marco had been the greatest explorer of his time, or any time before that.

When he was barely a teenager, he'd traveled from his birthplace in Venice all the way to China. His uncle and father had asked him to join them on their search for more lucrative trading partners.

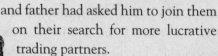

Some had said he was too young to go on such an adventure, but he'd ignored them. He wanted to see what lay outside the canals and countinghouses of Venice.

It had been the greatest decision of his life. The Polos had found gold and jewels, and plenty of them, but Marco had discovered much more than that. He had seen that the world was an enormous and fascinating place.

Marco coughed.

The priest, mistaking it for a death rattle, leaned over him expectantly. Marco smiled back faintly.

He shook his head. "Not yet," he mouthed silently.

The priest stood back up, bumping the bedside table and nearly toppling an ornate globe perched on a pile of well-worn books. The room was filled with such reminders of Marco's explorations.

Strange maps and exotic works of art hung from the walls. Hundreds of books in dozens of languages lay scattered on every available surface. Marco's sheets and robes were woven of the finest Chinese silk, decorated with scenes of his travels through Asia.

Marco coughed again, and the Mongolian princesses stitched into his collar moved and swayed, sadly dancing in time to the rise and fall of his chest.

Embroidered Persian camels marched up and down the length of the bed, reminding Marco of the camels that had carried him and his crew across many desert wastelands. He adjusted his aching body, ruffling the covers and creating sand dunes of linen in the pale fabric. Enormous, dark birds of prey swooped down his long sleeves. Marco thought of the vultures that had hovered over the bloody scenes of his many battles. Death had been part of his adventures as well.

And death was coming for him now.

Marco shared another faint smile with his loving family. His wife, Donata, smiled back. She knew Marco had secured a place for himself in heaven. They had loved each other deeply and had raised three lovely daughters.

Their two eldest daughters, Fantina and Bellela, were now married. It seemed as if the youngest, Moreta, might never marry, but it hardly mattered. No Polo daughter would ever know poverty. Even more important, Marco thought happily, they would know there was a world outside Venice.

Marco put his hand to his heart, which was growing weaker and weaker. His fingers paused over supple golden thread, the woven image of a smiling Kublai Khan. Khan, a Mongolian, had conquered China and ruled half the world. He had been the most powerful man on earth, and Marco had served him faithfully for nearly twenty years.

Marco remembered sitting at the foot of the great man's marble throne, regaling him with stories of his travels throughout the great Mongol Empire.

It was the khan's own impending death, thirty years ago, that had finally sent Marco and his relatives on the long journey back to Venice. Kublai Khan was revered as a god, so no one spoke openly of his illness—but the Polos could tell that he was growing weaker by the day.

Kublai Khan had especially liked Marco and his stories, and that had kept all the Polos in the ruler's favor. But there was no guarantee the next emperor would share the khan's fondness for foreigners.

They needed to get away before he died.

Then the khan announced that he needed trusted emissaries to deliver one of his princesses to Persia for an arranged royal marriage.

The Polos volunteered. Khan, perhaps sensing the situation, reluctantly agreed. They said good-bye and left the khan's palace behind. Not long into their journey, word came that their patron had indeed died in his sleep.

Marco coughed again. This time a trickle of blood formed on his lips.

Peter, his Mongolian servant, gently placed a handkerchief on Marco's mouth and wiped away the blood.

Peter had always been there for Marco. He'd been his personal assistant in Asia and had remained with him ever since. He had even stayed by Marco's side during the long and terrible journey home from Asia.

Marco shuddered, but it wasn't the pain this time. It was the memory of that horrible voyage.

That had been Marco's one great disaster. Along with the princess, he had also allowed a deadly cargo onboard. Hundreds of his crew had died. It had been his fault; it had *all* been his fault. Thankfully, only he and Peter knew the truth about what had really happened, and, in the years since, they had taken great pains to keep that secret safe.

Now Marco tried to share one final look with Peter. Marco had asked him to perform one last task—a task that would keep the past hidden forever.

He stared at Peter, but Peter seemed to be looking at Moreta. Was he avoiding Marco's glance?

4

Marco felt his weak heart leap. Had Peter not done what he'd asked? The horror of the thought gripped him. He lifted his head and looked at Peter again, pleading for reassurance.

This time Peter caught his eye and smiled. He nodded yes.

Marco lay back on his bed, relieved. Peter had done it; he had destroyed the final record of that journey. Marco felt ashamed that he'd ever doubted him.

The world would never know the truth. He could die in peace.

The priest must have sensed the end was near. He again leaned in close and whispered into Marco's ear, "Signor Polo, is there anything you'd like to confess? Any lies you have told?"

Marco laughed, and coughed, and then laughed again.

The people of Venice had loved his stories, but they'd never really believed him when he described all the wonderful and terrible things he'd seen. They scoffed when he told them of giant birds, and rocks that burned, and oil that seeped from the ground.

As he felt his spirit leaving his body, he raised his head and uttered his last words: "I have told only half of what I have seen!"

Marco Polo's lifeless body fell back onto the sheets. The great explorer had left on his final journey.

Venice, one year ago

Antonio Fusilli looked up from his desk.

Someone had just entered his inner sanctum—the

Marco Polo Library at the *Museo di Arte Orientale* in Venice—and Antonio was not impressed. First of all, this was a private library, with visits by appointment only. Then there was the way the person was dressed. His or her face, head, and body were completely hidden behind a large fedora, scarf, and trench coat.

"Do you not know that it is spring?" Fusilli called through the open office door. "Why do you dress so ridiculously?" Antonio himself was impeccably dressed, as always, and this person offended his fashion standards.

The figure turned toward him, but said nothing.

"Please leave," Antonio said. This place was more than an office for him. He was, after all, a descendant of Marco Polo. This was sacred ground.

Again, the figure said nothing. But this time a gloved hand emerged from the coat, holding a thick wad of euros.

Antonio relaxed his standards and rules a little. He got up from behind his desk and walked into the main hallway.

"Why do you offer me such a generous amount of cash?" He smiled.

"I want . . . the book." The voice was soft and scratchy. Antonio couldn't tell if it was coming from a man, a woman, or even a child.

"Book? What book?" Antonio shrugged, looking around. "This is a library. We have hundreds of books."

The figure grabbed Antonio by the neck and leaned in close to his face. The person was wearing a carnival mask! Outrageous!

"*Bruto*," the voice croaked. "Polo's secret notebook, you idiot. The one that he wrote in on his journey home from China."

Antonio felt a cold shiver run down his spine. "Polo decided the story of that journey was of no value," Antonio lied.

The figure hissed through the scarf. "*Silencio!* You know and I know that he kept a notebook *and* that it survived." The hold on Antonio's neck tightened menacingly.

Antonio gasped as his throat constricted, "If you kill me, you will never find it."

"So you admit it exists." The figure let go.

Antonio grabbed his throat, nodding his head in affirmation.

"Yes"—*cough*—"it exists," he said. "You can have one look, for five minutes. But it will cost you twice the euros you have offered."

Without flinching the figure unrolled an even larger packet of bills and placed it in Antonio's hand.

"This is four times as much," said the voice, "for fifteen minutes."

Antonio took a deep breath. "*Si, si,* fifteen minutes. But then you must leave and never come back."

"Agreed."

Antonio adjusted his tie. He gestured for his strange visitor to sit down in a small wooden chair. The chair looked ordinary enough, but it was actually the first step in Antonio's security system. The seat contained a sensor. If someone sitting there stood up, the sudden loss of weight would set off an alarm, summoning the police.

"Wait here and don't move," Antonio said. He made his way down a hall lined with bookcases. A vault door stood at the far end. Antonio looked back. The figure was sitting in the chair, reading a book.

Antonio took out a ring with three golden keys. He inserted the first key into the vault door. With a click of metal on metal, the door slid open.

Antonio looked back again. The figure was still seated, reading another book.

Antonio stepped inside the vault, letting the door almost close behind him. Then he gently lifted the edge of an ornate Persian rug. Underneath was a trapdoor. The second key opened that.

Resting inside the secret compartment was a golden box. It was decorated with emerald-eyed angels and mermaids, delicately wrought sundials, diamond-studded wind roses and carved sailing ships. Any thief who'd managed to get this far would grab the beautiful box, thinking it was the treasure. That, however, would be a mistake. The box was bolted to the floor; tugging it would release a spring-loaded knife.

Antonio chuckled. "Aimed right at *il cuore*—the heart."

The golden figures that adorned the top of the box were actually a clever combination lock. Antonio turned the arms on the wind roses and the sundial to the combination that he alone knew.

With a click the lid opened.

Antonio pulled out the final key and placed it into the lock on a small, plain tin box that lay inside. He turned the key and opened the lid.

Antonio leaned down and carefully lifted out the

real treasure: a tiny leather notebook. For centuries his family had kept it hidden from the outside world.

The great Marco's servant Peter had burned the original, according to Marco's instructions. But Peter had also betrayed his master's wishes and made a copy. Actually, he'd made two: one for himself, in his own Mongol language, and one in Italian, for Moreta, the Polo daughter he dearly loved.

"Ah, *amore*." Antonio sighed, carefully touching the cover. "You can be so cruel."

Moreta had had jewels and wealth. Peter had wanted to give her something no other suitor could offer: a glimpse into a part of her father's past that he alone knew. But when Moreta read the notebook and discovered the terrible secret that lay within, she had rejected Peter's love token and Peter himself.

Heartbroken, Peter had returned to Asia and disappeared, along with his copy of the notebook.

Then it was Moreta's turn to be heartbroken. She realized, too late, that she had rejected the one man she truly loved. And as much as she had hated the story the notebook told, Moreta could not bring herself to destroy it. It was her only link to the man she had lost forever.

Antonio knelt on the floor of the vault, holding the family heirloom. "With my apologies, dearest ancestor Moreta, I will now use this to secure my retirement."

Antonio knew that no one could unlock the notebook's secret in a mere fifteen minutes. He would end the day rich, and the mysterious figure would end the day disappointed.

Antonio stood up and turned around. He stopped cold.

The visitor blocked the vault's doorway, a gun sticking out from underneath the large trench coat. "*Santa Maria!*" Antonio gasped, staring past the barrel of the gun and back down the hallway to the empty chair. Except it wasn't empty. There was a neat pile of books where the visitor was supposed to be sitting.

"How . . . ?" Antonio gawked.

"Simple," the figure rasped. "I added one book after another as I slowly lifted myself off the chair. I happen to be an expert in weights and measures."

Antonio had to think quickly. He glanced around the room, trying not to let his panic show. There was one last alarm he could trigger: a button near the trapdoor.

"And what will you do now with the notebook?" he asked, inching toward the opening.

"You'll have to find that out in the afterlife. *Ciao*," said the figure as it pulled the trigger.

Antonio made a final lunge toward the alarm. The bullet narrowly missed the precious book, but it did not miss Antonio's heart. He fell, dead, his finger just grazing the button.

Alarms rang out and the vault door began to close. The figure leaped over to Antonio's body, grabbed the notebook and the money, and narrowly made it back through the door before it slammed shut.

By the time the police arrived, the strange visitor was long gone.

CHAPTER ONE

SALMON OR SALMONELLA?

Neil Flambé stood in his kitchen and took a deep breath.

Was perfection too much to expect? he wondered. He spoke slowly into his phone.

"Gunter, the salmon you sent me is just this side of rotten. I have twenty people expecting a fantastic fish dinner tonight. What they are not expecting is a side dish of FOOD POISONING!" The man on the other end of the call held the receiver away from his ear. He was Gunter Lund, a famous chef in his native Germany before burning out five years ago in a pitched battle with a stubborn batch of *bierwurst* sausages.

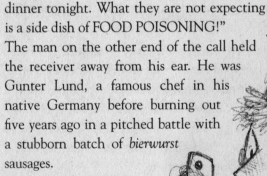

He'd moved to Vancouver to escape the stress and had started his own seafood distribution business. But clients like Flambé made him wonder if it wasn't time to go back to cooking. He felt a shot of pain in his stomach. His doctor had warned him about stress and ulcers.

It's not any fourteen-year-old who can talk to me in that tone of voice, he thought.

That was certainly true, but Neil Flambé was not just any fourteen-year-old. He had his own restaurant, his own line of cooking pans, and his picture was on the front cover of the latest issue of *CHEF! Magazine*, under the headline "Is There Anything This Boy Can't Cook?"

Neil Flambé was a star.

Another of Flambé's talents? He could make an ordinary cell phone sound like a megaphone.

"HELLO? GUNTER? Are you still there? I need a different fish!"

Gunter wanted desperately to hang up. Instead he tried another approach. "Neil, please calm down. The man on the boat assured me that he caught the fish this morning."

"Floating on top of an oil slick?" Neil yelled. "Listen, I have the top food critics from all the major newspapers coming for dinner, as well as the Spanish ambassador. If I serve that toxic fish to my guests, it will KILL THEM!"

"You're exaggerating, Neil," Lund said, struggling to stay calm. "It was fine when it left here. And it's only a few minutes to your restaurant."

Neil took a loud breath, prepping for another assault on Gunter's ears.

"But if you insist," Gunter continued quickly, deciding it was probably best just to give in, "I'll send over another fish right away."

There was a short silence.

"You'll send two," Neil said firmly.

Gunter paused. His stomach had started to churn, and he knew he'd need to pop another antacid or five when he finally got off the phone. Flambé was one of his best—or at least one of his best-paying—customers. He'd fork over plenty for a good salmon. The only problem was that he was a royal pain in the *zielscheibe:* the rear end.

Gunter rubbed his finger over his throbbing temple. "Yes, fine, two," he said. The line clicked and Flambé was gone.

"He doesn't even say *danke schön*," Gunter muttered angrily. He turned in his chair and yelled out the window to his partner Renée, who was sitting on the dock fixing her nets.

"I need two fresh salmon right away!" Gunter shouted. "Still flipping, if you can find any like that."

He burped. "And bring me some antacids, too."

CHAPTER TWO

PREP TIME

Neil clicked his phone shut and turned back to his chopping block. The fish lay there, its glassy eyes turning slightly opaque. Neil's extrasensitive nose told him this fish was not as fresh as it seemed.

Too bad. It had cost him an incredible $260. But there was no chance this smelly carcass was going to find its way onto his menu.

"Garbage!" Neil yelled at no one in particular.

"Chillax, cuzzin." The voice came from the rear doorway of the kitchen. "Man, you are wound tighter than my mom's hairdo!"

Neil turned and glared at his cousin. Larry was a few years older than Neil, hadn't shaved in a couple of days, and looked like he hadn't had a haircut in a couple of decades. His light brown hair fought to escape from underneath his chef's cap, and was winning the battle. He chuckled as he carried a crate of fresh asparagus into the kitchen.

"That fish has gotta be fresh, man. The delivery guy only dropped it off, like, ten minutes ago."

Neil closed his eyes and started to count to ten. He was trying to be patient, he really was. "Come here, Larry, and really smell this fish," he said. "See if you can stop yourself from throwing up."

"Oh, man," Larry groaned. "Here we go again with this whole 'extrapowerful sense of smell' stuff. What are you, a warlock? Harry Pots and Pans?" Larry laughed at his own joke.

As usual, Neil didn't.

Neil pointed at the fish. "Smell it."

Larry shrugged and walked over to the chopping block. He stuck his nose as close to the salmon as he could and took a big theatrical sniff.

"So?" Neil asked. "How does it smell?"

"Awful," Larry said.

Neil broke into a triumphant smile.

Larry winked. "But then again, I hate salmon." He laughed. "And hey, that smells like a fresh salmon to me."

Neil's smile was quickly replaced by a frown. "A truly fresh fish should hardly smell at all," he said.

"So what does bad fish smell like?"

"Bad fish smells like, well, *fish*."

"You mean like when you see a dead fish washed up on a beach, or like sometimes when you walk past the fish counter in a supermarket and you get a whiff and go whoa!?" Larry asked, walking his asparagus over to the large metal sink that stood against the kitchen's back wall.

"Exactly."

"Yuck. And you can smell *that* on this fish?"

Neil took another whiff. The faint scent of a fish going bad was stronger now.

"Yes," he said.

Sure, most chefs would miss it. Larry certainly had. The fish hadn't gone off enough to really kill anybody. But Neil Flambé held himself to a different standard, a much, *much* higher standard. And when it came to upholding that standard, his supersensitive olfactory nerve was his secret weapon.

"Why did I ever let you into my kitchen?" he muttered under his breath.

"Are you talking to the fish?" Larry asked as he carefully cleaned the asparagus in the sink. "Because that would be a little weird, even for you."

"Actually," Neil said, "I was talking to you."

"Ah." Larry nodded. "Well, in that case, we could start with the thrilling tale of how we got the restaurant. . . ."

Neil looked around at the peeling paint and the ancient fridge. It had not been Neil's first choice. In fact, it gave him a headache, and heartburn, just thinking about how Larry had picked the place.

"I'd rather not," Neil said.

"Okey dokey," Larry continued. "Then, on a more practical level, you 'let' me into your kitchen because there's no way my parents and yours would keep pouring money into Chez Flambé if I wasn't here."

Neil frowned. "True. Sad, but true."

"And," Larry added smugly, "I don't think the public

health department would be all, like, 'Hey, what a great idea! Let's let a fourteen-year-old kid run his own restaurant.' Face it, you need someone with experience."

"Experience?"

"Yes, experience. I worked at the world-famous Empress Hotel," Larry said proudly.

"You were a *dishwasher*."

"*And* I watched some of the best chefs in the business do their stuff."

"Ha!"

"And never underestimate the importance of clean dishes, chef boy," Larry added with a wink. "Keeping those nasty germs off the plates keeps them out of your clients' stomachs. And that keeps the boy genius out of court."

Neil rolled his eyes. He and Larry were like cream and lemon juice: mix them together, and you got spoiled milk. For now, he'd had enough.

"I have to cook," he said, turning his attention back to the fish. "Garbage," he repeated, staring down at the salmon. "It's not good enough to serve in my restaurant."

He grabbed the salmon by the tail and walked over to the back window. He managed to open it with his free hand and a crowd of well-fed cats in the alley jumped at the sound of the sliding wood. They quickly huddled together, licking their lips. Neil was a picky chef, and an open window outside Chez Flambé usually meant good eating.

"Here you go," Neil yelled as he tossed the fish into the alley. The cats lunged and fought to grab any bit of the gourmet fare.

Neil watched them for a moment. He'd tossed a

slightly overdone rib roast out the window the day before. He could still see the little bit of bone and string that remained. That dish he'd actually cooked. At least he hadn't wasted too much time on the salmon.

"See," Larry said, peering over Neil's shoulder. "It's good enough for cats, and they've got a great sense of smell."

"Not as good as mine." Neil clenched his teeth and slammed the window shut. "Now back to work—we've got customers coming."

"What can I do today, *mon capitaine?*" Larry saluted with a smile.

"Wash some dishes for a start," Neil suggested. "Then do what a good sous-chef does, and cut some vegetables, and onions. And grab the new fish when it arrives and bring it straight to me."

"Your command is my wish," Larry said, saluting again. He turned on his heel and headed back to the sink, whistling to himself.

Neil looked at the clock. Time to prep.

He'd make the mint sauce for the salmon later. First he needed to prepare the seasoning for his special dish.

CHAPTER THREE

POTATOES FLAMBÉ

Neil Flambé was in his element. Now that he was actually cooking, he could forget about the rotten fish. He ran his fingers along the handles of his favorite knives. They hung suspended on a magnetic rack above his stainless-steel countertops.

There were Japanese sushi knives that resembled miniature samurai swords. He had a large butcher's knife that looked like it could cut a whole cow in half. And he had a series of shiny steel knives of various sizes. They were all razor sharp and lovingly polished. They made the pale fluorescent lights of the kitchen gleam like sunlight.

Which one for this meal? Neil wondered. But he already knew the answer. There was only one knife that could calm his nerves after the skirmishes with Gunter, Larry, and the fish: the knife he'd had specially made when he was just ten years old. It had been forged in a centuries-old blacksmith shop in southern France and had been weighted perfectly for his hand and his alone.

Neil had undergone a growth spurt recently that had left him feeling gangly and awkward. But even still, this knife felt like an extension of his own body.

Neil pulled it down from the rack. Suddenly, he was like an orchestra conductor with his best baton.

He set a large maple chopping block on the stainless-steel counter. Larry was working away at the big sink at the back, but Neil had a smaller sink next to him. He placed a bowl of potatoes in the sink and covered them with water.

Neil's grumpiness disappeared as he started prepping the garlic. He didn't like chefs who sliced it all thin and uniform, especially not for this dish. He preferred irregular sizes. Some bits would give the diner a subtle hint of the herb, while others would suddenly explode on the tongue with a burst of garlic flavor.

He threw the garlic into a stainless-steel bowl.

"Some salt from Italy.

"Pepper from Indonesia."

Neil added herbs, picked just five minutes ago from the rooftop garden above his kitchen. He took some organic olive oil and splashed it with a slight touch of locally grown cranberry vinegar. The vinegar was his own brand, perfected in his basement with the chemistry set his parents had bought him in a vain attempt to encourage a less expensive career.

He swished the ingredients around in the bowl: the olive green of the oil blending perfectly with the fresh mint and rosemary and the slight red of the vinegar.

Neil rested the bowl on the counter and waited for the liquid to still.

"Ready for the potatoes." He always said that out loud, like a holy incantation.

Neil Flambé and the Marco Polo Murders

Over at the sink, Larry chuckled. "They're just potatoes, man. It's like rice—how different can you make them?"

Neil almost cracked a smile. Almost. "Yes, for most chefs—and two-bit dishwashers—potatoes are just a side dish. But not for me, not anymore."

For most of his life Neil had been unhappy with potatoes, both the ones he'd been making and the ones he'd been eating. He knew there must be a better way to make the humble tuber tremendous, and he figured it had to start with a better potato.

For months Neil had scoured the countryside, looking for his holy grail of spuds. He'd tried dozens of different types, from dozens of different farms, but he was never satisfied.

He'd almost given up the search when, one day, he took a wrong turn on his bike, on a residential street, right in the middle of the city. It was an ordinary street, like hundreds of others, with nothing to set it apart. Nothing, that is, until he smelled them.

He stopped his bike right then and there and stood, like one of those hungry cats in his alley, outside the window of a run-down old house. The wood-framed window was cracked. The paint was flaking off. A ramshackle fence ran under the window and down the side of the property. It was a dump—there was no other word to describe it.

But coming from inside this dump was the smell of someone cooking the most wonderful potatoes.

"Hm, too much pepper," Neil said, sniffing the air. "And is that *lemon juice?*" He sniffed again. Yes, definitely lemon juice.

21

Neil was not impressed. Lemon juice would completely overwhelm the starchy, subtle goodness of the potatoes. But it wasn't the dish that had caught his attention. It was the smell of the potatoes themselves. And someone was about to ruin them, with lemon juice! Neil jumped up on the fence and knocked on the window.

An old man was hovering over a pot of boiling potatoes, about to drop in a cup full of lemon juice.

"Hey, you in there!" Neil yelled, still banging on the glass. "Don't do it! Don't kill those potatoes!" The man was so shocked that he dropped the cup onto the floor.

"Thank goodness." Neil sighed. But the man wasn't fazed for long. He grabbed a broom and ran to window. It took only one push to knock Neil back onto his butt.

"What are you, some kind of a thug?" the man cried, shaking the broom menacingly. "You could have given me a heart attack. Now go away!"

"No, wait!" Neil yelled. "I'm a chef, a great chef."

"You've got to be kidding me," the man said. "You're just a kid."

Neil clenched his fist. *Just a kid.* He had been hearing those words his entire life, and he was sick of them. But he gritted his teeth and took a deep breath. He needed to get those potatoes.

"Look, sir, if I promise to make you the greatest potato dish ever, will you tell me where you got those spuds? That's all I want to know."

"Got them?" the man said. "I didn't *get* them anywhere.

I grow them myself." He pointed the broomstick in the direction of his own backyard. Neil looked over. The entire yard was full of potato plants, hundreds of them.

"So, Mr. Mini-Chef," the man said. "You gonna make me some dinner? Or do I have to wallop you again?"

Neil and Lu Ming struck a deal over that dinner. Neil smiled as he remembered the roasted garlic potatoes he'd prepared in Ming's dingy kitchen. Ming had even promised never to mix lemon juice with his potatoes again.

Neil had used a lot of subterfuge over the years to keep his secret spud supplier a secret. But it was worth it every time he saw the ecstatic grin on the face of a satisfied paying customer. After eating Pommes de terre Flambé, diners would sometimes forget the rest of their meal.

Neil pulled a handful of Ming's reddish brown spuds from the sink. They'd been sitting in the water just long enough to soften the skins. He took his paring knife and delicately scraped off the blemishes. No other bit of these perfect potatoes should be lost.

He'd barely started scraping when a blast of music yanked him out of his ritual. It was the theme from the old *Batman* TV show and it was coming from the chopping block he'd used for the rotten fish.

Neil stopped cold. It was his cell phone.

And it wasn't that oaf Gunter calling back, either. Batman was Neil's special ring tone. He'd never seen the show, but Larry had told him it was hilarious and had downloaded the song for Neil on the spot. "It's your own personal Bat signal," Larry said. And like the Bat signal, it rang only when something was wrong.

Neil sighed. The salmon would be here any minute,

and so would the guests. He had no time for this conversation right now.

He started back to work, but the phone kept ringing. With a sigh, Neil put down the potatoes and walked over to his phone. He scooped it up and flipped it open.

"Hello," he said without much enthusiasm.

"Flambé? That you?"

"Of course it's me. Who else would it be?" he snapped. It was, as he expected, police inspector Sean Nakamura.

"I don't know. Maybe I was hoping you'd lent your phone to a real chef," Nakamura said sarcastically. "Anyway, there's been another murder. We need your help."

Suddenly there was a knock at the back door. "The new fish is here," Larry yelled.

The potatoes stared back at him from the pot.

He could hear the front door of the restaurant opening. The Soba twins, Amber and Zoë, had arrived to prep the restaurant for dinner. The guests would be here soon, eager to claim the reservations they'd had to make weeks in advance.

"Flambé? You still there?" Nakamura yelled. "Flambé?!"

Neil calculated all the possibilities: the salmon, the potatoes, the guests . . .

"Give me twenty minutes," he said.

CHAPTER FOUR

POACHED
PERCH

The kitchen that Inspector Nakamura led him into was very familiar to Neil. He looked at the glazed tiles that covered the walls over the stain-less-steel ovens and counters. Each contained a picture of a different exotic, but edible, fish: mackerel, tuna, arctic char, mahi-mahi, tilapia.

Neil had been here dozens of times, visiting the man who'd made his magical seafood the talk of the town.

Lionel Perch was one of the best, with the emphasis on *was*. His grilled whitefish with sage and onion was the finest in the city, perhaps the country, perhaps even the world. Lesser chefs had been so discouraged after just one taste that they had quit cooking forever.

Lionel had once shown a five-year-old Neil the best way to know when a pan-fried fish was absolutely perfect.

"Flaky," he'd said, "so that you can just separate the layers with a fork. Then take it off the stove and let the internal heat finish the cooking for you."

And he'd explained how to time the sauce and the fish to be ready at exactly the same moment. It was a lesson in math, physics, and art that blew away anything Neil had learned at school in all the years since. Of course, Lionel had refused to show Neil everything. "After all," he'd said, asking Neil to turn away while he'd mixed his secret blend of spices, "if we all cooked exactly the same, we might as well be robots or work for McDonald's."

Neil had never told Lionel that he could smell the ingredients nonetheless. Lionel had mixed together maybe a tablespoon of fresh chopped sage, about one-and-a-half large cloves of garlic, a quick grind of pepper and one . . . no, two pinches of Italian sea salt. Neil could also tell that the whitefish was mackerel, almost certainly imported fresh from Asia on an overnight flight.

But now Lionel was lying dead on the floor. His face was contorted in a bizarre smirk, almost like a smile, and his face was turning blue.

"Looks just like the other dead chef we found last week," Nakamura said.

"Emily Almond," Neil said, crouching on the floor next to the body.

"Yeah, right, Almond. And, as you can see," Nakamura said, leaning in very close to Perch's face, "he has the same brown residue on his lips." He pointed with the tip of his pen and actually tapped the dead man's lips. An infinitesimal puff of brown dust rose up in the air.

Sniff. Neil took a deep breath through his nose. He could make out the slightest touch of something exotic . . . yes, a very good chai and some mysterious spicy overtone.

"It's the same spiced tea we found last week," he said.

"Masala chai?" Nakamura asked, referring to his notes.

"Yes. Black tea, water, and milk, with cardamom, nutmeg, a little cinnamon, and the slightest bit of cloves," Neil said, standing up. "And there's some kind of cumin. Which is odd because you don't often see cumin in a chai, especially if the cumin is really rich. And this cumin is richer than any I've ever smelled before. The tea is really aromatic as well. I can't place it either, and I've smelled more chai and cumin than anybody."

Nakamura rolled his eyes. The kid always had to show off. What the heck was he going to be like when he was twenty? Nakamura gave a little shudder. "And the other smell?" he asked.

Neil took another long sniff. "Yup, it's there again." This other smell was a complete mystery to Neil. "It's vaguely familiar, but I just can't pin it down." Neil didn't like that. He was used to knowing exactly what a smell was and how you could use it to make mackerel magnificent or anchovies amazing.

"The boys at the lab said they couldn't find anything on Almond except the chai spices and the cumin you mentioned," Nakamura said, looking closely at Neil's furrowed brow. "There's no poison they can detect. Are you certain there's something else there?"

But it wasn't doubt that was furrowing Neil's brow; it was frustration. Frustration he now aimed right at Nakamura.

"Am I certain?" Neil glared at Nakamura as he spoke. "No, I'm a complete idiot. Of course I'm certain! I can tell you the exact, and I mean the *exact*, combination, weight and even age of the spices in a Cajun jambalaya, from FIVE ROOMS AWAY! So yes, I think I'm *certain* that there's something else here." He took a deep breath before adding in a calmer voice, "I just don't know what it is."

Nakamura took a handkerchief out of his breast pocket and made a show of wiping saliva off his forehead. "Well, that last bit almost sounded humble," he said. He knew better than to wait for an apology.

"I'm going back to my restaurant," Neil said, walking toward the door. "The customers will be finishing their salmon right about now and"—he turned to Nakamura— "I want to be there for the applause."

Then Neil walked out, jumped on his bike, and started to pedal off.

"Come by the office tomorrow morning before school," Nakamura yelled after him. "I want to go over the evidence again, and maybe we'll visit the spice shops one more time."

Neil didn't even glance back, but Nakamura knew he'd be there. Neil Flambé hated to be stumped by anything—not incredibly elaborate recipes and certainly not this mystery smell.

He watched Neil disappear down the street, then returned to reexamine Lionel's body. With Neil—and his ego—gone, Nakamura could relax a bit and do a more precise examination. He started at the head. The bluish face, the strange smile . . . It was all the same as the Almond murder. He moved down the body. When he got to the hands, he stopped. He saw something he hadn't before.

Clutched in the dead chef's rigid hand was a scrap of lined paper. Nakamura carefully pried opened the hand and eased out the paper.

Nakamura sighed. It was in Italian, just like the note they'd found on Emily Almond. The contents of that note had been short and cryptic.

"The court at Daidu is always full of sumptuous meals," read the translation. *"The spices are wonderful. We have procured many for our eventual return home."*

Nakamura had assumed it was from one of Almond's recipe books: a diary, or something she'd else been reading when she died. It was written on a plain piece of lined paper. Nakamura had made note of it, though at the time he hadn't considered it much of a clue.

But now he'd found a similar note on another dead chef. That wasn't a coincidence.

"Hey, Stromboli," Nakamura called. "Come here and read this."

Sergeant Stromboli made his way across the kitchen and looked at the writing carefully. "It's in the same dialect as the other note," he said. "I'm pretty sure it says, *'We have the princess and our precious cargo. It is time to leave this wonderful land. It is time to go home. We shall deliver the princess to her court, and return to Venice. The great Emperor has blessed us with a tremendous gift—barrels of the most powerful gunpowder from his private store. This will garner a great price upon our return.'"*

"Venice?" Stromboli and Nakamura said together. "Emperor?"

"Princess?"

"Gunpowder?"

They stared down at Lionel, confused, but he was unable to help.

CHAPTER FIVE

CAPERS

Neil Flambé hadn't come by his cooking skills in any normal kind of way. And he certainly hadn't learned the craft from his parents. His father was renowned for his boxed macaroni and cheese. His mother was slightly less renowned for her spaghetti and ketchup.

Neil's parents were both very busy and important people. Eric Flambé was an ad executive, and Margaret was a lawyer. They'd never had the time nor the inclination to learn how to cook before Neil came along—and they had even less after.

The Flambés both felt incredible joy when their baby boy, sporting an endearing shock of red hair, came home from the hospital. But things had not gone well from the start.

Neil cried all the time.

Was he hungry? Then why wouldn't he eat? Maybe it was his mother's diet of cafeteria noodle dishes, fries, and coffee that was causing the tummy troubles, but Neil never did settle when he was breastfeeding.

They'd tried formula, but that just made things worse.

"He sure does spit up a lot," his dad would say as baby Neil leaned over the side of his high chair and added to the expanding white puddle on the kitchen floor.

"It's almost as if he doesn't like the taste," said his mother. "But that's impossible. He's just a baby!"

Whether it was because of his mother's diet or his own digestion, Neil also had trouble sleeping. He would lie down for maybe half an hour, whimpering in his sleep, and then he'd be up again. The Flambés just weren't ready for weeks and weeks, then months and months of a crying, milk-hating baby. To add to the despair, Neil *was* eating up hours they could have been using to bill clients.

They tried everything. Soothing music made him cry louder. Loud music made him scream. Dad was suddenly spending way more time at the office. Mom tried to go back to work, but nanny after nanny quit after just a few hours of watching the howling child.

One day Margaret Flambé had had enough. She had been in a court proceeding several months earlier where the complainants—all corporate executives—had been threatening to kill one another. At the time she'd thought that no one could whine and bawl like they could. But Neil was worse. "I need to go out," she yelled to herself, "even if it's just for one *second* of silence." She plopped her crying child onto his blanket on the living room floor, turned, and ran out the door.

It was a dangerous thing to do, but Neil didn't know that. All his baby mind knew was that he was sad and now he was also alone. He looked toward the door, still crying. His mother had definitely gone that way. He'd have to follow.

He started to walk. This being his first time trying, he wasn't very good. He stumbled and smashed his face, right on top of the TV remote. That hurt, and he cried even more.

Then he noticed something. The television was on.

Fortune smiled on the Flambés that day. For some unknown reason, the TV was tuned to PBS, not really a favorite of the Flambés Senior. It was showing an old Julia Child special on how to make a perfect *sauce beurre blanc*, or white butter sauce.

Neil turned his head.

He stopped crying.

When his mother came rushing back into the apartment a few moments later (having realized in a panic how foolish she had been), she stopped cold in her tracks.

There, sitting in front of the TV, was her baby. Neil Flambé was gazing up silently as Chef Child added the last cube of cold butter to the ever-thickening liquid. His hands echoed hers as he stirred his own imaginary sauce.

After that fateful day, Neil didn't cry anymore. He didn't whimper. He didn't whine. His parents bought every Julia Child DVD they could. They subscribed to the Food Network. Neil just stared at chef after chef on TV. He'd often mimic their actions, twirling his rattle like a whisk as the chefs made feathery meringues or fluffy omelets.

Life at the Flambés was suddenly good again.

Eric could take phone calls at home, so he wasn't at the office all day.

Margaret went back to work, because their latest nanny didn't quit.

Of course, there were new challenges.

They couldn't watch anything else on TV. Once, Margaret and Eric tried changing the channel. Neil screamed until they turned it back. He even got uneasy and started to whimper if the commercial was for anything other than cookware or food.

Eventually he would yawn and hit the power button on the remote. Then his parents knew it was bedtime. That caused some trouble at first. Although Neil now slept through the night, puckering his lips and smelling in his dreams, getting him to fall asleep was problematic. His parents tried reading him Dr. Seuss and Robert Munsch, but Neil just cried and whined until they stopped.

Then Papa Flambé had an idea. One day, on his way home from work, he stopped by a cookbook store and bought a couple hundred dollars' worth of magazines and recipe books. Now baby Neil fell asleep smiling as his mother and father slowly read the ingredients and instructions for exotic dishes such as cassoulet de mouton or eggs Florentine.

Getting Neil to talk had been a challenge as well. He'd never been a talkative baby (of course, who could tell through all the tears), but he'd even stopped saying "gorgle" and "glop-flopp." He just stared and stared at cooking show after cooking show, without saying a word.

His parents worried that this might be bad for him. His mother had once defended a case where a teenager had blamed a spree of carjackings on watching too much TV. Margaret was a good lawyer and had gotten her client off, but she hadn't liked him very much. Was Neil on his way to becoming a criminal?

But perhaps the biggest challenge was meal time.

The Flambés started their son on strained peas. The spray pattern on the wall showed what he thought of that. Then they tried broth. The official baby brands all ended up on the floor, or in Eric's face.

But then one Saturday Mr. Flambé passed an organic farmer's market. His skin usually crawled at the sight of all the hippie-dippies, with their lattes and their hemp headscarves and their facial hair, but on a whim he decided to stop. He bought an organic vegetable broth, homemade by some whacked-out farmer from one of the Gulf Islands. "The guy couldn't even figure out the right change to give back." Neil's dad had laughed when he came home with the glass jug of golden liquid.

They heated up the broth carefully, and placed it in their finest china bowl. They both leaned in closer as Margaret slowly inched the spoon toward Neil's mouth.

He took a big sniff. He opened wide. Margaret placed the spoon inside Neil's mouth and then she and her husband braced for the inevitable fountain of spew.

It didn't come. They both looked at Neil. He was swishing the broth around his mouth, a thoughtful look on his face. He swallowed . . . and looked at them . . . and that's when Neil Flambé said his first word. . . .

"Capers."

"What did he say?" his mother asked.

"Capers," Neil said again.

"Capers?" his father asked. "What the heck are capers?"

Neil started to get mad. "Capers, capers, capers," he said again and again, banging his fist on the tray of his high chair.

"Hurry, Eric," his mother said. "Go look it up!"

The Flambé family dictionary revealed that capers were the pickled flower buds of the caper plant.

"Gross," said Eric. "They look like little green rabbit poops. He wants these with his broth?"

"A baby can't eat capers," his mother said, horrified.

"CAPERS!" Neil cried louder.

"Okay, okay," said Mr. Flambé. "I'll get some capers."

A quick run to the grocery store later, and Neil Flambé was sitting contentedly in his high chair with his capers and broth.

The next time he spoke was a month later, when he dictated to his parents the exact recipe for a ham-and-cheese frittata.

CHAPTER SIX

GREEN WITH ENVY

Sean Nakamura stared at the array of pictures on his desk. It was a grisly sight: two of the city's greatest chefs, lying dead on the floors of their kitchens. First Emily Almond and now Lionel Perch.

Both had been poisoned, but no one could say how. The strongest lead was a mysterious smell that only a fourteen-year-old wunderchef wunderbrat could detect.

After Almond's murder, Nakamura had driven Flambé to every spice shop in the city, like a bloodhound trying to pick up a scent. No luck. So far, every lead had fizzled. Flambé seemed convinced that a spice, or a mix of spices, was creating the scent, and not an oil or liquid. "It smells too dusty," he'd explained. "A bit like the cumin, but as if something else is there too."

The pair had spent so much time combing the spice shops for clues that the other inspectors in the department were starting to call Nakamura the head of the Spice Squad.

Nakamura smiled to himself—it was kind of funny—but then he remembered how far they were from actually cracking this case, and he frowned.

"The smell is very faint," Flambé had continued, "and I can smell it on the victims. It's not on the counter, or anywhere else in or near the kitchen. It's almost as if it's coming from inside the chef."

"That's impossible," Nakamura had said.

"That's what they said about my first chocolate torte," Neil had replied. Nakamura had just rolled his eyes . . . again.

Nakamura continued to stare at the photos on his desk, his mind wandering back to the first time he'd experienced "The Nose"—the code name his department used for Neil Flambé. It had been during the Jade Green murder: a case that had looked like a real slam dunk.

Jade Green had been one of Vancouver's many up-and-coming chefs. On the day of the murder, however, Jade had been cooking at home. Someone had stabbed her right in her own kitchen with one of her own knives. When her sister Olive had arrived for dinner, she'd found the body and called the police. Nakamura was put in charge of the investigation.

The crime scene wasn't anything too complicated. Jade's body was lying next to the stove, which made sense since she'd obviously been preparing dinner when she was killed. The killer had even left the sauce on the heat. Nakamura took a look at the bubbly liquid.

It was a puttanesca sauce—one of the smelliest pasta sauces in the world—packed full of olives, fish, anchovies, basil, and oregano. Some of the sauce had spilled out of the pan and onto the stovetop. Nakamura wondered if there had been a struggle or if Jade was a messy cook. He made a note of that, then took a picture and turned off the heat.

Next, he examined Jade's body. It was still slightly warm, as if she hadn't been dead long. But the heat from the stove could also explain that, which made it next to impossible to determine the exact time of death.

The knife lay on the ground next to the body. Nakamura picked it up and placed it in a plastic evidence bag.

Then he spoke to the sister. Olive Green had tears streaming down her face as she told Nakamura that she suspected Jade's husband, a mechanic named Otto. According to Olive, Otto was terribly violent and had threatened to kill Jade before. She also said that he came home for lunch every day and demanded fresh food.

The police brought Otto in for questioning.

At the station, Otto admitted to Nakamura that he had come home for lunch, but he claimed that Jade was alive when he left. He swore that he would never hurt his wife. After more questioning, he just shook his head back and forth, muttering, "No, no, no." He refused to say anything else.

Nakamura looked at his suspect closely. Otto had a vacant stare and a sweaty forehead. He kept closing his fingers into fists. Nakamura figured he was probably in shock. Nakamura had noticed something else as well.

Otto had fresh sauce stains all over his shirt.

Nakamura arrested him on the spot.

It seemed like an open-and-shut case, so they had rushed to get the trial over with. Neil's mother had been hired to represent Otto, who just sat in his chair, staring blankly as the police department's forensic experts laid out the case against him.

Then, on the final day of witness testimony, Margaret had brought Neil to court. The babysitter had gotten sick, or some such thing. Anyway, the kid couldn't have been more than nine.

Olive Green took the stand.

Neil had been really fidgety, sitting behind his mom on the lawyer's bench, until the lawyers started asking Olive about the evidence—especially the part with the puttanesca sauce. Just as Olive Green described walking into the room to see her sister dead on the floor, the kid stood up and pointed right at her. "That lady is telling a lie," he said. The whole courtroom went silent.

The judge looked at the kid and smiled one of those "please stick a sucker in your mouth and shut up" smiles. "I'm sorry, sonny," he said, "but this is a court of law. You must behave yourself or you'll have to leave."

The kid just crossed his arms and said, "Excuse me, grandpa, but there are more holes in her story than in a block of havarti cheese."

Nakamura could have sworn he heard the judge's jaw hit the top of his table. The man clutched his gavel menacingly, but then seemed to decide that the best way to shut the kid up might be to humor him instead of clubbing him.

"Fine," he said, leaning back in his chair. "Please tell everyone here what those holes might be, young lad."

Neil pointed at the evidence table set up in front of the witness stand. "Well, first of all, there's that picture of the sauce and the stove."

Nakamura and everyone else turned to look at the picture of the murder scene.

Neil continued. "Olive says her sister was killed at lunchtime, and that she was making the sauce when she was killed. But that's a gas stove on medium heat. There's no way there would have been any sauce left if it had been burning that long at that temperature. So Jade must have still been preparing it *after* her husband went back to work. Anyway, a puttanesca takes only about an hour to make, so the timing is way off."

Now the judge was listening. "Go on," he said, leaning forward.

"Then there are the clothes that Otto guy was wearing when the police picked him up."

The clothes lay on the table next to the picture. Neil took a big sniff.

"They don't have any trace of oregano or basil on them. They would have if Otto had handled the murder weapon. And the murder weapon was clearly the knife his wife was using to cut those herbs. I can still smell the residue from the basil and oregano on the blade, at least the part that's not bloody."

The judge looked down at the knife. It was on a table with an "Exhibit A" tag tied to the handle. The clothes were labeled "Exhibit c5."

"Do you mean to tell me you can smell those herbs on that knife from way over there?"

Neil shrugged. "It's a gift," he said. "I have others."

Nakamura had watched as the kid's mother just stared at him, a smile starting to form on her lips. She was about to get her client off with some seriously reasonable doubt.

But the kid wasn't done yet.

"Actually, the *sister* still has traces of the spices and the puttanesca sauce in her hair."

"She did find the body," the judge said, "so we know she was in the kitchen."

"Oh, please," Neil replied, looking slightly annoyed. "I'm not an idiot. She has more than just the trace amount *that* would leave. She used a natural lavender emulsion to shower, but I can still make out the olives and onions, and especially the anchovies. It takes more than a couple of weeks to get the smell of those out. Especially when you add too many."

Nakamura, the judge, and everyone else turned to look straight at Olive. Her face was twisted with rage.

"Olive," Otto cried from the defendant's table. "Why?"

Olive Green stood up in the witness box. "Why? Because I always loved you," she screamed at Otto. "But you married her! My own sister! AND SHE WAS MAKING MY PUTTANESCA SAUCE!"

Then Olive turned her glare on Neil. "If I ever get out of jail, I'll make a puttanesca sauce out of you, you little rat."

Neil just yawned. "I'd obviously be much better as an alfredo sauce, you hack."

After the bailiff cuffed Olive and let the grieving husband go, Nakamura waited for Neil and his mother outside the courtroom.

"Hey, kid," he'd said. "Nice work. But what about the stains on Otto's shirt? How do you explain those?"

"Pepper sauce, you ignoramus," Neil replied. "I think if you do a little *more* police work, instead of just

a little, you'll find that he had a chicken roti for lunch that day."

Neil's mother gave him a huge hug. "Can I buy you some ice cream to celebrate?" she asked.

"I'd prefer some duck confit from Pierre's," he said, and then they walked outside.

Nakamura chuckled as he remembered that day. The Nose was something else. He wasn't sure what, exactly, but definitely something else.

Since the Green trial, Neil's parents had let him work on other cases—as long as he was handsomely paid and kept out of the public eye.

Curious about their new boy wonder, the police had run tests on the kid to find out how he ticked. It turned out Neil Flambé was born with an incredibly sensitive olfactory nerve, or nose. Over the years, he'd helped Nakamura crack at least five counterfeit spice rings, and arrest and convict a gang of street vendors who were passing off minced cat as 100 percent all-beef sausage. But, despite their past successes, in this current case they were still stumped. Neither Sean Nakamura nor Neil Flambé was any closer to figuring out the mystery of the murdered chefs.

Nakamura looked at the clues he'd laid out in front of him. It didn't take him long, since there were hardly any.

Almond and Perch had both been alone in their kitchens, and both had been killed on days when their restaurants were closed. The doors had been unlocked from the inside, which suggested that the chefs knew the killer, or were at least expecting him or her. There were traces of spiced Indian tea—chai—on the lips of the dead chefs. There also seemed to be some cumin. Exotic and rare, yes—but poisonous?

And of course there was the mystery smell only Neil could discern. Was it a poison? If so, why hadn't the lab turned up any trace?

There were a few fingerprints, but they didn't match anything the police had on file. There were no clothing fibres.

Nakamura stared at the two scribbled notes.

Emperor, Venice, Princess. It was all tweaking some long-lost memory, but Nakamura couldn't quite place it. He'd been to Venice on vacation, about a year ago. He'd gone to the Doge's palace. He'd taken a gondola ride. He'd eaten some great food and even visited a couple of museums. But he wasn't much of a history buff, so this wasn't really his field.

The clock struck six.

"I'm stumped," Nakamura said to his empty office. He carefully placed the notes and photos back into their evidence box and locked it in his desk. He got up, grabbed his coat, and made his way to the place he always made his way to when he was stumped: Master Tojo's sushi restaurant on Broadway. He could think there, and it was the only place in town where he could get sushi as good as his father had made back in Japan.

CHAPTER SEVEN

LARRY, LARRY, QUITE CONTRARY

The clock above the kitchen door struck midnight. The last customer had just left Chez Flambé, decidedly heavier of hip and lighter of wallet—but smiling contentedly.

Neil sat down on a stool next to the counter and watched Larry, Amber, and Zoë clean the kitchen. It was not a fun job, which was why Neil had no desire to help. "One of the advantages of having your name over the door," he'd told Larry, explaining why the head chef's night was done once the cooking was done.

"My name is Flambé too!" Larry said. "So I guess I can be a lazy slob like you!"

Neil frowned. "Being a lazy slob is what you do best already. Maybe it's time to try something new."

Larry was a Flambé, but in Neil's opinion he was not a very successful one. Sure, Larry was the "adult" listed on the deed, but calling Larry an adult was a bit of a stretch. He stayed up too late. He drove a motorcycle. His sketchy friends would sometimes show up at the back door, blaring rap music from their headphones. Larry almost always spent his money before his next paycheck and had to bum cash from Neil.

"Please? I've got a date tonight" was his usual excuse.

Neil just couldn't understand why Larry was satisfied with being a dishwasher or a sous-chef. Larry wasn't stupid—not at all. He would often stop Neil in his tracks with tidbits of knowledge on all sorts of subjects, from philosophy to music to history.

"I'm always interested in what the pretty ladies are interested in," he'd explain. "There are lots of pretty ladies, so I read lots of interesting things."

Larry wasn't lazy either. He'd work hard, if he cared enough. It was more like Larry was, well, not *ambitious* enough to be a Flambé. Neil thought of their parents. His own were, of course, very successful. Larry's parents were chemistry professors. They were always working or teaching or doing research for some big company or other. They were rarely home. Larry joked about how they forgot his birthday, his high-school graduation . . . his name.

Neil hardly ever saw his parents either. But that was okay. He was busy too.

Neil wanted to be famous. He wanted to be rich. He wanted to be . . . perfect.

Larry just wanted to be Larry.

When it came to food, Larry wasn't totally useless. He made an excellent white sauce, and was even good on the grill. Neil was *almost* considering letting him handle some Kobe beef steaks . . . and those cost about a hundred dollars a pound.

But it seemed that whenever Neil was just about ready to let Larry do more of the cooking, Larry would do something to suggest that he was thicker than a badly made gravy.

Like the time Neil had come into the kitchen and caught Larry making pre-fab boxed rice in his best risotto pan.

"Hey, man, you've gotta have an appreciation for the common things in life," Larry had said defensively.
"That's a five-hundred dollar hand-hammered copper pot . . . made in Italy!" Neil had yelled in disgust. His voice climbed higher and higher as he shrieked. "It's ruined!"

"Oh," Larry had said. "Well, do you want some rice? I made two packages."

Neil had almost cried.

The only thing that seemed to get Larry *really* motivated was a pretty face. Larry was always joking or showing off in front of the ladies. He was doing it now with Amber and Zoë.

Larry had taken the leftover vermicelli noodles from dinner and plopped them on his head. "Hey, look," he said, gazing at his reflection in a freshly polished wok. "I'm a Pasta-farian!"

Amber and Zoë doubled over with laughter. "Does that mean you like Ragu music?" Amber laughed.

"Hair-larious!" Zoë added.

At this rate, it was going to take them hours to finish cleaning the kitchen.

"Can you keep it down, please?" Neil said. "I'm trying to plan the menu for tomorrow."

Larry threw the noodles into the compost bin. He winked at Amber and Zoë, who were still giggling, and they all got back to work.

Neil tried to concentrate despite the clattering of the pots and pans and the metallic clink of the cutlery. Neil wasn't the sort to rest on his laurels. Yes, tonight's potatoes had been a hit, but they were done a full three minutes before his boeuf Bourguignon. That was the sort of miscalculation he found unacceptable. He needed to be better tomorrow.

"And the fenugreek in the lamb stew was way too strong," he muttered out loud.

Over at the sink, Larry just shook his head and smiled. Neil was a little nutty sometimes. Larry had tried

both dishes, and they had blown his mind. He'd often wondered how you could give two people exactly the same meat, spices, and cookware, and one would make something approximating a dead rat (that would be him) and the other (Neil) would create a dish that could bring tears to your eyes.

"Well, anyway, boss," Larry called out as he stacked the rest of the dishes into the washer, "it was a good night for the bottom line. I figure we took in $5,638.79 tonight. Almost enough to cover our costs!"

Neil took a quick look at his figures. Larry was right. Neil shook his head.

"How did you work that out so quickly?"

"It's just math," Larry said. "I'm lazy, not stupid."

"You had me fooled," Neil responded.

Then Neil stood up so suddenly, his stool crashed to the floor.

Amber and Zoë jumped in surprise, dropping the dishes they were in the process of drying.

"Oh crap!" Neil shouted.

"Sorry, Neil," said the twins in unison. (They did that a lot; Neil assumed it was a twin thing.) "Sorry." Neil yelled often, but he rarely used anything that resembled bad language. He must have been really mad about the dishes. "You can take that out of our wages," they said together.

"No, no, no." Neil waved them off. "Larry said, 'It's just math.' I totally forgot! I have a math test tomorrow morning!" He was out the door within seconds and on his bike, pedaling for home.

* * *

School had always been a challenge for Neil Flambé. He wasn't bad at it: He was just so tired all the time. A chef's life is busy. A successful chef's life is nuts. Add in a secret side job as a human bloodhound, and it's nearly insane.

Neil liked the challenge, of course. It was like a life-long episode of *Hell's Kitchen*. You had to be ready for anything, and the results needed to be great. When push came to shove, Neil always decided it was the cooking that would get the lion's share of his energy. School was way down on the list of his priorities.

The other thing that made school tough on Neil was the class neanderthal, Billy Berger. He'd had a hate-on for Neil since their first lunch recess in kindergarten. Billy's lunch bucket had contained a pack of chips, a bottle of spray-on cheese, and a packet of Twinkies. Neil had practically lost it, laughing. "You'll be dead of a heart attack before you're twelve," he'd said.

Billy took a look at the scrawny kid who was sitting there laughing at him. "And you'll be dead in five seconds if you don't shut up," Billy replied. "What are you eating, geek? Bean sprouts and tofu?"

"No. But I'm willing to share what I have if it will get you to eat something besides that garbage."

Billy watched with growing annoyance as Neil carefully unpacked a thermos of pesto risotto ("I made it fresh this morning before school"), crusty bread ("picked up at Terra's Bakery on the way over—Andre has such an amazing gift for yeast"), and fresh snow peas ("just at the height of the season"). When Neil pulled out some weird hand-held contraption to grate his own fresh parmesan cheese, Billy had had enough.

"Hey, geek," he said, grabbing Neil's gourmet grater, "why don't you eat normal food? You trying to tick me off or something?"

Billy grabbed the risotto and threw the bowl against the wall. Then he took the baguette and cracked it in two over his knee. By the time the cafeteria supervisor arrived he was shoving the snow peas, one by one, up Neil's nose.

Neil ate with the teachers after that. They said it was to protect him from bullying. That might have been true at first, but it wasn't long before the teachers were enjoying Neil's particular way of saying "thanks for saving my life": extra risotto and gourmet cheeses. Within days, they had let Neil install his own hotplate in the teacher's lounge, just so he could experiment with different kinds of crêpes.

Becoming a teacher's pet did nothing to endear Neil to Billy, and Neil got pretty fast at dodging Berger's hammy fists and ferocious kicks in the hallways between classes.

The final straw, though, came when they entered high school. Billy had long since given up bringing any lunch to school. Instead, he made his parents give him enough coins to buy five bags of chips and a cola from the vending machine.

One day, near the beginning of eighth grade, Billy made his way over to the bank of glowing machines, put in his coins, and automatically pressed his favorite option: B15—corn bugles. But what came out the bottom of the machine was about as far from corn bugles as a person could get. Inside a clear recyclable container was a red tortilla. The label read: "salmon and brie wrap with fresh British Columbia mint."

"What the fudge?" Berger said. He looked up at the other selections. There was lamb and camembert on pumpernickel (C23) and a Greek salad with Denman Island goat feta (F12). C23 and F12 were supposed to be taco chips and Twinkies!

At that moment, Neil came up behind him.

"You don't seem happy with the tortilla, Berger. Would you prefer panini?" Neil asked. "They're just putting a grilling machine behind the counter."

"What the heck did you do, you freak?" Berger asked, forming his fingers into a fist and crushing the tortilla in the process. Flecks of salmon and vinaigrette oozed between his fingers.

"Oh, please. Look how unhealthy the old food was," Neil said. "I'm just trying to help ignorant slobs like you eat real food, since you obviously can't help yourself."

Neil noticed that Berger's face was turning as red as the wrap he was crushing to a pulp in his hand. He looked like he was about to try the same technique on Neil's head, but Neil didn't flinch.

"Don't try it, Berger," Neil said, looking him right in the eye. "There's a camera crew following me around today. They want to chronicle a day in the life of the city's newest restaurateur. I'd hate for the footage to become evidence in a court case. Besides, I'm faster than you. You'd probably have a coronary running across the room. Enjoy the salmon. Unlike you, it's fresh."

Neil walked calmly away from Berger and toward the white light of the waiting camera crew.

He didn't see the murderous look in Berger's eye as Berger pounded his fist into his palm. He also didn't hear Berger vow, through gritted teeth, "Oh, you're gonna get yours, Flambé. Somehow, someday, you're going to get yours."

CHAPTER EIGHT

FOWL PLAY

Neil sat on one of the stools that usually gathered dust in the kitchen of Chez Flambé. He leaned on the stainless-steel countertop, trying to keep his eyes open. The stools were usually pushed to the side of the kitchen—there's little time for sitting when you work in a busy restaurant—but Neil needed to sit for a while. He hadn't slept much, and the math test had not gone well. Neil couldn't understand why he had to know things like how to measure angles or figure out whether Janie traveling in a train from city A would arrive before or after Jimmy who was traveling from city B and at a different speed. Who cared?

He used real math in the kitchen every single day, every time he measured ingredients or felt for the perfect weight of a fish filet portion. He knew his customers would always give him an A+ for that. But sadly for Neil, his math teacher wanted numbers, not noodles.

And now he had an English assignment to finish: "Write a poem that expresses how you feel about the seventeenth-century wool trade."

Neil banged his head on the countertop and moaned.

The Batman ring tone sounded out loudly, echoing off the kitchen walls. Neil closed his notebook and pushed it to the back of the kitchen counter. He welcomed the break from his assignment. So far he'd written, "You've got to be kidding me!" and "Yuck!" He wasn't expecting an A+ on this assignment either.

He flipped open his phone. "Neil here."

"Another dead chef," Nakamura said. "Paul LeBoeuf. You know his place?"

"Yes." Neil sighed. "I'll meet you there."

Neil clicked the phone shut. He knew Paul LeBoeuf's place very well.

He looked at the clock. Dinner service was still a few hours away. He wrote a note for Larry, asking him to start the dinner prep. He taped it to the kitchen door, then got on his bike and rode off.

As he pedaled, he thought about Paul LeBoeuf. Neil had to admit he admired him as a chef. LeBoeuf was a world-renowned maker of free-range pâté de foie gras. The delicacy is usually made by fattening up geese with a tube and a lot of food. It's not pretty. Neil had once visited a farm where the producers stuffed food into the geese, then didn't let them move for days, and then extracted their livers. It's a process known as gavage.

LeBoeuf always said it was more like *savage*—a truly

horrible way to treat an animal—and he refused to buy force-fed goose livers. One autumn day, as he sat on the porch of his farm, he noticed that the geese were getting fatter all on their own. It was part of their preparations for flying south for the winter.

Nature, that wonderful provider, had presented LeBoeuf with an ethical source of fatty liver. He also found there was a large number of people out there who wanted to enjoy their pâté without a side dish of guilt. That realization had made him a lot of money.

At first, visiting critics from France refused to believe LeBoeuf when he showed them pictures of the fat but happy geese that populated his tiny farm in the Fraser River Valley. They would taste his foie gras and refuse to believe it had come from anything but the traditional method.

But LeBoeuf was adamant. He'd even named his latest restaurant EthicalEats, as an expression of his passion for fair food.

Neil looked up at the sign as he parked his bike and made his way through the door and into the kitchen. LeBoeuf was lying on the ground next to a well-adorned counter of fresh goose livers. Someone had very unethically poisoned him.

LeBoeuf had the same twisted smile on his face as the other two dead chefs, and his face was the same shade of blue.

Nakamura led Neil through the evidence they'd gathered so far. "LeBoeuf unlocked the door from inside. He'd been alone, as far as we can tell."

Neil took a sniff of LeBoeuf's lips. "Chai and cumin," he said. "Same as the others."

"Is the tea involved somehow?" Nakamura asked.

"Possibly," Neil said. "But a lot of us drink Masala chai when we're brainstorming new food combinations. It's kind of a thing with the chefs here in Vancouver. The good ones, anyway."

"How cute." Nakamura chuckled. "Like a club of old ladies playing bridge." He adopted a high-pitched voice. "Oh, please pass me two sugars, sweetie, and perhaps some of that scrumptious clotted cream."

Neil ignored Nakamura and took another big sniff. "The other smell is there, too," he said with a sigh.

Nakamura looked at his notes. "There are no fingerprints here, other than LeBoeuf's. Weird. Not even the staff's fingerprints are around."

"It's called *cleanliness*," Neil said with a note of disdain in his voice. "A chef has to make sure that each day starts with the kitchen as clean as possible. You should really stop wasting time on expensive lab tests."

Nakamura pointed a finger at Flambé and started to say something. Then he stopped. When the Nose was right, he was right.

"Hey, you know something?" Nakamura said, looking at Neil with mock wonder. "Now that I think about it, a chef would make a great criminal."

"A burger flipper, maybe, or a line-order cook. We real chefs have more important things to do," Neil replied.

Nakamura just shook his head as the photographer snapped photos of LeBoeuf's rather large body. "I wonder what a foie gras made from *his* liver would taste like," he said.

Neil stood up. He didn't say a word to Nakamura. He just walked out of the kitchen.

"Hey, sorry, Nose," Nakamura called after him. "I didn't mean to offend you or anything. It was just a joke!"

But Neil wasn't worried about Nakamura's lame sense of humor. He'd been around the inspector long enough to know that Nakamura was never going to quit his day job to become a comic.

Neil just needed to think.

He walked through the kitchen's double doors. They eased shut behind him on their compression spring hinges. Chrome vanadium, Neil noticed. Very nice and very expensive. LeBoeuf always did have a great sense of detail.

In fact, everything at LeBoeuf's EthicalEats was top-notch—over-the-top even. The tables were antiques that Paul had bought at auctions from all over the world. The chairs were intricately carved by French craftsmen. The linen was *actually* expensive Irish linen, not plastic or some cheap knockoff.

No one but a chef knew how hard it really was to make a restaurant profitable and to keep it that way. You were always a couple of slow weekends away from going broke, no matter who you were. So you had to impress the patrons with the food *and* the atmosphere. Paul LeBoeuf consistently did just that. At EthicalEats you felt like you were having a meal in Napoleon's private chamber.

Neil thought about his own little place. Most of the tables were metal. The linen was some kind of cloth, but Neil wasn't exactly sure which. The chairs were bought wholesale at an estate auction, and Larry was constantly gluing the joints to keep them from squeaking too much when diners cut their steaks.

Of course, the whole state of affairs was Larry's fault in the first place.

Neil looked again at LeBoeuf's elegant dining room, made even more spectacular by the sun setting on the mountaintops across the water.

This was supposed to be Neil's restaurant.

CHAPTER NINE

ETHICALEATS?

A year and a half ago, Neil had finally had enough of being a child prodigy on display. He'd done most of his cooking on TV talk shows and at private parties for his parents' clients. His parents didn't appreciate the food so much, but their clients sure did.

Neil was kind of like Mozart, touring the world for command performances but always looking for a permanent concert hall. It was time to strike out on his own.

Neil picked out a great location for his first restaurant. It was right on the water, and the dining room featured huge windows that caught the last golden rays of the sun setting on the distant mountains. It would seat two hundred for dinner service. There was even a brand-new kitchen with all the best stoves and grills and walk-in refrigerators that money could buy. It was expensive, but it was worth it; a fitting setting for the miracles-on-a-plate that Neil was going to prepare.

But Neil wasn't the only one with his eye on the place. The agent said another chef was looking too.

Neil needed to sign the lease

fast, and he needed to grease the wheels a bit. This was the dirty underbelly of the cutthroat world of Vancouver restaurant real estate. The agent was willing to let Neil sign first, *if* he provided a nice down payment: $5,000. in cash. That was on top of the whopping lease. And the other interested person was coming at ten the next morning to sign. Neil had one day to come up with the money.

That's when Larry entered the picture.

Neil couldn't go to his parents. They were willing to help bankroll the restaurant, but his lawyer mom would have freaked at the mere suggestion of a bribe.

Neil had saved some money, but because he was still underage, he couldn't access his own bank account without his parents' approval. Neil broke his piggy banks, even the one that was shaped like the famous Savoy Hotel in London. It had been a gift from the head chef there, Andre, after Neil had taught him a superior way to prepare a perfect crème brûlée. Andre had even stuffed a few euros inside after Neil agreed to keep the fact quiet.

He came up with a grand total of about $1,200.

Neil was stumped. He didn't really have any friends to speak of. Usually, that was fine with Neil. He preferred the company of food. But it didn't give him too many financial options at the moment. You can't bum money from a head of lettuce.

He briefly debated forging his dad's signature, but decided against it.

There was always Angel, but Angel gave all of his money away to charity. And besides, things with Angel were . . . well . . . complicated.

In the end, there was only one person whom Neil could call. He picked up his cell phone and dialed Larry. As cousins, Neil and Larry had never been close, but Neil knew that Larry knew "stuff"—like how to turn small amounts of cash into larger amounts of cash. Of course, Larry was equally adept at turning large amounts of cash into smaller amounts, but that was a risk Neil would have to take. Desperate times and all that. . . .

"Hey, it's Julia the Child!" Larry snickered into the phone. His voice sounded a bit rough.

"It's three in the afternoon!" Neil feigned shock. "Did I wake you from your beauty sleep?"

"Who needs more than a couple of hours when I'm already so naturally beautiful?" Larry asked. "So why the early start to my day?"

Neil explained the situation.

"Don't worry about it a bit," Larry said. "Just give me the thousand bucks and I'll get that down payment for you."

"How?" Neil asked. Then he added quickly, "Never mind. It's better if I don't know. Then I can't give evidence at your trial."

Larry just laughed. "Don't worry! I won't do anything stupid. Let's just say that I'm feeling lucky."

Neil was feeling closer to ill than lucky as he clicked his phone shut. He had a sense that this wasn't going to turn out well, but it was too late. Larry was at the door an hour later to grab the money.

"It'll take me a while to drum up the cash, but I'll be at the restaurant tomorrow morning."

"At nine thirty sharp," Neil added quickly.

"Is that a.m.?" Larry choked.

Neil frowned.

"Just kidding." Larry patted Neil on the head. "Don't sweat it for a second. I'll be there." Then Larry hopped on his Harley, revved the engine, and drove off.

Neil was at the restaurant at nine. The real estate agent let him in and stuck out his palm faster than a waiter looking for a tip.

"It's coming" was all Neil could say as he sat down at the desk the agent had set up near the glorious picture windows. "I can sign the lease now and give you the money by ten." Even the seagulls outside seemed to laugh at that one. The real estate agent just tapped his fingers on the desk and frowned.

"I don't think so," he said.

The contract sat on the desktop, waiting for the five thousand bucks to show. Neil noticed the spot for the name of the leaseholder was still blank.

The clock ticked in the background. 9:30. No Larry.

9:45. No Larry.

9:55. Neil wondered which of his knives would be the most efficient for revenge.

9:59. A knock at the door. Neil jumped up and ran over. He opened the door so quickly, the man on the other side almost fell in. It wasn't Larry. It was Paul LeBoeuf.

He was the other chef! And Neil could tell by the bulge in his vest pocket that he'd been able to get the money together.

"Neil Flambé!" Paul had called jovially. "What are you doing here? Come to see my new home?"

"Um." Neil fudged around for a second, fighting

back a mixture of embarrassment, sadness, and anger. "I was just looking at the stove. I'm thinking of buying one like it for my new place."

"*You* are opening a restaurant!" LeBoeuf seemed both impressed and a little condescending. "Where? At a daycare center?"

Neil hesitated as he looked wistfully around the room. "It's a secret," he said.

"Ahhh," Paul smiled. "Well, *bon chance, mon ami*. It's a rough life you know. And ruthless. But, *alors*, I have a business transaction to attend to now. *Au revoir*." He stepped aside to let Neil leave.

Neil's face was as red as an overcooked lobster. His dream restaurant was about to slip away. He looked back through the picture window of the restaurant and saw LeBoeuf place a thick envelope on the desk. He signed the lease with a flourish.

Neil turned away, climbed on his bike, and rode off. There were tears in his eyes and murder on his mind.

Halfway down the street he heard the distinct low hum of a Harley motorcycle engine. Sure enough, there was Larry . . . barreling toward Neil at top speed. He had a big smile on his face and he seemed to be singing.

Larry was so wrapped up in his own happy place that he didn't see Neil until the last second. Hoping to avoid "death by Larry," Neil jumped off the bike. That was a good thing too, because his bike slid under the front wheel of the Harley before Larry could stop. By the time the brakes kicked in, the bike was a twisted, tangled mess.

Larry cut the engine. "Whoa, close one!" he said.

"Where *were* you?" Neil growled through clenched

teeth. He took off his bike helmet and threw it at Larry. Larry ducked. The helmet sailed over his head, landed in a nearby ditch, and sank in the mud.

"You never were much of an athlete," Larry said, watching the helmet disappear. He handed Neil a motorcycle helmet. "Now hop on, cousin of mine. Have I got a surprise for you!"

"Where's the money I gave you?" Neil said.

"Well, that's part of the surprise, obviously," Larry said.

Neil didn't see anything obvious about it at all. "I don't appear to have any other way to get home," Neil said, glaring at his wrecked bike. Larry looked at it as well. "Hey, that was a clunky old bike anyway. I've got a better one at home. You can have it. I don't need it now that I have the old hogster here." He tapped the side of the motorcycle's gas tank. Neil climbed warily on the back, and they were off.

It only took Neil a couple of minutes to realize that they weren't heading toward the west end of the city where his family lived. They were heading toward the *east* end of town, and not the best part of the east end either. Neil half wondered if Larry had lost more than the thousand dollars and had made some deal to deliver a famous kid chef to some kidnappers.

"Where are we going?" Neil asked over the roar of the engine.

He wasn't one hundred percent sure, but he thought Larry said, "Bombay." That didn't make him feel any better.

Finally, Larry stopped the bike in front of a grocery store and what looked like an abandoned thrift shop. Some sketchy-looking characters milled around outside.

"Where are we?" Neil asked. All of a sudden, his kidnapping idea didn't seem so crazy. What happened next did nothing to calm his nerves.

"Oh! One more thing," Larry said, pulling a white napkin out of his backpack. Before Neil could say no, he was blindfolded.

"Take my hand, cousin," Larry said, and he started to lead Neil down the street.

"If you got yourself into some kind of trouble, Larry, you can just ask my parents for the ransom." Neil spoke quickly, trying to calm his nerves. "You don't need to involve any crooks, you know. . . ."

Larry just chuckled. "Almost there" was all he said.

And then they stopped. "Now for the surprise!" Larry yelled, and he pulled the blindfold off Neil's eyes.

Neil flinched, expecting a punch from some grown-up version of Billy Berger to flatten him and keep him in line.

But Larry just stood there and said, "*Voila!*"

Neil blinked. Larry was standing in front of a run-down storefront. There was so much grease and dirt smudged on the window that it was impossible to see inside.

A faded plastic sign above the door read "Wong's Fish 'n' Chips." A notice tacked onto the door said "Closed." Someone had written "Thank goodness" in the grime.

"What the heck is this?" Neil asked. "A joke?"

"No joke, cuz," Larry said. "It's our restaurant!"

Neil said nothing. He just stared, incredulous.

"It's true," Larry said with an enormous smile. "I kind of won it in a card game last night. That's where the money went. It paid for this! Not a bad investment for a thousand bucks, eh?"

As if on cue, the sign came off its hinges and crashed through the glass door. A pigeon and a couple of smaller birds flew out the hole, followed by two cats and what looked like a very scraggly rat.

"Luckily, I have a few hundred left over to pay for the door. The glass looked pretty scuffed up, anyhow," Larry said.

Neil was almost too shocked to speak. "I had a place picked out already. I needed the money to pay for THAT PLACE."

"Yeah, but that's the best part!" Larry said. "You see, I play a game of poker every Monday night with a bunch of chefs. And last night I was winning and winning, and usually I quit when I'm a little ahead, so one of the guys asked me why I was so eager to keep playing. So I told him, 'I'm trying to help my cousin raise some dough to grease the wheels on a restaurant deal.'"

A terrible realization was starting to dawn on Neil. "You don't happen to play with a chef named Paul LeBoeuf, do you?" Neil asked.

Larry was taken aback. "Yeah! You know him? Of course you know him! But he gave me some great advice."

Neil's head started to pound.

"He said it was crazy to start out in the restaurant

business on a big scale. Do you even know what the taxes on that other place are?"

"I know LeBoeuf does," Neil said sadly.

"Thousands!" Larry said. "'Start small,' he said. He even had a mortgage for the perfect place, he said. I handed over the seven thousand dollars—"

"SEVEN THOUSAND?" Neil coughed. Now he knew where LeBoeuf had gotten that bulge in his coat pocket.

"I told you I was doing well," Larry said. "So I handed over the seven thousand, and he signed this place over to me. We own it! He said you'd do a way better job than he would have with this 'cause he's so old and all and this place needs a little work. We can get your mom to handle the legal stuff later and get your name added on as an owner as well. Cool, eh, partner? Welcome to Chez Flambé!"

Neil realized now that Larry hadn't said "Bombay" when Neil had asked him where they were heading. He had said "Chez Flambé." Bombay would have been preferable right now.

Neil stared at Larry with utter disbelief.

"I know," Larry said, completely misinterpreting Neil's mood. "You're touched. It's like a fairy tale come true. Your own place! And it's small so you won't even go broke running it."

"You're right," Neil said finally. "I *do* feel like I'm in a fairy tale. It's called Jerk and the Beanstalk!"

"Hey, don't forget there's a lot of golden eggs and a totally hot magic harp for the hero at the end of that story." Larry shook a set of keys in Neil's face, still smiling. "So, should we take a look inside?"

Back in the sunset-lit elegant dining room of Paul

LeBoeuf's place, Neil shuddered as he remembered the bugs, the cobwebs, the grease, and the ancient ovens. Someone had even left behind a wok filled with some mummified noodle dish. The wok was so fused to the stove they'd had to chip it off with a hammer.

Tens of thousands of dollars in renovations later they finally opened to rave reviews, for the food. Patrons still didn't visit Chez Flambé for the atmosphere. *Not yet anyway*, Neil thought. He promised himself that would change. He wondered if there'd be an estate sale for LeBoeuf's furniture. "At least your eats were ethical," he said, looking around the deserted dining hall.

"Hey, Nose," said a voice behind him.

Nakamura had followed Neil into the dining room.

"There's one other thing I should tell you about these murders," he said, looking at his feet. "I should have mentioned it before, but it wasn't really up your alley, so to speak."

He handed Neil a small plastic bag, the kind police use to keep evidence clean. Inside was a crumpled piece of paper

"What's this?" Neil asked. "A recipe? No thanks, I have plenty."

"It's a clue, genius," Nakamura said.

"It's in Italian, *idiota*," said Neil, looking at the writing.

"You really are the master of the obvious, aren't you?" Nakamura said. "I just wanted you to see it. The killer left notes like this on the bodies of Almond and Perch, too. This one is a bit longer, though."

"What does it say?" asked Neil. He could only make out a couple of words, like *oche* and *mucca*, Italian for "geese" and "cow." He knew those from cookbooks.

Nakamura looked at the quick translation Stromboli had scribbled in his notebook and read it out loud.

"We have been stranded off the coast of Dai Viet. Ships have come out to trade with us and we have bargained for great amounts of spice, especially a cardamom of such rare quality that we will earn much for it upon our return home. There are also geese and cows to eat. The people here, it is said, can summon storms at will. The Khan has attempted to conquer them many times and has been unable to do so. It has been said the place is cursed. I pray that this is not true."

Neil looked at the paper more closely. "Can I take a sniff?" he asked.

"Of course," Nakamura said. "Just don't touch it."

Neil opened the zip top carefully and took a slow whiff. He could make out the faintest scent of the cumin and even some of the chai spices . . . but no trace of the other smell. "Same smells," he said, zipping up the bag. "Are the notes related to the murders in any obvious way?"

"Well, this one mentioned cardamom. The note on Perch talked about a princess, but nothing about food. It did talk a bit about gunpowder."

"What about Emily's?" Neil asked.

"It mentioned a feast and some place called Daidu, but it was pretty short."

"I don't see a pattern," Neil said.

"Neither do we." Nakamura shrugged.

"I assumed that," Neil said, "but when *I* can't figure it out, it's serious."

"Ha, ha, ha," Nakamura said dryly.

"Why leave notes at all?" Neil wondered.

"Well, I've done a lot of homicides," Nakamura replied. "It's likely a dare. Killers sometimes like to bait the cops; it gives them an extra thrill. They want to leave clues that they can piece together, but the cops can't. We do eventually. Killers have huge egos—not as huge as boy chefs, mind you, but big enough. Eventually they get cocky and screw up."

"Well, that's one thing they *don't* have in common with boy chefs," Neil said, turning to leave.

"Look, Neil." Nakamura's tone softened a bit, and he put his hand on Neil's shoulder. "I know we ask an awful lot of you."

Neil narrowed his eyes and stared at the inspector. Was Nakamura actually trying to be nice?

Nakamura continued, "This is a lot of heavy stuff for a fourteen-year-old to handle."

Neil stiffened. Nakamura wasn't being nice; he was being condescending. Another "hey kid" moment was coming on. Adults really ticked him off sometimes.

"You are an amazing help," Nakamura continued, "but is there anyone you could ask for advice on identifying these spices, these strange smells? Someone with more experience? Angel, maybe?"

Now Neil pulled his shoulder away completely. "Why don't you contact him yourself?" he asked coldly.

"Well"—Nakamura shuffled and looked at the floor—"he kind of won't talk to me right now."

"Why not?" Neil was a little surprised. Angel wasn't

the type to get into arguments or hold grudges.

"Well, I kind of busted him for raising all those goats."

"You're kidding?" Neil said.

"He lives in an apartment building in the middle of downtown, for crying out loud! The neighbors complained."

Neil frowned. "You've known about those goats for years."

"Yeah, I know. Angel makes this amazing cheese he sometimes gives me. . . ."

"What? To keep quiet? Isn't that a *bribe*?"

"Actually," Nakamura said, smacking his lips. "It's more like a brie." He quickly went on. "This time one of the stupid goats jumped the fence and was munching on some neighbor's heritage rose bushes. He complained. What was I supposed to do?"

"Look after a friend, maybe?" Neil asked—but as soon as he heard himself say it, he felt ashamed. "Friend" wasn't a word that took up residence in Neil's mind very often. It was less common for it to travel from his mind all the way to his mouth. Neil wasn't even completely sure where that thought had come from. Still, he kept talking, "*Especially* a friend who gives you gourmet cheese."

"Look who's talking!" Nakamura said, tossing his kindness back out the window. "Mr. Warmth himself! Chef Chuckles!"

Neil glared at Nakamura and walked back into the kitchen. He wanted to be angry, he really did. Angry was easy, and he was good at it. But right now he was just kind of confused.

Neil sighed. He had vowed never to speak to Angel again.

But maybe Nakamura was right. Neil had believed he could solve the mystery of the secret smell on his own, if he just tried hard enough. He looked at Paul LeBoeuf's body again. Three chefs dead, and he was nowhere near finding out how or why. He might even be next. A chill ran down his spine at the thought.

It hurt Neil to admit it, but he was stumped. He was going to need help. And there was just one place he could go for that.

CHAPTER TEN

GINGER, GARAM MASALA, AND GUITAR

Angel Jícama sat on his living room floor, playing an airy tune on his guitar. His father had crafted the instrument from the trunk of a tree that had been struck by lightning in the backyard of their home in Cedros, Trinidad. Or was it Oaxaca, Mexico? Or was it Madagascar? Angel told different stories to different people. Did it really matter?

It was the same with food. Does a real curry come from the Orient? Or India? Or the Caribbean? Or can it come from all places and no places at once and still be a curry? All that matters is that it is true to itself.

Angel passed this thought around in his head while his nimble fingers strummed out a breezy tune. The guitar took him back to his childhood—practicing music in the garden, his mother chopping fresh chilies in the kitchen. She would add a dash of garam masala, some cardamom and a few cinnamon sticks to a boiling pot on the wood-fired stove.

All the smells came together in a wonderful symphony of scent—the spices, the chicken thighs, the ginger, the smoke, his mother's rose-petal perfume—but even from outside the kitchen window Angel could tell them all apart.

His mother stirred the mixture with spoons and spatulas that his father had also carved from the branches of the fallen tree. Angel could feel their movements echoed in the wood of his guitar—the strumming outside and the stirring inside matching each other perfectly. All things together, all things connected, all things in harmony.

Angel's music changed as his memories moved and danced through the years. He hummed along with his mix of rhythms and melodies . . . now calypso, now mariachi, now rock and roll.

He still had his mother's spoons, but he never used them. He didn't want to lose the smells that still clung to the worn, blackened wood. He would sometimes take them out of the special carrying case he had made and pass them under his nose before setting to work on his own special dishes. "It is always good to remember the people who have helped you get to where you are," he had told young Neil that first day in their kitchen, "if you want to have any idea where you are going."

"Who are you?" Neil had asked. "Obi-Wonton Kenobi?"

He was a cocky kid, even then. And, despite Angel's best efforts, he had gotten cockier over the years as he grew older and progressed in cooking prowess.

Angel strummed some more, now picking out an old B. B. King blues tune as he remembered reading in the paper about a seven-year-old kid who could make his own beef Wellington from scratch, and win awards for it as well.

The world of haute cuisine would be a dangerous place for a kid with those kinds of skills. Angel knew that first hand. He'd called up the Flambés and asked to meet their son. He wanted to help Neil avoid the pitfalls of a life dedicated to making great food.

"We've tried to cure him of this cooking bug," Neil's father had said over the phone. His voice rose in pitch as he listed his concerns. "It's costing us thousands of dollars a month. How many other seven-year-olds have a five-star gas range and a meat locker? We've had to move out of our condo and into a house just to find room for all this stuff! Do you know what the real estate market is like right now?"

The Flambés sounded panicked. Angel had assured them that he could talk to the boy about finding more balance and less brashness in his future. Simplicity. That would be his gift to them. It would start with dinner and a conversation at his house.

"What should we bring?" Eric asked.

"Well," Angel explained. "I make only one dish a year. This year I'm trying to make the perfect paella."

"What kind of pie?"

"Not a pie," Angel said. He was beginning to realize that Neil's fondness for gourmet eats was not shared by his parents. "Paella. It's pronounced *pie-ay-ah*. It's a sort of a Spanish rice stew. I'm trying it with shellfish tonight."

"Oh." Neil's dad sounded a bit let down.

Angel smiled to himself. "I can make a side dish of french fries and hot dogs, if you'd like."

"Sure!" Eric said quickly. "Do you have ketchup and mustard?"

"Um, no," Angel said.

"Cool," Eric said. "We'll bring some of that."

"Wonderful," Angel said, chuckling to himself. "And I have some refreshing lemon punch that will go perfectly. It's a *limonata* that I make myself, but friends tell me it tastes just as good as the stuff from Italy. See you at seven."

They had arrived half an hour early.

The boy seemed excited at the possibility of meeting a world-famous chef. The parents weren't really sure who Angel was, but Neil seemed to know everything about him: how he cooked only one dish a year, but how thousands of people around the world begged to be invited to his home to enjoy it.

Angel would spend twelve months or so experimenting and reworking the chosen dish. Then, once he was certain it was as close to perfect as he could manage, he would announce a date for the dinner.

Only fifteen a year were given the privilege of attending. Twelve of them paid, and paid dearly—although Angel gave almost all the money away to the city's food banks. The others at the table were Angel's special, non-paying, guests. They were usually people who gave something back to the world. One year it was the head of *Médecins Sans Frontières*. Another year the guest of honor was Mother Teresa.

"And this year you're working on paella!" Neil had said, smelling the paprika, rice, and rosemary. "When's the big dinner?"

"I don't know yet," said Angel. "Soon, I hope."

"The trick to the dish," Angel told him as they stood together by the gas-fired stove, the paella simmering and bubbling slowly, "is to find the perfect balance of taste, texture and"—Angel looked straight into Neil's eyes—"smell."

"Smell?" Neil repeated, astonished. "You have that too?"

"My ability is not as powerful as yours, obviously," Angel said.

"How do you know I have it at all?" Neil asked. "Because," Angel replied, "to have such an advanced gift for proportion and taste at such a young age, you must have a sensory ability far advanced from that of so-called normal people."

"But why is mine stronger than yours?" Neil asked, all the while chopping some cilantro and thyme.

"Well, I don't know *why*. But I know that it's true. I wasn't able to make my first great demi-glace until I was

twelve. I read that you made one two years ago."

"I am pretty good," Neil said with a smug smile on his face. "A kind of demi-glace demi-god, in fact."

"You are blessed with a great gift. The question is, what will you do with it?"

"I'll become famous," Neil answered calmly.

Angel sighed. "I was like you," he said. "Arrogant. Just as determined to know everything, to try everything, to excel at everything. I traveled the world over, cooking ribollita better than the Italians in Tuscany, soufflés better than the French in Lyon, and roast duck better than the chefs in Beijing. I excelled at them all, but my heart was always restless."

"But you were the greatest chef of all time!" Neil exclaimed. "You were great at everything!"

"But I was not happy in here," Angel said, touching his chest gently.

"Your cooking gave you heartburn?" Neil asked.

"No." Angel rolled his eyes. "I was unhappy. And I hurt people as well."

Angel suddenly wore a look of pain.

"Do you have heartburn now?" Neil asked.

"*No!*" Angel said with exasperation. "I was remembering something from my past."

"Oh. Did you cut somebody's finger off by mistake?"

"No."

"Give somebody famous food poisoning?"

"No."

"Rob a bank?"

"NO."

"Well, what *did* you do—kill somebody or something?" Neil asked.

Angel didn't answer. "I had to be the best, and that was all that mattered. My success was judged by how many Michelin stars I earned and how many glowing reviews I garnered. Other people's lives and loves were not important. Finally, I realized the crazy existence of the celebrity chef was a complete sham. I sold my restaurant in Rome and left the world of cooking behind."

"Wow," Neil said slowly. He couldn't conceive of such a thing.

"I traveled the world, looking for a better way to cook, a better way to live," Angel continued. "It took me years, but I found it."

"Where?"

Angel touched his chest again. "Here," he said. "Right where I started. I found it in the hearts of Burmese peasants and their simple but joy-filled family meals of rice and broth. I found it in the crusty bread, cheese, and grapes that the farmers in northern Italy have after their long days in the field."

"Cheese and grapes?" Neil said with disgust. "Give me a break! I wouldn't even serve that as a side dish. At least not without a really good vinaigrette and sorrel salad."

Angel smiled gently.

"Simplicity is the answer," he continued. "Not showiness. Now, each year I pick one dish and one dish alone that comes from a place I have visited. I get to know it. It becomes a friend. Sometimes it becomes an enemy that I wrestle with. It is all I will make here in my monk's cell, I suppose you could call it, all year. Each year I begin with the hope that I will finally perfect a dish. That has yet to happen, but I am at peace with the journey. And peace is what everyone, in the end, has to find in life."

"I'd be satisfied with a piece . . . of really good Italian veal," Neil said.

"You'll see," Angel said, smiling.

"But," Neil asked, "what happens when you do finally achieve the perfect meal?"

Angel looked wistfully at the pan of slowly cooking rice. "I suppose once I have done that, I will just die." He looked at Neil and smiled. "Now keep chopping that cilantro."

The memory ended and Angel stopped playing. He had lost the melody all of a sudden. Neil Flambé had learned much about the art of cooking in Angel's kitchen, but he hadn't listened to him, not really. Neil learned to simplify his repertoire, his ingredients, but not himself. Finally, they had a nasty fight. It was over Neil's first experience with the shadiest side of international cuisine.

Neil had just turned thirteen. He had a new restaurant of his own and he needed money. He was invited to take part in a cooking duel, to be held in Venice. The richest man in Italy, Lorenzo Buffoni, had heard of this Neil Flambé and was offering cash if he could outcook his personal chef.

Angel had known that this day would come. He, too, had been lured by these offers of money and glory. He'd ended up like a gunslinger in the Wild West. Ingredients got more elaborate. Techniques got more risky. Eventually every chef in the world wanted to take him on. It was the part of his old life that he hated the most.

"It's dangerous," Angel had said to Neil.

"It's totally cool!" Neil countered. "Especially because I know I'll win."

"They are stupid events," Angel said, slamming his fist on his maple cutting board. "They appeal only to the showy side of your nature."

Neil had seen Angel worked up before, but never like this. He tried to calm him down. "I heard through the grapevine that you used to be quite a dueler yourself. There's a lot of cash up for grabs."

"It is a waste of your talent," Angel said slowly.

"Why do you hate duels so much?"

Angel frowned. "Do you know how this man Buffoni got all his money? He's in the mafia. This is a cook fight for gamblers and criminals. These are not the people your gifts are meant for. Have you not listened to anything I've told you in the past six years?"

Neil soldiered on. "I'm going. I'm allowed to bring one cook to help me. If I win, I can finally buy a new stove for the restaurant. You know how much I need that if I'm going to stay in business. Will you come with me?"

Angel lowered his eyes. "No."

Neil was clearly hurt. He'd been certain Angel would help him once he knew what was at stake. He could even feel tears starting to well up in his eyes. He knew Angel could see this as well, and that made him angry. "Well, then. I guess I'll win without you." He walked to the door. "Larry says he'll join me."

"If you go to Venice," Angel said, "you will regret it for the rest of your life."

Neil opened the door. "Who needs you, anyhow," he said angrily. "Sitting here with your little basic dishes and cushy recipes. You had your time in the fast lane, why can't I?"

Angel said nothing.

"You're washed up," Neil said before he could stop the words.

Still Angel said nothing. Neil slammed the door behind him. That had been one year ago.

Angel sighed.

And now Neil was back.

"Come in," Angel called as he carefully placed his guitar back on its stand. "I can smell your teriyaki marinade through the door."

The door opened slowly. "And you still use too much ginger," he said as Neil's red-topped head peered into the room.

CHAPTER ELEVEN

ANGEL OR DEVIL?

I t's late," Angel remarked.

"I just closed up a few minutes ago," Neil said, still in the doorway. "And I was standing out on the street for a bit."

"How was Venice?" Angel asked.

"I have a new stove," Neil said. "Although not as top-of-the-line as I'd hoped. That crook Buffoni didn't pay as much as he'd promised. I won. Then he told me there was a fee for all the food he'd provided. He made a very convincing argument. At least the guy next to him with the gun did."

Angel said nothing.

Neil went on. "You can say 'I told you so' if you want. But it was still a thrill."

"Congratulations" was all Angel said. "You are now a full-fledged member of the

world of high gastronomy. I hope it treats you better than it treats everyone else."

"Angel," Neil said, shuffling his feet. He wasn't quite sure how to say what he wanted to say.

"There is no apology necessary," Angel said, leading Neil in and closing the door.

"Apology for what?" Neil scoffed. "I just wish you'd been there instead of Larry. I made this excellent braised rabbit in a quince marinade. It was world-class. But if you'd been there, it would have been sublime. Buffoni would have been so impressed, he would have given me all the money."

Angel lifted a skeptical eyebrow.

"Well, anyway," Neil said. "I wish you'd come."

"Apology accepted," Angel said. "Now, no more duels in your future?"

Neil shrugged. "Let's leave that for some other time. I didn't come here to have another fight. I need help on a case."

Angel lifted his eyebrow again, in surprise this time. "Is this about the murders?"

Neil nodded.

"I've followed what little the papers can tell us," Angel said. "I'll do whatever I can. It's sad to see such great chefs gone, but you've seen the dark side of this world now. Even chefs as likeable as Emily and Lionel can have enemies."

Neil thought for a moment about how unlikable *he* could be. How many enemies had he made in his short life? Olive Green, Billy, possibly Gunter . . . maybe even Angel. Neil had amassed a mental list of about ten when Angel interrupted.

"So, what can I do for you?" Angel said.

Just then Neil noticed a smell. It was faint, but it was definitely coming from Angel's kitchen—a mixture of basil, oregano, tomatoes, and . . . cumin. Neil froze.

"What's this year's dish?" Neil asked.

"Why?"

Neil looked at Angel. It was always hard to read what he was thinking. "I'm just wondering. The cumin smells kind of . . . familiar."

"I'm doing something a little different this year," Angel said. "Not just one dish, but five. Actually, the menu was inspired by your trip to Venice."

"How do you mean?" Neil asked. "I don't smell a lot of cumin in Italian cooking."

"No," said Angel, "although in a quirk of the language cumin is sometimes called Roman caraway."

"Uh-huh," Neil said. "I still don't see the connection."

"The connection has to do with a famous Venetian, not the place itself or the food per se. Perhaps you've heard of Marco Polo?"

"The game you play in the swimming pool?" Neil asked.

"Um, no," Angel said. "Didn't you have to study Marco Polo in school?"

Neil did a quick mental scan of his bookshelf at home. Not the twenty or so shelves that held his various cookbooks, but the tiny one where he kept his books for school. He could vaguely recall a book with Marco-something-or-other written on the cover. He was supposed to have done a report on it for history. He hadn't

read it, though. In fact, if his memory served him right, he'd handed Ms. Carlin a quail-and-cranberry wrap instead of the essay. She'd given him an A-.

"Sort of," Neil said finally. "Why?"

"Well, I followed Polo's route through Asia on one of *my* journeys," Angel said.

"Does he live in Asia?" Neil asked.

"He did," Angel said, frowning. "About eight hundred years ago. Would you like the short version?"

"Always."

"Polo was a great explorer and merchant from Venice. He traveled through Asia in the service of Kublai Khan, the head of the Mongol Empire—today's China."

"This Khan guy was rich?"

"Incredibly. They also say he had somewhere in the neighborhood of a thousand wives."

"A thousand chefs would have been more useful."

"Possibly. At any rate, when Polo got back to Italy he described the interesting people he'd met, the places he'd seen, and the foods he'd eaten. A lot of people thought he'd made up the stories, they seemed so fantastic."

"Like what?"

"Palaces and streets of gold, giant birds of prey that could carry an elephant in their claws, kingdoms on mountaintops, paper money instead of coins, exotic spices. Lots of things Polo said that he saw there seemed unreal. In fact, up until recent times British school children who told a lie were accused of 'pulling a Marco Polo.' Now we know he was talking about condors, Tibet, and the Khan's glorious retreat Xanadu."

"So what happened to Polo?"

"You really should do your homework," Angel said.

Neil gave a loud sigh.

"He traveled a route that is often referred to as the Silk Road," Angel continued. "It was the route that brought trade and knowledge from the East to the West. Polo was one of the trailblazers. During this time Polo amassed great wealth and knowledge. After seventeen years of service to the khan, he was given a final mission. He and his uncle and father were to deliver a princess to her future husband."

Neil's ears perked up. "A princess?"

"Yes, the princess Kogatin. She was to marry King Argon of Persia. But the trip there was fraught with peril. No one knows exactly what happened, but hundreds of Polo's crew died. They were so late that King Argon was dead by the time they arrived."

"So what happened to the princess?"

"When did you get so romantic?" Angel asked.

"Just wondering, that's all," Neil said with a shrug. He was no romantic.

"She was married to one of Argon's sons. Life wasn't always so great for the women in these stories, I'm afraid. But the wedding was a great event, and there was an enormous feast, I'm sure. Can you just imagine what they would have eaten? Polo didn't describe that particular meal, but he generally loved to write about the different foods of the world. He was always going on and on about noodles, and breads, and exotic meats, and rice, and fruits, and. . . ."

"I get it," Neil said. "On and on and on. Sounds familiar. Maybe you should simplify your storytelling."

This time Angel gave a loud sigh. "Arrogant *and* impatient. I often forget you are just a kid."

Neil looked annoyed, but Angel just gave a good-natured laugh. "Anyway, when you went to Venice it made me think of Marco Polo. I decided to do a meal based on his travels. Smoked fish, Beijing noodle, Tibetan flat bread, and a really good curried rice, possibly served on a banana leaf, for authenticity. Peasant fare, I think you'd call it."

"If that," Neil said with a snort.

"I promise it will bring tears to your eyes, *if* I invite you to dinner."

"Which you have yet to do. That's four dishes, by the way. You said five. What's for dessert?" Neil wondered.

"I haven't decided yet. I'd love to do something from Polo's journey home. But as I said, he was very quiet about that part of his life."

"Or maybe not," Neil said. "This whole thing you mentioned about the princess makes me think there's a connection between your meal and the murders."

"Are you accusing me of something?" Angel asked with a chuckle.

"No," Neil said, but he didn't laugh. *At least, I don't think so,* he thought as he once again caught the faint aromatic whisper of the spices. "It's just that Nakamura found notes on the bodies of Emily and Lionel. One mentioned stopping in a place called Dai Viet and these magic storm makers who lived there and ate spices. Then there's a bit about heading back to Venice with a princess and some precious cargo."

"Certainly sounds like Polo," Angel said. "But I read his account of his journeys dozens of times on my own travels over the Silk Road, and I never read any passages like that."

"So someone is copying his writing style?"

"Maybe . . . or maybe not. This is twigging a memory." Angel scratched his forehead. "There is a legend. . . ." His voice trailed off.

"A legend about . . . ?"

"It's a legend a friend told me," Angel said, a faraway look in his eyes. "A very dear friend. Her name was Chabui. That was the name of Kublai Khan's favorite wife, by the way."

"Fascinating," Neil said dryly. "How about the legend?"

"She saved my life, you know," Angel continued, with a small chuckle. "I had taken a very misguided journey across the Gobi desert, and I collapsed at the edge of Chabui's village from severe dehydration. She gave me food and water and a place to recover. We hit it off really well right from the start. She came with me on the rest of my journey."

"Oh, brother!" Neil said, rolling his eyes. "And the legend?"

"Well, she said she was a distant descendant of one of Marco's servants. There was a family legend that Polo had kept a private journal of the tragic journey home to Venice, but that the book was cursed. It was rumored to have disappeared after Polo's death. The legend said that if it were ever discovered, it would lead to heartbreak."

"You think the killer discovered this notebook?"

"Oh, I don't know about that," Angel said, laughing. "Chabui said the whole thing was just a story her family told to scare the kids. She said no one really believed it."

Neil frowned. "Nakamura likes facts, not stories. But I guess I should tell him about all this Polo stuff, anyway.

Still, no matter where the notes come from, they don't point to any kind of pattern I can make out and they don't tell us what's killing the chefs."

"What can you tell me about that?" Angel asked.

Neil hesitated. He sniffed the air again. The aroma of the spices was still hanging in the air.

"Where did you get that cumin you're cooking with?" It wasn't the exact cumin Neil had smelled at the crime scenes, but it was awfully close.

"Ulan Bator," Angel said. "Mongolia. Chabui's family grew it."

"Not a very common crop for that part of the world," Neil said.

"They were talented farmers. That's one of the reasons she traveled with me, and not just on the Silk Road. We made our way through the entire Far East looking for exotic seeds and plants."

"It sounds like it was a wonderful time."

"It was. She also gave me something special as a token of our friendship." Angel walked over to an intricately carved bookshelf and reached for the very top. "I don't know what it is, exactly, but we used it to press herbs on our travels. It's written in a dialect of Chinese that I can't understand. Chabui couldn't read it either. She said she had found it among her mother's belongings after she had passed away. She'd never seen it before, but assumed it was a family heirloom. She passed it on to me as a gift, and I have treasured it."

Angel handed Neil a very, very old book. The outside was soft black leather with the faint traces of some barely visible carved characters. Neil turned to the first page.

"It's all in Chinese characters," he said. He thumbed

through the rest of the book. The pages weren't paper—they were thicker. Neil thought they smelled like something from an animal.

"It's parchment, made from sheepskin," Angel explained, catching Neil's look. "It's odd actually, because they've had paper in China for thousands of years. So this must be European in origin, despite the Chinese."

"If it's written in Chinese," Neil said, remembering something Larry had told him, "I think you're supposed to start reading from the back."

He flipped the book over and opened it again. Some leaves and spices were pressed inside to dry.

The smell rushed at Neil like a dagger. *This* was the smell. *This* was the smell he'd detected at the murder scenes.

Neil stared at Angel, a look of shock on his face.

"What's wrong?" Angel asked.

"Um, nothing," Neil said. It was too much information, both physical and emotional, to process all at once. His imagination swirled.

Could Angel be the killer? Had he handed Neil the notebook as a clue, like the notes the killer was leaving on the bodies? Was he daring Neil to connect the dots?

"It's late," Neil said. "I really need to get some sleep. I have an exam in the morning, and, um . . . I need to prep for a big dinner." He made his way to the door.

Angel looked at Neil. "Are you feeling okay?" he asked.

"I'll call you tomorrow," Neil said, and he hurried out the door and downstairs.

He'd cycled six blocks before he realized that he'd tucked the notebook into his coat pocket.

CHAPTER TWELVE

TUNA TROUBLES

Angel, a killer?" Larry said incredulously. "Are you completely nuts?!"

Neil handed Larry the notebook. "Smell this," he said.

"Not this again. You know I don't have your super nose—'able to detect a foul chicken in a single sniff,'" he said. "My nose is much better looking, but not as, well, *exceptional* in the sensory department."

Larry hated to say anything that might feed Neil's already massive ego, but he'd never seen Neil so bothered before. He wanted to keep him as calm as possible, because Larry also knew there would be a patented Neil Flambé flame out coming just as soon as his cousin noticed the broken—

"What happened to the window?" Neil asked.

—window. The front window had been smashed into a million pieces. Larry had done his best to cover the opening with some tablecloths and duct tape, but the result resembled a quilt an auto mechanic might have made. A one-armed auto mechanic.

"Well, let's just say it was a funny start to the day."

"Let's NOT say that," Neil said. "Instead, why don't you tell me what the heck happened to this window?"

"Fish," Larry said.

"Fish?"

"Tuna, actually."

"A tuna broke the window?"

"Yes." Larry nodded. "Well, someone threw a tuna through the window."

"Threw a tuna?"

Larry nodded again.

"How big was this tuna exactly?"

"Oh, it was big."

"Is it still around? Because I'd like to beat you over the head with it."

"See, that's another reason I don't like fish," Larry joked. "Too violent."

Neil didn't laugh. "Will you please just tell me what happened?"

"First of all, nothing was stolen. And second of all, it wasn't my fault. All I know is that I turned up for work this morning and there was this shady character hanging around outside."

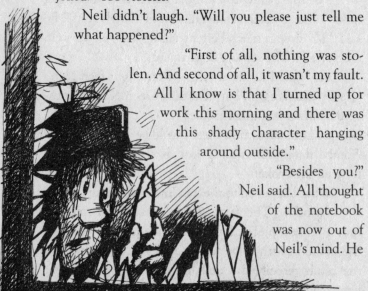

"Besides you?" Neil said. All thought of the notebook was now out of Neil's mind. He was calculating how much it would cost to fix this mess before dinner service began.

"Ha-ha. Anyway, the person was wearing this enormous coat and this big black fedora. Didn't say a word. Just watched me open up the shop."

"And you called the police, right? *Please* tell me you called the police." Neil said. "There are a lot of dead chefs around, you know. Perhaps you've read the papers."

"I know, but, well," Larry said, "a lot of sketchy characters live around here."

"Yes, thanks again for doing such a bang-up job scouting this prime location."

Larry ignored this latest insult and continued. "So I figured it was nothing too out of the ordinary. Then, just as I was at the back door getting the vegetable delivery, I heard a loud crash. I ran out to the front and saw a giant tuna on the floor and the window smashed."

"Did you call the police then?"

"Well, I was going to."

"And you didn't because?"

"Well, because of the vegetables."

"Did you say *'vegetables'*?"

Larry nodded. "Um, do you want me to tell you about the vegetables?"

"What?!" Neil's head was pounding.

"Is that a no?" Larry was secretly relieved.

"No! I mean, yes . . . I mean, tell me about the vegetables!"

"Well, I'd just finished taping up the window," Larry said, "and I went back to unpack the vegetables. I opened the boxes, and everything inside was rotten."

"Rotten?" Neil asked.

"Well, someone had poured some rancid tomato sauce all over them. I washed off as many as I could, but a lot of the leafy ones were soaked. I'd just finished when you got here."

Neil took a sniff of the air. "It's puttanesca sauce," he said. "With way too many anchovies." An image of Olive Green threatening him from the witness stand flashed before his eyes. "I have to make a call," he said, heading toward the kitchen. "Actually, a number of calls."

"Neil," Larry called after him, "do you have any enemies I should know about?"

Neil had a tiny office in one corner of the kitchen. It was a place to meet clients, to make phone calls. It also housed a small safe. He pulled Angel's notebook out of his pocket. What were the leaves he'd seen inside? He knew the notebook was important, and he was anxious to take a closer look, but the broken window, the tuna, and the image of Olive Green were more urgent concerns.

"You'll have to wait," he said to the book. He opened the safe and placed the notebook inside, on top of a small amount of cash, his most treasured recipes, and maps to the secret locations of his best suppliers.

Neil stared for a moment into the blackness of the safe. His mind was racing. The tuna could have come from any number of people. If Angel was the killer and had noticed that Neil had the notebook, he might have sent it as a warning. He thought for a second about calling Angel to apologize for his weird exit, just to see how Angel sounded, or if he said anything suspicious.

But no, Neil wasn't quite ready to talk to Angel again. Not yet. Their first meeting in a year had left Neil with too many questions and suspicions. He'd asked Angel once before if he'd ever killed anyone. Neil had been seven at the time and he'd meant it as a joke, but Angel never had given him a direct answer. If Neil asked him the same question now, what would Angel say?

Or had the tuna come from Gunter Lund? He and Neil had had another blowup just a week ago over the price for Alaskan crab. Maybe Gunter had finally flipped his lid. Neil closed the safe and grabbed his phone. He dialed Lund's number.

"Allo," came a woman's voice.

"Bonjour, Renée," Neil said. "I'd like to speak with Gunter."

"Ha-ha! Wouldn't we all. All I know is that I showed up for work this morning and 'e had left a note saying 'e was on a vacation 'to rest his nerves.'"

"Do you know where he went?"

"Even if I did, I wouldn't tell *you*. Why do you think 'e *needs* a vacation?!" And she hung up the phone.

Neil stared at his phone for a second. Gunter needed a vacation because of *him*? Anyway, Gunter wasn't ruled out as a suspect in the attack of the tuna, but until he got back, Neil would have to follow some other leads.

Why tuna? he wondered.

Tuna wasn't Neil's preferred fish—not once he'd mastered salmon and perfected the proper and safe way to cook fugu, the Japanese puffer fish that would kill you if you didn't prep it properly.

Neil leaned against his desk. He thought back to the worst tuna dinner he'd ever had. It had been four years ago, when he was ten. He'd been cooking with Angel for three years and had been gaining a reputation as a "must-have" guest on daytime TV. His parents decided that it was time for a very rare family vacation.

They had chosen Paris. Neil was looking forward to visiting the home of great cuisine.

Before he left he went to say good-bye to Angel. Angel told him to look up an old apprentice of his, a woman named Carlotta Calamari. She and Angel had been quite close, possibly even romantic. They'd had a falling out. Neil didn't get the whole story, but he was able to piece bits of it together from Angel's chats in the kitchen. Carlotta used to help Angel prepare his special meals. Then, one day, he'd caught her using some store-bought chicken broth and cheap dried spices. Neil knew enough about Angel to realize that this was an unforgivable crime. Angel and Carlotta had separated, both professionally and personally.

Carlotta wasn't out of the business for long. She moved to France and set up her own restaurant, Chez Miscellaneous. Angel suggested they give it a try.

"What you really want is a spy to let you know if your former girlfriend is any good at cooking, is that it?" Neil had asked.

Angel had just smiled a mysterious smile. "She was always very talented, but she never learned to trust her ingredients. Carlotta thought she could cut corners to increase her profits. She was good enough to get away with it, most of the time. I'm curious to see if she's learned anything or if she's still sacrificing her gifts for gold."

It had been the latter, as it turned out, and as Angel probably suspected.

At first, Neil liked the look of Chez Miscellaneous. A sign outside the door showed two Michelin stars. The Michelin tire company releases an annual guide of the best restaurants and hotels in the world. The critics remain mostly anonymous and are incredibly powerful.

Michelin stars are like Olympic gold medals. One is a triumph. Three is almost unheard of. Chefs will do almost anything to keep them. The famous French chef Bernard Hirondelle once heard a vague rumor that Michelin was going to downgrade his restaurant from three to two stars. Distraught, he'd armed himself with his best kitchen knives and started taking revenge on every set of Michelin tires he could find.

Three days and hundreds of punctured inner tubes later, police finally tracked him down as he prepared to storm the company's headquarters with a meat cleaver and a flaming shish kebab.

The two stars at Chez Miscellaneous were promising, and Neil had high expectations as he walked across the marble doorstep and into the large dining room.

The restaurant was simple but elegant. Blue-and-red-tile mosaics covered the floors and walls. It looked classy. Neil had just started thinking of setting up his own place and he was looking for ideas. He was impressed.

The menu was eclectic and ambitious. Carlotta offered everything from steak tartare to chicken Kiev to something called crepinettes de porc.

"What are those dishes, dear?" his mother had whispered to him, using her menu as a shield.

"In general terms," Neil replied, "Raw hamburger, cheese-stuffed chicken, and tiny pork chops."

"No macaroni and cheese?" Eric said.

"Um, no," he answered. He took a deep breath and inhaled the scent of the dishes that were making their way out of the kitchen. Pretty good.

Then Neil's mother spoke seven fateful words. "I guess we'll have to be adventurous." She took another close look at the menu. "Oh, look Eric, they have something called salade niçoise. We visited Nice. It was lovely, wasn't it, honey? I'll start with that."

Neil was shocked. This was a bold move for his mother. Salade niçoise was one of those deceptively simple dishes. There were only a few ingredients: fresh vegetables (usually beans, potatoes, and lettuce), tomato, hard-boiled eggs, anchovies . . . and tuna. And not just any tuna. It had to either be fresh or the ridiculously expensive canned Ventresca tuna.

Mixing those varied ingredients seemed easy, but doing it well was a real test for a chef. Too much tuna, and the salad would taste like a tuna-fish sandwich. Too much oil, and everything would go limp. Too many vegetables, and it would taste like rabbit food.

A few minutes later Neil heard the kitchen doors swing open and saw the waiter carrying the tray with their salads.

"That was fast," Margaret said, impressed.

Too fast, Neil thought, with some apprehension.

In fact, as soon as the dish left the kitchen, Neil had smelled it. Mixed in among the odors of the spices and vegetables was the unmistakable smell of . . .

"Canned tuna!" Neil yelled, shocked. He stood up

and pointed at the approaching waiter. "That salade niçoise is made with cheap canned tuna!"

The dining room went silent. No forks scraping against plates, no ice clanking in glasses—total silence. Neil looked over at the kitchen doors, which were still swinging gently open and shut, open and shut. Suddenly, like a gopher in a chef's hat, a young woman's head popped up and peered through the round glass window. A shock of black hair fell over her wide dark eyes. Even from this distance Neil could detect a bead of sweat forming on her upper lip.

She scanned the dining room with a look of panic on her face, until her eyes locked on Neil.

He knew right away that she was Carlotta Calamari. He also knew that *she* knew that *he* now knew her terrible secret. She was still a fraud.

Neil saw her mouth form the words "oh no," and then her face disappeared. He heard a furious scream and the sound of pans being thrown against the kitchen doors. He didn't want to think about how much money was being irreparably dented in there. Then again, Neil thought, if she was skimping on tuna, she was probably using some cheap aluminium cookware she'd bought at a dollar store.

An impeccably dressed man at the table next to Neil's turned to him. "*Excusez-moi*, young man," he said, "but what deed you say about ze food?"

"I said the salade niçoise is made with cheap canned tuna." He took another sniff of the air. "It smells like some no-name brand. I'll bet a lot of dolphins died to put that on a plate."

"'Ow can you be so certain?" asked the man.

"I'm always right," Neil said matter-of-factly. He walked over and grabbed the dish from the waiter and brought it back to the man. "Here, smell it yourself."

The man took a long, low sniff of the salad. Then he took his fork and tasted a small bit of the flaky fish.

"Hmph," he said at last. "Zees ees shocking, absolutely shocking." The man pulled a red notebook out of his pocket. The inscription on the cover said *Guide Michelin*. Neil watched with wonder as the man tsk-tsked to himself and jotted down notes in the book.

Suddenly, there was a tremendous crash. The kitchen doors swung violently open, and Carlotta rushed toward Neil with a carving knife clutched in her right hand. Like a charging bull she knocked over tables and chairs, some still holding surprised diners.

She arrived at Neil's table in seconds, drew the knife back and prepared to plunge it into his body. Frozen to the spot in shock, Neil saw his brief life pass before his eyes. Wow, he thought, that was a really good bolognese sauce I made last year.

The Michelin man saved him. At the very last second, he grabbed a butter knife and leaped in front of the charging Carlotta. In a flash, they had begun a duel.

"'Ave you never heard ze saying, 'Ze customer, 'e eez always right'?" the man said as he repeatedly deflected Carlotta's knife away from his heart.

Carlotta screamed in a rage and threw herself again and again at the man. "I just want to get at the boy!" she yelled.

"I'm glad I didn't mention the frozen beans," Neil called out, doing nothing to calm the situation.

Carlotta screamed even louder, if that was possible,

and made one last desperate attempt to reach Neil. It was exactly the opportunity the Michelin man needed. He flicked his knife against hers with a lightning-fast twist of his wrist. Carlotta's knife flew into the air and lodged itself in the stucco ceiling with a *twang*. Carlotta took a swinging punch at the man's head, but he stepped nimbly aside. She lost her footing and tripped, crashing into the table and knocking herself out cold. The impact must have loosened the knife from the ceiling because it fell down, hit a chair, flipped, and pinned Carlotta's jacket to the floor.

The man took a silk kerchief from his pocket and calmly wiped the sweat from his brow. He turned to Neil. "She weel be lucky to 'ave even one star after zees fiasco," he said. "But I 'ave not introduced myself. My name is Jean-Claude Chili."

Neil's eyes opened wide. Jean-Claude Chili's name was legendary in the cooking world. He had been an Olympic fencer, a gold-medal winner for his native France. But his true love was great food. He had even quit fencing at the height of his career to devote his life to finding the finest restaurants in the world.

"I would like to thank you for exposing to me ze fakery of zees chef," Chili said.

"Thank you for saving my boy," Margaret said, wiping bits of salad and dressing from her head.

"*De rien*, it was nothing, madame," Chili said with a bow. Then he turned back to Neil. "You 'ave a gift for food, young man. What eez your name?"

"Neil Flambé."

Chili took out his notebook and wrote the name carefully inside. "We shall meet again," he said.

Back on the floor, Carlotta awoke with a low moan.

Neil and the others turned toward her. She tried for one more lunge at Neil, but the knife held her in place. The front doors swung open as the police arrived. Neil looked around for Jean-Claude Chili, but he had vanished.

As Carlotta was carried away in handcuffs, she looked at Neil. "I'll get you for this, Flambé," she said.

"What are you going to do?" Neil said. "Attack me with a can opener?"

Carlotta just growled.

Now it was four years later and a tuna had crashed through Neil's window. *At least it wasn't canned*, he thought.

He shook his head, closed the safe, and turned around to grab his cell phone. Larry was standing in the doorway. "You okay, Neil?" he asked.

"Ask me after I talk to Nakamura," Neil said as he dialed.

Sean Nakamura picked up on the first ring.

"Hello, Nose. What can I do for you?"

Neil told Nakamura about the tuna, the puttanesca sauce, and Carlotta Calamari. He explained his suspicion that the notes on the dead chefs were related to Marco Polo. He was about to fill Nakamura in on the notebook Angel had given him, but at the last second he stopped. Was Angel really involved? Neil found it impossible to believe. He didn't want to put Angel under unnecessary suspicion. The man had helped Neil become a great chef. He had shown him how to run a top-notch kitchen. Didn't Neil owe him something, even if it was just a little bit of time and a little benefit of the doubt? Neil needed to answer more questions on his own before he got the police involved.

Instead of mentioning Angel, Neil just said, "I may be getting closer to figuring out where the mysterious smell is coming from."

"Keep sniffing around," Nakamura said, "and keep me posted."

As it turned out, Nakamura also had some news. "I'm just looking on the international police database." Neil could hear the clicking of a keyboard in the background. "This Carlotta Calamari you mentioned was last seen two years ago. She'd spent a few months in jail for trying to knife you and that food critic. When she got out, her restaurant had gone bankrupt. It apparently lost all of its Michelin stars."

"No surprise there," Neil said.

"Hold on," Nakamura said. Neil heard more typing. "This is interesting."

"What?" Neil asked.

"Well, according to the database, Olive Green was released from prison around the same time as Calamari. Green got early parole."

"For murder?!" Neil didn't even try to hide his surprise.

"Well," Nakamura continued, "it appears that her sentence was drastically reduced for good behavior."

"Let me guess," Neil said, thinking of his own strategy for getting by in school. "She reformed the prison cafeteria."

"For the prisoners *and* the staff. It says here the warden's nickname is now Fat Charley. And it looks like she brought peach melba to her successful parole board hearing. No one has seen her since she was released either."

Neil sighed. Things were getting even more compli-cated. Olive Green could have attacked the vegetables with the puttanesca sauce. Carlotta Calamari could have thrown the tuna through his window. Either one—or even Angel—could be a serial chef killer.

"And did you say something about Polo?" Nakamura asked.

"Yes."

"As in Marco Polo?"

"Yes. Those notes seem to be some made-up Polo passages or something."

"How do you know that?"

"I don't, not for sure, anyway. Let's just say I did a little homework on Polo, and Daidu was a fortress in ancient China that he visited. He was also carrying a princess back to Venice at one point."

"Well, this is interesting." Nakamura typed some more. "When I key Marco Polo into the database, it actually comes up with an open case file from a year ago in Venice. Some guy at a Marco Polo museum was killed under mysterious circumstances."

"A chef?"

"No, a librarian. Weird." There was a long silence as Nakamura read the file on his screen. "It looks like this guy in Italy was shot, not poisoned. And there was no note on his body," Nakamura said. "I'm going to call the Italian police. I'll let you know what else they have to say."

Neil clicked his cell phone shut and walked out of his office.

Larry had set the salvaged vegetables on the counter. Neil could tell with one sniff that they were still infused with anchovy aroma.

"Larry," he called out. "Get that garbage out of my kitchen . . . and I'm not just talking about your haircut."

"I guess you're feeling better." Larry smiled, gathering the vegetables from the sink.

"Get a new truckload of vegetables over here, pronto, and then get me the number for that window installer we used last time."

"Aye aye, sir," Larry said with a salute.

"And one other thing," Neil said. "Get me a fresh tuna and some anchovies from Gaston's. We're adding salade niçoise and pasta with puttanesca sauce to the menu tonight. No one intimidates Neil Flambé."

"Or Larry Flambé! We're in this together!"

CHAPTER THIRTEEN

INTIMIDATION ...
AND ISABELLA

The school year was wrapping up, and Chez Flambé had gone a few weeks without flying fish or sabotaged string beans.

Nakamura had contacted the Italian police. The victim in Venice was named Antonio Fusilli, a well-known playboy. But that was about all they knew. There was nothing missing from the official inventory of the Marco Polo library, so they assumed he'd been murdered by one his many jealous lovers.

Nakamura had told them about the Polo, or at least Polo-esque, notes. Italian police agreed that it might be more than a coincidence, but they couldn't figure out the connection. They had all agreed to keep each other in the loop.

Meanwhile, Gunter Lund had returned from his vacation. The police had questioned him about the tuna. "If I were going to throw something through a window, it would certainly not be a fish!" he had said. "What a horrible waste of food."

The officers were suspicious about how many antacids Gunter had popped during the interview, but they couldn't find any evidence that he was involved. He'd even sent over a shipment of fresh prawns to Neil that afternoon, as a sign that he was still in business.

Neil continued to be troubled by the aromas he'd picked up in Angel's apartment, but he still couldn't believe Angel was involved. He must have been mistaken about the spices he'd smelled. He'd have to check the notebook more closely. He meant to do that almost every day, but between prepping for final exams and prepping for dinner service, he'd had no time to do anything else. The same went for his half-formed idea of taking the notebook to a university professor for translation.

As for school, Neil was going to end the year with pretty good grades, although Ms. Cinnamon had given him a C+ in Home Economics, which Neil found kind of hilarious. Of course, he spent most of that class sitting in the back snorting at whatever recipe Ms. Cinnamon asked them to make that day. The comment "Is that supposed to be a lemon tart or a foot fungus?" had actually gotten him sent to the office.

He almost laughed out loud at the memory. Here he was in the kitchen of his own restaurant, prepping for tonight's fully booked dinner service. A C+? He didn't think so! Neil chopped some fresh endive and threw it into a bowl. There was one other bit of weirdness that gnawed on him as he gently sautéed some pine nuts in butter: Billy Berger.

Berger had stopped threatening to kill Neil every

time he saw him. A few times he had even been down-right chummy. Just the other day he had come up to Neil in the school library and asked, *politely*, if he could borrow some notes. What the heck was that all about?

Neil needed to give the whole Berger issue some more thought, but like Angel's notebook, it was something else he'd have to leave on the back burner, so to speak. At least for now.

Neil put the pine nuts aside. The customers had started to arrive. Amber and Zoë were flittering from table to table taking orders. Neil wanted to take a look at the room before the orders came rushing in. It was kind of a game for him. He could usually tell by looking at the people who would order the steak, the salmon, and the more exotic pasta dishes. He'd sometimes wow the twins with his accuracy when they made their way back into the kitchen.

Neil wiped his hands on a towel and pushed open the door. The room was full (of course) and he was sure there would also be a long line of wannabes outside, praying for a cancelled reservation.

His eyes swept across the room as he made his mental calculations: three steaks by the window, a Cajun-rubbed-chicken pasta in the corner there. Then his eyes came to rest on the table under the Emily Carr painting. Neil had bought the painting of the giant red cedars in the flush of his first month of actually making money on the place. He had it hung in a place of prominence, over the best table in the house.

And now his eyes were glued to the person sitting in the chair right under the painting's largest cedar.

Neil didn't usually mingle with the guests, not until

after they'd eaten and he was sure of some grateful pats on his back. (His presence usually spurred bigger tips for the twins as well, which also meant fewer demands for higher wages.)

But as soon as he saw the girl sitting with her back to the wall, he felt an irresistible urge to mingle, combined with an equally irresistible urge to run back to the kitchen. The result was that he was rooted to the spot, staring stupidly.

The girl had dark wavy hair that was pulled back into a braid. One lock had fallen out, and she delicately used a finger to slide it back in place. Her eyes were deep and dark and large, the color of pure cocoa. While the rest of the people at her table chatted and laughed and looked at the menu, she just stared quietly at her plate, occasionally offering a polite smile and a nod.

Neil also noticed that she smelled fantastic, like fresh lavender on a misty June morning.

Neil felt a tap on his shoulder. It was Larry. "I just came out to find you. We've got orders to fill." Larry looked at Neil's face. "Uh-oh," he said, "I've seen that look before. Did you just spot a nice savoy cabbage or something?" Larry followed the line of Neil's gaze. He let out a slow whistle. "A girl! *Now* you're cooking with ingredients I know something about!"

Neil didn't say a word.

"And clearly it's an area where you are completely and utterly and pathetically lost. Here, start moving." Larry gently pushed Neil from behind, straight toward the table.

"Sorry, sir." The words came from a large shadow that passed quickly in front of them. Neil looked up to see an unsmiling man with a bald head, sporting sunglasses and a large scar down the left cheek. The man also had an earbud in his left ear and a suspicious bulge in his chest pocket.

"Let me handle this, cuzzin Casanova," Larry said, stepping in front and gazing up into the man's sunglasses.

"Excuse me, Quasimodo," Larry said, "but the master chef here would like to say hello to his guests."

"The name is Jones, sir," the man-mountain said. "And I'm afraid that Miss Tortellini does not speak to cooks, sir."

Neil stood there, open mouthed. Isabella Tortellini? The world famous perfumier, here in his restaurant? She had only recently moved to Vancouver from her native Italy. There'd been a whole article about her in the Life section of the paper. Neil even knew of her father, a famous chef from Torino. He'd died in a mysterious accident involving a deep fryer. No one knew what had happened. That was more than a decade ago, when Isabella was just a child. In the article it had explained that, after her father's death, she had refused to ever speak to a chef again. She was sixteen now, and had kept her vow of silence.

Neil finally found his voice. "This is *my* restaurant, gorilla," he said to the unmoving man-mountain, "and I'll say hello to whomever I please."

"You go, grill," said Larry as Neil advanced.

"Fine," said Jones, not moving. "We will just leave, sir."

Neil stopped. He could see Isabella's face through the crook in Jones's arm. She was so . . . lovely. She smiled slightly and caught his eye. Then she saw his chef's hat. Her smile quickly turned to a frown, and she bowed her head.

"No, no. You can stay," Neil said, walking backward toward the kitchen, "But please, let me cook a special dinner for her. Tell her there's no need to read the menu. I'll choose the dishes. And I promise that I won't try to talk to her again."

Neil and Larry retreated to the kitchen. Neil looked around in a panic. What to cook? What to cook? If he couldn't speak to Isabella with words, he would speak to her through his food.

He did a quick mental inventory of his pantry. "The potatoes, definitely the potatoes," he muttered. He snapped his fingers. "And the penne appetizer to start."

"Gonna wow her socks off, eh Neil?" Larry patted him on the back. "Good for you, dude. Chicks dig complicated men."

Penne mantecati con carciofi e ricci di mare wasn't just one of the longest names on the Chez Flambé menu—it was also one of the most complicated dishes. It involved fusing the diverse tastes and textures of pasta, artichokes, and seafood, all on one plate.

"Larry, you're in charge of the beef and the fish," Neil yelled. "I've already prepared the sauces and marinades. You'll be great."

"A compliment?" Larry asked, shocked. "You're not thinking straight. You must be in love!"

Neil ignored that, although he had to admit that he wasn't exactly sure what he was feeling right now. (Come to think of it, he'd been in that situation a little too much lately.) All he knew for sure was that he wanted to impress Isabella.

Neil started chopping the slightly poached

artichoke, the key ingredient in the sauce, while Larry took the first order of steaks off the grill.

Neil sniffed the air as his knife blazed through the rest of the vegetables. "They need two more minutes on that side," he called over. Larry dutifully put the steaks back on the hot surface until they were just right.

Neil mixed his ingredients and heated his best skillet. All the pieces now joined together into a wonderful combination of color, texture, and flavor.

Just as Neil was about to take the dish off the stove, his cell phone rang out the theme from *Batman*. "Not tonight, Nakamura," Neil said as he ground fresh pepper over the top. "Not tonight."

The dish was ready. Neil took special care to prepare the plate so that it would look as good as it would taste. "Just right," he said as Amber and Zoë came in to grab the dishes.

They went back out into the dining room. As they delivered the various orders, there were cheers from a number of the tables, but Neil's eyes were fixed on only one. Isabella took small bites of the pasta, and even seemed to enjoy it, but she never smiled. In fact, she even left a bite or two untouched.

"Wow, that's the first time I've seen someone leave any of the penne on their plate," Larry said cheerfully, sidling up beside Neil at the window. "She must have *really* good taste." Larry poked Neil in the ribs. "That's bad news for you, cuz."

"Stupid, stupid, stupid," Neil said, banging himself on the head with a ladle. "She's had this dish at Marcelo's in Milan a hundred times! I need to make something new, something exciting."

"Stop banging yourself with that ladle," Larry yelled. "I'm getting a headache."

Neil stopped. Suddenly, over the ringing in his ears, he could hear Angel's voice in his mind. "Keep it simple."

Neil decided, finally, to listen.

He didn't need to wow Isabella with complex mixes and mash-ups. He needed a dish that was true to itself. He needed to make sautéed prawns à la Flambé.

He'd made this dish hundreds of times and had never been completely satisfied. If he were to go radical like Angel had, Neil knew this would be the one dish he would have to perfect. Well, tonight was as good a night as any to try for that perfection.

Neil grabbed a warm plate and laid a foundation of his best rice on the bottom. A sprinkle of lemon, and it was ready for the perfect topping.

Neil was like a man possessed as he fired up the stove and placed the pan on the open flame. "Just a touch of olive oil," he said after waiting a few seconds for the pan to warm. He watched as the oil expanded across the surface, then he threw in the chopped onion. It sizzled. Neil took a long sniff.

"Almost," he said, and he carefully counted out five more bits of onion and threw them in. Another sniff. "Better."

He added just the right balance of salt and pepper.

"Wait for it," he said as the aroma reached his nose. "NOW!"

He threw in just a small amount of finely chopped garlic, then a fraction more salt and pepper.

He waited, and waited . . . and just as the garlic turned golden he threw in the prawns. *Gunter, you old rat,* Neil thought. *These better be the best prawns you've ever sent me or I'm going to give the rest of my business to Marlin Beach.*

A slight bit more salt and pepper, just a dusting. Neil's nose was tingling with the sensation now. Just before the prawns were finished, he added a dash of soya sauce and then a tiny spritz of fresh lemon juice.

And then . . . he sniffed.

Not yet.

And then . . . he sniffed.

"Now!"

Neil threw in a small pat of unsalted butter.

He gave the pan a final swish to mix everything together. Tiny spits of butter splashed over the side and the flames licked the pan. With a flick of his wrist the dish was off the pan and onto the plate.

He rang the bell.

"Table seven, pronto!"

Neil watched through the door as Amber carried the plate to the table. Isabella took a deep breath as the scent of the simple dish reached her. Her eyes opened wider than Neil could have believed possible. Even the others at the table were watching her now. She took a fork and gently picked up a prawn. She opened her mouth just slightly and took a tiny bite. She started chewing—delicately, Neil thought, not like some of the people he'd seen in his place who seemed to be half cow.

Now what is she doing? Neil thought in a sudden

panic. Isabella put her fork down and lifted her napkin to her face. *Oh no*, he thought. *The prawns are poisoned! She's going to spit them out. Gunter, I'm going to kill you!*

But instead, Isabella lifted the napkin to her eyes. She started to shake.

"Um, I don't think she's laughing," Larry said, rejoining Neil at the window. "Boy, you do have a way with women. Maybe you should stick to noodles."

"Oh my god," Neil said out loud, backing away from the door. "What have I done? I've ruined everything."

He sat down on a stool and put his head in his hands. Neil had failed.

Self-doubt, even the first inkling of it, was new to Neil. How was he supposed to react? Should he pretend that it didn't matter to him—just shrug and shake it off? Or would he have to accept that even the best cooks aren't perfect? He was at a total loss.

A knock on the kitchen door interrupted his thoughts, and Jones stomped in. *Uh-oh*, Neil thought, and he braced for a smash to the jaw or bullet in the head.

Instead, Jones stood in front of him and said, "Sir, Ms. Tortellini would like a word." Before Neil could reply, the bodyguard stepped aside and in walked Isabella, the traces of tears still in her eyes.

"Signor Flambé," she said. "I just wanted to say thank you."

For the second time that night, Neil Flambé was absolutely speechless.

CHAPTER FOURTEEN

BUMPED OFF AT THE BISTRO

Sean Nakamura dialed again and again. Nothing. Neil was refusing to pick up.

"Another chef dead, and he's not answering his phone," Nakamura yelled at no one in particular.

"Should we wait any longer before taking this stiff to the morgue?" Stromboli asked. He and Nakamura were standing in the foyer of the Ungava Bistro. The chef and proprietor, Gaston Ungava, was lying dead in the kitchen. The details were much the same as the other crime scenes: the unlocked door, the traces of tea, and the faint hint of cumin on the victim's lips. The same tortured smile marred the chef's blue, lifeless face.

And there was another note.

"We have progressed to Great Java, but have become marooned by yet another terrible storm. There are cattle and geese to catch and eat if we are to be here long. There are also spices here that are plentiful beyond belief; nutmegs and cumin and pepper are among the produce of the island. The princess is well. The cargo, even more precious to me, has been

somewhat damaged. The crew is now moving the
barrels of gunpowder to shore to keep them safe."

"This is great literature and all, but what the heck does it have to do with killing chefs half a world away?" Nakamura said with more than a hint of frustration.

Stromboli shrugged.

"Hey, Inspector," another officer yelled. She was standing by the back door of the kitchen.

"What is it, Singh?" Nakamura hoped it was good news for once.

"You might want to come see this." Singh was using a pair of tweezers to hold something up to the light. Something small. "It looks like our killer finally made a mistake," she said with a smile.

Nakamura made his way over and looked closely at the object in the tweezers. Singh was holding up a single strand of hair. It was bright red.

Nakamura pulled out his cell phone and tried, again, to call the only redhead he knew personally.

"He's not answering—again!" Nakamura yelled. "What the heck could be so important?"

CHAPTER FIFTEEN

SO IMPORTANT

Neil and Isabella had time to exchange only a few words in the kitchen before Neil had to get back to work and she had to get back to the clients she was entertaining.

"It was not so good to make me cry when I am trying to close a very lucrative business deal," she joked. Even her voice was lovely, Neil thought, with a beautiful Italian cadence. It was like music.

Neil wasn't quite sure what to say. He went with what he knew: cooking. "I read that your father was a great chef," he said finally. "Really good with pasta."

"Yes. I haven't had a meal that wonderful since . . . since *mio padre* died." She said this calmly, but a tear rolled down her cheek. "I vowed never to speak to a chef again. My father broke our hearts, leaving us so suddenly and so soon. But there was something in the meal you presented to me that made me want to . . . to make an exception."

She focused her large chocolate eyes on Neil.

Neil could feel his face turning red. His brain froze and he fumbled out the words, "I know your father died in a fire, but, um, how did it happen exactly?" Immediately he felt like kicking himself.

Even Larry let out a theatrical sigh as he tossed the vinaigrette for the salad.

"I mean," Neil stammered, "only if you want to talk about it, that's all."

"It was a duel," Isabella said. She stopped her explanation suddenly when she noticed the strange expresseion on Neil's face. "Are you feeling well?" she asked.

Neil coughed. "Um, yeah, fine. A duel you say?" Neil swallowed nervously. "How, um, weird."

"There was nothing weird about it," she continued, angry now. "It was stupid and tragic. I remember my mother pleading with him not to go. But he was a stubborn man. He said we needed the money, but he really wanted the glory."

"Yeah, ha-ha . . ." Neil laughed nervously again. "Glory is not all bad, you know. It lets you charge a lot extra for a two-dollar spaghetti sauce."

"Glory was all that mattered to him, like it matters to all chefs. Like it mattered to the chef who killed him. If I ever meet that man face to face . . ." Isabella's eyes flashed for an instant. The she turned to Neil and smiled. "I apologize. You are a chef as well, and I have insulted you. But I must return to my table."

"Can't you stay awhile longer?" Neil said.

"I'm afraid I cannot," she said. "The people at my table are very important clients. I am trying to convince them to stop using chemicals and to use only natural scents in their perfumes."

"And the orders are backing up!" Larry called from the grill.

"I hope we get a chance to talk later," Neil said. "And I'm glad you liked the prawns."

Isabella stopped at the door. "I loved them," she said before letting the doors swing closed behind her.

"Wow," Larry said over the steaks. "What a dish. And I'm not talking about the prawns, by the way."

"Shut up," Neil said.

"Of course, you're a real charmer," Larry went on as he stirred the soup. "Can I steal some of your lines? 'I liked your dead dad's pasta.' 'Duel? What's a duel?' Smooth baby, real smooth."

"Shut up," Neil said.

"You might be in for a rough married life. Did you notice how angry she got when she was talking about that chef who killed her dad?"

"Shut up," Neil said.

"It was like that scene from the opera, *Rigoletto*. *'Vendetta del pazzo!'* Revenge of the fool!"

"Shut up," Neil said. Then he stopped. "Wait a second. You mean to tell me that you know Italian?" Neil asked, incredulous.

"Si," Larry said.

"We were in Venice together. I never heard you speak Italian."

"I believe your three bits of advice to me when we got there were 'One: shut up. Two: shut up. Three: shut up and cook.' So I took you at your word."

Now that Neil thought about it, Larry had been uncharacteristically quiet on that trip.

"Wait another second," Neil said. "You speak Italian *and* you listen to opera?"

"Yeah. Don't you remember a couple of years ago

when I was dating that soprano, Mirella Birra?"

"Well, then," Neil replied. *"Stai zitto!"*

Neil's cell phone rang again. Batman. He looked at the line-up of order slips Amber and Zoë had brought in during the past few minutes.

"Stai zitto," he said to the phone. "You shut up too." He turned it off.

An hour later Neil personally delivered dessert to Isabella. It was his blueberry-and-lavender sorbet, and she had almost cried again.

"It is very much like the gelato my father made for me when I was a child," she said, her eyes misting.

"I learned some tricks when I was in Venice last year," he explained.

"You were in Venice? So was I," she said. "I was there for a conference on the natural aromas of Asia's Silk Road. Why were you there?"

"Um." Neil hesitated. "Uh, vacation." He quickly excused himself and headed back to the kitchen to help Larry wrap up the service.

Isabella popped back in as she was preparing to leave. "Shall we chat again?" she called through the kitchen doors.

"Sure!" Larry called back from the back of the kitchen. "Anytime!"

Neil glared at him. "Actually, I'm really busy these days," Larry said quickly as he started loading dishes into the dishwasher. "Maybe you and Neil should get together instead."

"Well, chef Neil." Isabella smiled. "What do you say?"

"Sure. I'd like that," Neil said. "A lot, actually."

"Good," said Isabella. "Monday. You are closed?"

Neil nodded.

"Then I'll pick a nice place. I'll call you Sunday with the details."

Neil wasn't sure if that was a question or not, so he just nodded dumbly.

"What just happened?" Neil asked Larry. They watched as Jones opened the door of a waiting limousine and Isabella waved good-bye through the window.

"I think you just got asked on a date by a total babe," Larry said.

"I'm going home," Neil replied as Isabella's car turned the corner and disappeared. Neil was in a bit of a daze, and he was exhausted.

"I'll clean up here, Tiger," Larry said.

Neil was halfway home when he remembered that he and Larry needed to work out the orders for tomorrow's menu. They had to call them in first thing. He reached into his pocket for his cell phone. It wasn't there.

"Rats," Neil swore. "I must have left it in the kitchen after I turned it off."

He turned his bike around and pedaled back. The lights were still on inside the restaurant, which was odd. Amber and Zoë had cleaned the dining room and gone home for the night before he left. And Larry should have finished his cleaning by now.

Neil let himself into the kitchen. Larry wasn't there. Neither was Neil's phone. *Maybe I put it on my desk,* he thought.

He walked to his office and opened the door.

And there, seated at the desk, was Larry, with the safe wide open behind him. Larry looked up, shocked. Neil's eyes nearly popped out of his head. Larry was reading Angel's notebook!

"I can explain," Larry said.

CHAPTER SIXTEEN

LARRY EXPLAINS

"You're telling me this is Marco Polo's diary?" Neil repeated what Larry had just told him, trying to digest the information. "That it's not just an old family legend?"

"What's not just a legend?" Larry asked.

Neil told Angel's story about the lost Polo diary to Larry.

"Maybe this is it," Larry said.

Neil didn't answer. Something else was bugging him. "Let me get this straight," Neil said, a mystified look on his face. "*You* can read Chinese?"

"Technically, this isn't Chinese," Larry replied. "It's Han'er, a medieval predecessor of what we tend to call modern Chinese, or at least Mandarin, which is the official language in China. Han'er was the language of Mongolia, the place Kublai Khan was from. He was Marco Polo's boss, you know."

"And you can read it?" Neil was still skeptical.

"With some effort, and a good dictionary." Larry gestured toward an imposing book that lay open on the desk. Angel's notebook looked tiny next to it. "I've been translating it in bits and pieces after work ever since you brought it in here. I didn't want to say anything until I had a better idea of what it actually says."

"Wait, wait, wait." Neil held up his hands and shook his head in disbelief. "HOW can you read Ham'er?"

"It's HAN, not HAM. Is everything about food for you?" Larry sighed. "Don't you remember that girl I was dating, Shu Li?"

"Um, shocking as it might seem, I've stopped keeping a chart of all your former girlfriends."

"Yeah, I ran out of ink, too," Larry said with a grin. "Anyway, she was studying medieval Chinese history. And she had the most beautiful hair." Larry looked wistfully into the air.

Neil snapped his fingers. "Focus!"

"Well, anyway, I learned some Han'er to help her with her PhD. That's basically the story, at least the parts you need to know," Larry continued, winking. "As for the notebook, I've only translated the first few passages, but they're pretty interesting."

Larry told Neil about Polo's description of the princess, eating whitefish with some emperor, and being marooned off the shore of Java.

"That matches the notes," Neil said, thinking out loud.

"What notes?" Larry asked. Neil was about to explain when he stopped, his mouth half-opened. How trustworthy was Larry, really?

"Before I tell you anything else, maybe you can

explain to me how you got into the safe. WAIT, let me guess. It has to do with some ex-girlfriend who was a bank robber."

"You met Lisa?" Larry asked, surprised. "She did teach me a lot, but not how to crack a safe. Truth is, I was standing behind you once when you opened it."

"And you say you've been translating the notebook ever since?"

"No. I saw you open the safe weeks before you brought the notebook here."

"So you've been into the safe before?"

"Um, yeah. Lots of times," Larry admitted sheepishly. "I've actually been reading some of your recipes."

"WHAT?!!" Neil was so mad he walked out of the office and back into the kitchen. Larry was reading his recipes? He kicked over one of the stools.

"Listen, Neil," Larry said, following after him. "You're not the easiest boss to work for, you know. You're pretty demanding. Actually, you're *not* pretty when you're demanding. You can be kind of a jerk."

"I hold you to a high standard. But it's no higher than the one I use for myself." Neil was now marching up and down the aisles between the counters, waving his arms. "The customers hold us to that as well. I don't plan on going easy on anybody!"

Larry looked at Neil and grinned. "That's not what I meant. It's just that you're hard to impress."

Neil stopped and glared at his cousin. Was Larry more sneaky than he seemed? "So you're stealing my recipes and selling them to the highest bidder? Getting back at me for being too demanding, is that it?"

Larry was clearly hurt. "I would never do that," he

said, sinking back against the counter. "I'm just trying to be more of a help in the kitchen. This is kind of my place, too, you know."

"Aha! Maybe your plan is to get rid of me and take over?" Neil was really angry now. There were lots of valuable things in that safe.

"I just want the place to succeed, that's all. Do you honestly think I could run a kitchen on my own?" Larry asked, staring intently at Neil. "Honestly?"

Neil debated this. Larry *had* been showing more flair around the kitchen lately, but not enough to run the place. Maybe he *was* just trying to help.

Larry smiled at him. "I mean, remember the time I used that expensive pasta pot to tie-dye a T-shirt? And when I used the stove to dry my rubber boots?"

"That's why we needed to go to that duel in Venice—to get money for another one," Neil reminded him.

"Yeah, so clearly I still have a whole lot to learn about chef-ing. That's all I'm trying to do."

Larry was right about his skills, Neil thought. He still wasn't head chef material, not by a long shot, and there was no way this place was going to make money with mediocre food. They needed each other.

"Don't worry," Larry said. "My evil plan is to usurp you in a couple of years, not today." He patted Neil on the shoulder. "Partners?"

Neil reminded himself that Larry could read the notebook. At the very least that would save him a trip to the university. It might even help him crack the case and determine whether or not Angel was implicated.

"Keep translating," Neil said. "I'll finish cleaning the kitchen."

"You got it!" Larry beamed as he made his way back into the office.

CHAPTER SEVENTEEN

SUSHI AND NOT-SO-SWEET DREAMS

Sean Nakamura sat in his office and waited for his cell phone to ring. His head bobbed as he fought off sleep.

The Nose must have picked up his messages by now, so why hadn't he called? In a few hours the morning papers would have the news of the latest murder on the front page. Nakamura had hoped to do some work with Neil before there were even more reporters crawling all over the crime scene.

That's one hope dashed, he thought as the clock on his office wall ticked closer to three in the morning. His eyelids felt heavy. He tried to concentrate on the clock, or his phone, but that just made him sleepier. His head bobbed down again, and his chin touched his chest. His eyes closed completely.

He heard his father's voice.

"Sean," his father was saying. "Sean. Have some lunch."

His father was still alive? He was cooking!

"This must be a dream," Sean said.

His father said nothing.

Sean's father had been a great sushi chef in Japan. When he was in his twenties he had come to North America to start his own place. Sadly, that was before North Americans were ready to eat raw fish or anything green with a name like wasabi. Mr. Nakamura had ended his career making deep-fried chicken balls and sweet-and-sour pork in an "authentic Chinese café." He'd become so bitter by the end of his life that he'd refused to let his son even consider pursuing a life in the kitchen.

Sean caught a glimpse of himself in the polished glass that separated his stool from the counter where his father was making sushi. He was a young boy again.

Sean banged his chopsticks on the counter in anticipation.

"Dad?" young Sean asked. "What are you making me?"

"A wonderful meal of fish and rice, wrapped in nori," his father answered.

"YAY!" Sean cried.

His father beamed.

In the dream his dad was happy again. His knives flittered and flipped through the air as he chopped and arranged the sushi on a long bamboo tray. Then, just as he turned around to present the wonderful food to his hungry son, a dark figure slid into the room. Sean couldn't make out who it was. The figure offered Sean's dad a drink of tea. Sean could smell it. It was a masala chai.

"NOOOOO!" yelled Sean, but it was too late. His father sipped from the cup, and then sank to the floor.

The sushi turned into sweet-and-sour ribs and fried rice. It smelled like grease.

His father disappeared and the figure laughed. Sean felt a cold sweat pour down his face.

Now he and the figure were swimming in a giant vat of miso soup. Sean couldn't see. He called out "Marco" and the figure replied with "Polo," but try as he might Sean couldn't catch him.

Then Sean was sinking, sinking. The figure was laughing at him, laughing and then suddenly singing. *"Yorn dish bjorn, der ritz der get der goo."*

Nakamura woke with a start. It was the Swedish Chef song from *The Muppet Show*. Sean had downloaded it as his special ringtone for Neil. He always got a kick out of the image of Neil making meatballs in a puppet suit, and was almost always chuckling when he answered the phone. This time, however, the dream had rattled him too much.

"You called?" Neil asked.

"Listen, Nose, there's been another murder."

"Who?"

"Gaston Ungava."

Neil said nothing.

"Didn't you and Ungava have a big fight last year?"

"He hijacked a load of very expensive fish—some arctic char that was headed for my place."

"Had you visited him recently?"

"No," Neil said. "Certainly not since he stole my fish. Why? What are you suggesting?"

"Nothing, nothing," Nakamura replied quickly. "Just routine police work. Dotting the i's and crossing the t's.

I tried to get you earlier. I was hoping you could come over and examine the crime scene."

"It was a really busy night."

"I was also worried about your safety."

"I'm touched. Was Ungava killed the same way as the others?"

"As far as we can tell, yes."

"And was there a note on his body?"

"Yes." Nakamura read the note into his phone.

"We have progressed to Great Java, but have become marooned by yet another terrible storm. There are cattle and geese to catch and eat if we are to be here long. There are also spices here that are plentiful beyond belief; nutmegs and cumin and pepper are among the produce of the island. The princess is well. The cargo, even more precious to me, has been somewhat damaged. The crew is now moving the barrels of gunpowder to shore to keep them safe."

"Sounds like another Polo passage for sure," Nakamura said.

"But there's no real lead about the murder weapon or motive," Neil added.

"Look, Neil," Nakamura said. "It's late and we've closed up the crime scene. I'm pretty sure you would have picked up the same smells. Everything else is the same. Get some sleep and drop by the precinct tomorrow. I'd like to talk to you some more about the case."

"Actually, I can't make it tomorrow," Neil said. "We're hosting a big private party for some Hollywood types. Saturday's busy too. How about Sunday?"

"Sadly, I will be at work, so I guess that'll have to do. As long as you promise to actually answer your phone if I call over the weekend."

"If I'm not in the middle of a soufflé or a béchamel sauce," Neil said.

"I'll take that as a qualified yes."

"One other thing," Neil said. "When I come in, can I bring Larry?"

"For what? Comic relief?"

"Well, he's certainly funnier than you," Neil replied. "I'll explain on Sunday."

"Okay. See you then," Nakamura said. He hung up the phone. He'd decided not to ask Neil directly about the hair they'd found at Ungava's place. The lab would have a DNA profile in a few days. Meanwhile, he would give Neil the benefit of the doubt. There were lots of redheads in the city. And one hair didn't prove anything.

Sean Nakamura was too tired to go home. He let his head slip back down onto his desk and hoped his smiling dad would return in his dreams.

CHAPTER EIGHTEEN

PASTA AND PETS

"Did you know that when Marco Polo returned home to Venice, no one recognized him?" Larry asked. His elbows rested on the counter as his eyes scanned a big red book with an engraved picture of Polo on the cover. "Isn't that cool?"

"Did you know those slices of garlic are cooking too quickly?" Neil yelled. "Those are movie stars out there in the dining room! They feed braised gourmet lamb shanks to their pets."

"You mean they're crazy?" Larry asked, not taking his eyes off the book.

"Yes, and rich, so we have to be better than good tonight. Let's concentrate."

"Some of Polo's distant relatives had even taken over his house!"

"I mean concentrate on the *cooking*," Neil said.

Larry had thrown himself into the story of Marco Polo with both feet. Every time he came across a reference in Angel's notebook

142

that required some background, he'd run to the nearest computer or to the library to sign out more books on Polo's travels. In the kitchen his eyes darted back and forth from cookbook to library book.

"This is so cool! Polo traveled with his dad and his uncle. They'd been gone so long, everyone at home assumed that all three of them had died. And when they finally did show up, they were dressed in these tattered old clothes."

"I thought Polo was rich," Zoë said as she grabbed the appetizer plates. The twins were hooked on the snippets of the exotic story that Larry was adding to the daily routine of work, but they were rarely in the kitchen at the same time. They'd compare notes at the end of their shift to piece together the narrative.

"That's the best part!" Larry said. "Once they convinced people that they *were* the Polos, they took off the ratty clothes and cut open the stitching. Out fell hundreds of diamonds, sapphires, rubies, and other gems."

"So they'd only dressed poor to keep people from robbing them on the way back home!" Amber said as she came in and grabbed the cheese platters.

"Poor is what we'll be if you burn that pasta and we get stiffed on the bill," Neil said.

This type of private party was a new venture for Chez Flambé. Vancouver was well-known as home to some of the richest—and most demanding—stars in the movie business. They had a lot of money and loved to try new foods. There was always a kind of movable feast going on, with the stars hopping from place to place looking for new culinary thrills.

But they liked to be pampered. You had to serve

them the best of the best, the priciest of the pricy. You didn't actually make money on the meal itself. You just hoped for a big tip at the end. Neil knew chefs who'd lost bundles on these dinners, but he also knew chefs who'd made thousands.

Now Neil was feeling the pressure.

Larry shook his frying pan with one hand and turned the page with the other. "Did you know that Marco Polo was jailed when he got back from Asia?" he called out over the spitting oil. "Venice and Genoa were at war, and Polo was heading up a Venetian war galley. He was captured during a battle and thrown in jail. This is so cool! If he hadn't been thrown in prison, we might never have even *heard* about his travels!"

"Throw in the tomatoes now or I'll throw you out the window!" Neil hollered. Larry threw in a bowl full of freshly chopped tomatoes and tossed them in the pan. Neil was busy with his trademark potatoes on his side of the kitchen.

"See, Polo ended up sharing his jail cell with this guy named Rustichello," Larry continued, while adding a healthy dose of chopped basil and some sea salt to the bubbling sauce. "Rustichello was a romance writer. They had lots of time to kill sitting around the cell, so Polo told him all about his travels. Rustichello knew a good story when he heard one and convinced Polo that they should write down the whole thing. Polo even had his personal dairies sent to him from Venice."

"Fascinating," Neil called back. "Now fire up the grill again. Zoë just brought in an order for five Kobe steaks."

"Get this! Polo already had lots of practice telling

people about himself. He used to sit for days in the Mongol court, regaling Kublai Khan with tales of the wonders he'd seen. It was kind of a standing imperial order that Polo had to come to the palace everyday with a new story." Larry looked up from the book with a giant grin and a flourish of his hands. "Hey! I'm like a modern day Marco Polo!"

"Does that make me the modern Kublai Khan?" Neil asked.

"I guess it does!" Larry said.

"Then I order you to put the book down and concentrate on your cooking."

"Yup, you are just like Khan. He could be a tyrant too."

It had taken him more than a week, but Larry had translated almost half of Angel's notebook. It chronicled Polo's journey home in great detail. But the language was hard and it was slow work.

"You know what's really weird?" Larry asked.

"You," Neil said.

"Ha-ha. No. I mean weird about Angel's notebook. It's way different from the official version of the story that Polo and Rustichello put together. They just kind of skip over the whole journey home from China in a few words. But in Angel's notebook Polo describes everything about the trip."

"Like what?" Amber called over her shoulder as she grabbed a tray of pasta dishes.

"Well, like where they stopped, what they ate. Polo

wrote down lots of stories the locals told him on the way. There are long descriptions of pirate attacks, and there's this cool story about a battle involving ten-foot-long spears. Lots of references to gunpowder too."

"Just like a couple of the killer's notes," Neil said, when he saw that both twins were in the dining room and out of earshot.

"Yeah." Larry nodded. "But the killer left out all sorts of stuff that Polo talks about in Angel's notebook . . . like the stories and some of the meals."

"There must be some hidden method or pattern to the choices, but what is it?" Neil wondered out loud as he chopped some leeks.

"Unless it's just some total nutball who's picking the passages at random," Larry suggested.

"Nakamura seemed pretty convinced that the killer is leaving clues that tie together," Neil said. "Some sort of pattern that the killer is daring us to discover."

"And so we shall!" Larry yelled, turning his attention back to his books.

Neil didn't mention an odd discovery *he'd* made about Angel's notebook. A couple of days before, Larry had walked over to Neil to show him something from the beginning of the notebook. He'd opened it right in front of Neil. It was the first time Neil had seen the notebook opened to the first page since he'd been at Angel's.

Once again, Neil had noticed a smell. But it wasn't quite the same this time.

When Neil had opened the book in Angel's apartment the mystery smell had been unmistakable. But when Larry opened the notebook in their kitchen, the smell was gone. Instead, the pages smelled more like the spices in a chai, but *only* like that.

Neil checked the book and saw the same spice leaves pressed between the pages. He was perplexed. Had he been mistaken about the notebook? Was Angel concocting the poison in his kitchen? Had he been wrong about the origin of the smell? Or was he just plain wrong about what he'd smelled at Angel's in the first place?

"You know the weirdest thing about Marco Polo, and I mean the *weirdest* thing?" Larry called out as he threw some pasta into the saucepan. "In all his official writing with Rustichello, about all his years in Asia, Polo doesn't once mention having tea! He was in China, for crying out loud!"

"And in Angel's notebook?"

"He mentions it all the time. He visited tea shops, drank tea when he was marooned in Java, drank tea with Kublai Khan."

"So why not mention it in the official version?" Neil wondered.

"Dunno," Larry said. "Weird though, eh?"

"Yes." Neil nodded. "That's definitely weird." Neil had an inkling it might not just be weird but important as well. Unfortunately, he was yanked out of this thought by the smell of an overcooking slice of bacon—Italian pancetta, actually—right under his nose.

"We have seventeen more orders for the pasta carbonara," Amber called as she walked through the kitchen doors.

"Seventeen orders at the *same time*?" Neil yelled. "How many people are out there?"

"It's not for the people," Amber said as she headed

back to the dining room. "London Marriott just arrived and brought her dogs."

Neil's arms fell limply to his sides.

Larry started laughing so hard he doubled over. "You've arrived in Hollywood now!" he forced out between guffaws. "Cooking for the pets to the stars!"

Neil's cell phone went off. Batman again.

"It's Purina on the phone," Larry said, still bent over with laughter. "They want to know your secret recipe!"

The phone kept ringing.

Zoë walked in. "That guy who hosted the Oscars last year wants a side dish of mushroom risotto."

"Let me guess," Larry said with a laugh. "For his pet goldfish?"

The phone kept ringing.

Neil put down his knife and rubbed his face with both hands. He'd promised Nakamura he'd answer the phone, but now he had ten minutes or fewer to feed perfect pasta to poodles and make a rich risotto for a superstar. He ignored the call.

"Get me more pancetta from the fridge," he said to Larry.

"Woof, woof!" Larry called, sticking his tongue out and panting.

"Good doggie!" Amber said. "Go fetch the bacon. Go get it, boy!"

Neil felt his shoulders slump as he heated every pan he could fit on the stove. He couldn't wait for the night to be over, but that was hours away.

CHAPTER NINETEEN

HOLLAND DAZE

I don't believe it," Nakamura said as he flipped his cell phone shut. "He lied to me. The Nose lied to me!"

Nakamura was standing in the kitchen of yet another dead chef—Johann Cruyff. He'd moved to Vancouver from the Netherlands only a few weeks ago. At the time, he'd been quoted in the paper saying that he wanted to be part of the most exciting culinary scene in the world.

"Got a little too exciting, maybe," Stromboli said as he walked over to Nakamura.

"How?" Nakamura said, baffled. "He hadn't even *opened* this restaurant yet."

"Dunno," Stromboli shrugged. "Anyway, here's the transla-tion on the latest note." He handed Nakamura a slip of paper.

"We have arrived in Ceylon. The people are idolaters, but make trade with anyone. We must procure more goods. The food has become scarce. The crew have broken into the barrels of our precious cargo and mixed everything together. There is now much sickness and death. Many have gone mad. The Princess tried the mixture as well, and almost died. But she has now regained her health so there is no fear of reprisal when we arrive in Persia."

"So Marco Polo got into some trouble on the way home," Nakamura said to Stromboli. "A Google search last night told me that within ten seconds. And what's with this mixture stuff?"

"Stuff from all the barrels, I guess," Stromboli said.

"Yes, but what was *in* the barrels?"

Stromboli just shook his head. "I just translate the notes, I don't understand them. Singh did find another red hair near the back door."

Nakamura sighed. He was still waiting for the lab results from the first hair.

"And there are more prints on the note," Stromboli said. "The guys at the lab have only done some quick tests, but they think they might be the same as the prints on the note they found on LeBoeuf."

"But no match to anything in our database?"

"Nope. Nothing we have on file."

"How about the Italian police? Do the prints match anything *they* have on file?"

"Nope. In fact, they say they didn't find any prints at their crime scene."

"Or mysterious spices." Nakamura scratched his

head. This all made no sense. Cruyff was Dutch. Polo was Italian. The killer was . . . who knew? Possibly a redhead.

Yet there they were, all coming together, in Vancouver. He looked around the room. The brown residue was there. Cruyff's face was blue and twisted into an eerie smile. Those details were consistent with the murders here, but not the one in Italy. Were they related? What the heck was going on?

He tried Neil again.

Finally, on the fifteenth ring of the fifteenth call, Neil answered. "Sorry about that," he said. "I had to make some dog food."

"What?"

"It's not important. I've only got a few seconds before I have to get dessert ready. What do you want?"

"Johann Cruyff is dead."

"Seriously?"

"Yes. Why 'seriously?'"

"Well, I was just talking to him yesterday."

"At his place?" Nakamura asked.

"Yes. He called me up and asked me to come over. I'd eaten at his place in Amsterdam once. He made these wonderful crêpes and this amazing curried lamb. I guess he remembered me and wanted to show me his kitchen and the gas stove he'd just bought."

"Nice stove?"

"Better than mine, that's for sure," Neil said. "I think that's why he wanted me to see it. He seemed like a bit of a show-off."

"How unlike a chef," Nakamura said sarcastically. "Did you notice any strange smells in the place when you were here?"

"No," Neil said. "He hadn't really done much cooking. The stove was brand new. And I certainly didn't smell anything like the stuff we're looking for. I was only there a couple of minutes."

Nakamura wrote down the details in his notebook. "Can you come over and take another sniff?"

"I can't, not right now," Neil said. "It's crazy tonight."

"Later? We are paying you a retainer, you know."

"It might be crazy for a while. I can't leave."

"Because of all the dog food you're making?"

Before Neil could answer, Nakamura heard Amber's voice in the background, "The chihuahuas are demanding more chili con queso."

"Ugh!" Neil said. "Look, I gotta run. Larry and I will see you Sunday." He hung up.

Nakamura clicked his phone shut.

"Stromboli," he said with a sigh, "I guess we can clean up around here. The Nose isn't coming."

Stromboli nodded and signaled to the other officers to start collecting the evidence.

As Nakamura watched his officers work, he felt a knot in his stomach. Neil had always come when Nakamura called. He sometimes stayed for just a minute or so, but he came. Why was he so difficult to pin down all of a sudden?

"Pin down," Nakamura said to himself slowly. "*Pin* down." An idea was forming in his mind. "Pins!" he yelled.

"What?" Singh and Stromboli asked.

"Never mind." Nakamura put on his coat, hat, and gloves. He lifted up the yellow police tape that crossed the doorway and stepped outside.

"Where you heading, boss?" Stromboli called after him.

"I've got an idea," Nakamura called back. "I'm off to buy a map."

CHAPTER TWENTY

SUNDAY MORNING ... WAY TOO EARLY

Neil opened his front door. Larry leaned against the outside wall, snoring.

"Wake up," Neil said, jabbing him in the side with his finger.

Larry slowly straightened up and shuffled inside.

"Two questions," Larry said as Neil shut the door behind them. "One: Did the lovely Isabella call this morning? Two: Do you have any coffee? It's way too early to be awake."

They were on their way to meet Nakamura. Larry had just arrived to pick up Neil, and he looked a little worse for wear.

"It's eleven a.m.!" Neil said.

"Please stop yelling," Larry squeaked, holding his head.

"Well, get used to it, because Nakamura is going to freak if we don't get there soon," Neil said as he led Larry into the kitchen.

"As for Isabella: Yes, she sent me a text message. I'm

meeting her tomorrow night at seven at this little Indian place on Commercial Drive."

"That's great. Really, I'm just interested in the coffee," Larry said. "I only asked about Isabella to be nice."

"Gee, thanks," Neil replied. "I think my mom and dad left some behind after they went to work."

"They work on Sundays?"

"They always work."

Larry moved quickly and within seconds, it seemed to Neil, he had quaffed two full cups of strong black coffee.

"I finished Polo's book last night," Larry said, clearly more animated than he'd been just moments before.

"Angel's notebook?" Neil was impressed.

"No," Larry said, with a wave of his hand. "Sorry. Not yet. I finished the official version that Polo wrote with Rustichello. It's weird. He ends the whole book with about a dozen stories of various kings and princes being poisoned. He hardly mentions poison at all in the first three hundred pages, then all of sudden these guys start dropping like flies."

"Does he say what kind of poison?"

"No, but he was clearly obsessed with the idea. He does mention once that the locals had an antidote of sorts. They'd make the poisoned guy eat dog poop."

"You're kidding," Neil said, disgusted.

"I don't think it actually was an antidote, per se," Larry went on. "I think it just made the guy throw up before he'd absorbed all the poison."

"Good to know. In case you or I get poisoned, we still have lots of dog poop on the carpet back at the restaurant."

Neil thought of the rather crazy party that had wrapped up early in the morning on Saturday. The good news was the guests were suitably impressed with the food and the service and had paid Neil well. The bad news was Neil and Larry and the twins didn't sleep at all as they hurried to get the restaurant ready for Saturday evening. They'd also had to shell out some cash to have a carpet cleaner come in on a weekend morning to get all the hair (and other material) off the floors. After the overtime and cleaning costs, Neil wasn't sure it was all worth it.

"Never again," Neil said, shaking his head.

"Oh, relax," Larry said. "It was fun watching you cook for pets. And the star of that TV sitcom . . . Um, I forget the name of the show. You know, the one about the good-looking neighbors who sort of don't get along, but really, underneath, they like each other?"

"That really narrows it down," Neil said, rolling his eyes. "Let me guess, 'laughter and zaniness ensue.'"

"That's the one!" Larry said with a huge grin. "Anyway, she gave me her phone number. We have a date the next time she's in town."

"Congratulations."

"Thanks. And we made some good coin. I saw it in the safe."

"I'm changing that combination tonight," Neil said, shaking his head. "All right, Larry. You're caffeinated?"

"Yup."

"You have the notebook?"

"Yup."

"Let's get this over with."

Half an hour later, Sean Nakamura welcomed them

into his office. The first thing Neil noticed was that
Nakamura had taped a large map to his wall.

Large letters on the bottom read "The Travels of
Marco Polo." A red line on the map marked the route
Polo had traveled to China and back.

"Hey," Larry said. "That's a great Polo map! Where'd
you get it? I've been looking for one all over the place."

Nakamura raised an eyebrow, "Really? Why?"

"I'm sort of researching Polo's life. For the investigation. Hey! Can I get a deputy badge or something?"

Nakamura turned to Neil. "Can you please explain
what's he's babbling about?"

"We've got something to show you," Neil said, and
he nodded at Larry.

Larry pulled Angel's notebook out of his backpack
and placed it on the desk. Nakamura turned it over and
opened it up.

"What is it?" he asked. "A recipe book? It looks
Chinese."

"It's the journal Marco Polo kept during his voyage
home from Kublai Khan's court," Neil said.

"It's where the killer is getting the stuff for the
notes," Larry added.

"WHAT?" Nakamura's voice bounced off the walls
as he dropped the book on the desk. It was as if someone
had just told him he was holding a live grenade.

"This is the killer's?"

"We don't think it's THE journal the killer is using,"
Neil said quickly, "but it does contain the same text as
the notes. Maybe it's a copy or something. Larry's been
translating it bit by bit."

"From Chinese?"

"Ah, not exactly," Larry started to explain. "It's actually in Han'er. That's a—"

Nakamura held up his hand with a jerk.

Larry stopped.

"So hold on . . . ," Nakamura said. He put a finger to his temple and spoke slowly, "Let me ask this carefully. How long have you had this book?

"A couple of weeks," Neil said.

"WHAT?!" Nakamura yelled so loud that Neil felt his chair shake.

"We didn't want to show you until we had some idea of what it actually said," Neil said.

"And what *does* it say?" Nakamura stood up and leaned his knuckles onto the top of his desk.

"Well, until yesterday," Larry said, "I had only translated things you'd already seen in the killer's notes, so there was no real reason to tell you stuff you already knew."

"Oh, really," Nakamura said.

Larry went on. "But I'm on a bit now about a stop in Ceylon and—"

"And buying barrels of food?" Nakamura finished his sentence.

"Yeah," Larry said. "How did you know?"

"That was the note on Cruyff's body. If you'd told me before, maybe it could have helped me save him."

"Oh, come on," Neil scoffed. He was getting angry now. "Can you even conceive of a way to link that note to Cruyff?"

"It was on his body," Nakamura said.

"I mean the *content* of the note," Neil said. "Have you figured out how any of the notes connect to any of the dead chefs?"

Nakamura had to admit he was stumped. "We're still working on that," he said, "but I have a theory." He lifted his knuckles off the desk and straightened up. He rubbed his mustache. "And that book you've *finally* brought in might help."

"How?" Larry and Neil spoke at the same time.

Nakamura pointed at the far wall. "Well, it brings me back to this Polo map."

They all walked over to the wall.

"I've used pushpins to mark all the places named in the killer's notes," Nakamura said. "Daidu is the Mongol name for Beijing, as it turns out. Great Java is what Borneo used to be called. Ceylon is Sri Lanka. Notice anything?"

"Yes," Neil said. "They're all near Polo's homeward journey, but they don't match up with the red line that's printed on the map."

Neil took his finger and traced the red line. Little drawings of ships decorated a route that started in Daidu, but then passed through Sumatra. The pin Nakamura had used to mark the first stop from the killer's notes was stuck off the coast of Java. "Those places are hundreds of miles apart," Neil said. "How could the mapmakers get it so wrong?"

"Well, it's not totally crazy," Larry said. "Remember, Polo and Rustichello didn't waste much ink on the journey home—just a few lines. Historians have done their best to discover the true route, but they've never agreed on Polo's exact journey."

"Um, yeah," Nakamura said, stunned. "Thanks, uh, Professor."

"He comes up with stuff like that that a lot," Neil said. "You get used to it."

Larry beamed and gestured toward the map. "But you can see that the killer *is* going in the right sequential order."

"How do you mean?" Nakamura asked.

"Well, imagine there's a red line that goes through your pins. It would be a straight line, from Daidu toward Venice. The killer's not skipping around or going backward and then forward. The killer is choosing the notes according to the direction Polo took home, if not the exact route on this map."

"So that's where the notebook comes in," Neil said. "It tells us the *real* route Polo took home!"

"Exactly." Larry nodded enthusiastically. "It's the route that Polo didn't reveal, for whatever reason, in the official version."

"And if we know where Polo *really* headed next," Nakamura added, looking at the map closely, "we can at least try to guess where the killer is headed next."

"That's only if we can figure out how the place references in the notes relate to the chefs," Neil said, staring intently at Nakamura's pushpins.

"*Before* they get killed," Nakamura said.

"Why don't you just stake out all the restaurants in Vancouver?" Larry asked.

"Do you know how many chefs there are in this city?" Nakamura replied. "Thousands. And there are dozens from each place Polo could have visited on his way back to Venice."

"I thought Cruyff was Dutch," Neil said.

Nakamura nodded. "But when we searched his

personal papers, it turned out he was actually born and raised in Sri Lanka. It used to be a Dutch colony."

"And Sri Lanka was known as Ceylon in Polo's days," Larry said. "I don't know where Polo headed to next. I had to stop translating because of that visit from the petting zoo we had the other night."

Neil didn't say anything. Cruyff was from Sri Lanka? This was tweaking something in his memory. But he was interrupted by Nakamura.

"So I just have two questions left for you," he said, sitting back down behind his desk.

"First of all, Neil"—Nakamura pulled an evidence bag from his top drawer —"can you take a whiff of the latest note?"

Nakamura opened the bag and held it under Neil's nose.

"It's the same smells," Neil said.

"Okay. Second question: Where did you get this notebook?"

Neil had been worried this question would come up. He shuffled his feet. "I'd rather not say. At least not right now."

"This is a police investigation, Nose," Nakamura said. "I've got five dead chefs out there!"

"I know," Neil said, avoiding Nakamura's gaze. "But it's personal."

"Fine," Nakamura said, shaking his head. "But I'm seizing this notebook right now." He picked it up and slid it into his drawer. Then he turned the key and locked it.

"But we're not done translating it!" Neil cried.

"It's evidence," Nakamura said firmly as he stood up

and walked toward the office door. "And we'll get a real expert in to translate it right away."

Neil didn't say anything. He just stared with his mouth open.

"You're sure you won't tell me where you got it?"

Neil shook his head.

"Then you stick to the smells, and let the police deal with the rest of the investigation." Nakamura opened the door and showed them out.

Neil sat down on the precinct steps, dejected.

"Why so bummed, Neil?" Larry said, slapping him on the back.

"What are you talking about?" Neil just stared at Larry, too upset to yell. "They took the notebook! Why aren't *you* bummed?"

"I knew Nakamura was going to pull something like that," Larry said. "Cops always do. That's why I was more bagged than usual this morning. I was up all night making photocopies."

CHAPTER TWENTY-ONE

LARRY WALKS AND TALKS

Sunday was a light day for most restaurants, but not Chez Flambé. Neil didn't open for brunch, so the demand for dinner tables was still revved up.

And because dinner service was earlier, Neil was often more frantic than usual about getting prepped early—which usually meant Larry had to work harder than usual. But this Sunday was different.

"I'll do all the prep work," Neil told Larry. "You lock yourself in the office and don't come out until you're finished translating the notebook."

"Okay, but why the rush?"

"I've got a theory," Neil said, "but before I call Nakamura again I want to be sure."

Larry had restarted his translating work around noon, right after they'd returned from the police station. Neil watched the clock nervously as it inched closer and closer to dinner. He'd been too busy to check on Larry's progress, but he was going to need his assistant back soon.

Finally, right before five, Neil couldn't wait any longer. He knocked on the office door. Larry didn't answer. Neil turned the handle. It was locked.

"Larry?" he called. "Larry, are you okay?"

Still no answer. What if he'd been poisoned by the notebook? Neil had seen Larry lick his fingers when he turned the pages—maybe he'd picked up poison from some residue on the sheepskin.

Neil wasn't sure what to do. His only set of keys for the door was on the inside with Larry. He looked at the lock. He was sure Larry could pick it with a chopstick. In fact, he probably had at some point or another. But Neil was no good at that kind of thing. He ran over to his knife rack and grabbed the thinnest—and cheapest—paring knife he could find.

He rushed back to the door and stabbed at the lock. He shoved the blade in between the door and the frame and lifted the knife hard. There was a *click*, and miraculously, the door swung open.

Neil rushed inside. He looked under the desk, half expecting to see Larry slumped on the floor, his face turning blue. But Larry wasn't there. The tiny window beside the cabinet was open and a slight breeze rustled the papers on the desk. Neil looked at the safe. It was closed. Luckily it was also bolted to the wall.

Suddenly, Larry's face emerged in the window.

"Oh, hey, Neil," Larry said. He put a hand onto the frame and pulled himself up and through.

"'Hey, Neil'?" Neil said, incredulous. "What the heck are you doing? Where were you?"

"Well, I got through a bunch of the notebook, and then I just needed some fresh air, so I slipped out the window and went for a walk."

"Oh, that's logical," Neil said, shaking his head. "Why didn't you come out through the door?"

"Where's the fun in that?" Larry said, walking over to the desk.

"That's it? That's your explanation?" Neil said. "You're kidding!"

"Nope." Larry shrugged. "Now let me tell you what I've been able to translate so far." He gathered his notes and some pens. "I also grabbed a map like Nakamura's while I was out."

"You went for a heck of a trek."

"Yeah. It was invigorating." Larry headed out to the kitchen counter and unfurled the map that he'd tucked under his arm. It already had fresh circle stains from a coffee cup and looked a little crumpled.

"Stopped for a coffee as well?" Neil asked
"Of course." Larry smiled, pulling a pencil from somewhere in his hair. Then he pointed to the map and drew a circle around Ceylon. "Now, this is as far as I'd translated when Cruyff was killed. The official *red* line on the map says Polo headed to this spot in southern India." Larry pointed to the bottom tip of the country and a city named Cail. "But the notebook you got from Angel says he actually headed farther north up the east coast to a place called Kavali." He circled the city. "Kavali, by the way, has been known for centuries as one of the rice bowls of India."

Neil didn't respond. "Rice bowl," he muttered, chewing meditatively on his lip. "Eastern India!" He quickly walked over to his cell phone and dialed Nakamura.

The inspector answered on the third ring.

"Why are you always laughing when I call you?" Neil asked.

"I was just reading a funny book," Nakamura lied. The image of Neil as a Muppet was still floating before his eyes. "What can I do for you?"

"I know the killer's next target," Neil said confidently. "It's Vinjay Daloo."

CHAPTER TWENTY-TWO

DINNER AT DALOO'S

Nakamura had personally signed the order for the sting operation at Daloo's. It wasn't going to be cheap. Usually, the police would order burgers or a pizza during a stakeout. Daloo had insisted he would rather be killed than allow that to happen. He offered to cook for the officers, at a twenty percent discount. Otherwise, no sting. Nakamura couldn't believe it, but Daloo insisted.

As a result, twenty undercover cops were about to be treated to a world-class Indian meal on the police force's tab. He'd had to beat back the volunteers with a stick.

But the Nose made a very convincing argument. Larry had somehow determined that eastern India was the next stop on the Polo tour, and this had confirmed a theory Neil had been working out. He'd explained it to Nakamura over the phone not an hour before.

"The killer is targeting chefs from each region that Polo actually visited," Neil blurted out almost as soon as Nakamura had answered. "Not the best chefs, mind you, but the second best."

"Second best?" Nakamura said.

"Well, the chef who cooks the second-best meals from each region."

"Who's the best?"

"Me, you dolt" Neil said matter-of-factly. "Emily Almond was from Beijing, known as Daidu. That was the starting point for the return journey."

"Okay, I'm with you so far," Nakamura said.

"Good, because it's about to get tricky."

"Okay."

"It's not just *where* the chefs came from," Neil continued as slowly as his jumping nerves would allow, "but also *what they cook*."

"Explain that a little more, please," Nakamura said.

"Okay. Emily was from Beijing, so that makes sense, right? But Lionel wasn't from anywhere in Asia. That's what had me stumped before. But it turns out there *is* a link between Lionel and the place that's named in the note the killer left on his body."

"And that is?"

"I should have figured out the connection earlier!" Neil said. "I gave the killer too much credit."

"Okay, Nose. Check the ego trip, slow down, and spell it out for me, please."

"All right. Lionel wasn't from Asia, but his food—or at least his *specialty*—was. I could tell by smell that Perch *always* used imported whitefish. According to Larry, Polo stopped on the island of Hainan. Have you ever tasted mackerel from Hainan? It's exquisite."

"All right. So the killer is choosing victims based on either where they came from or where their specialty came from?"

"Yes."

"Okay, but what about LeBoeuf? He was French and cooked French food, like that goose liver pâté."

"True. But according to Polo's private notebook, Polo went from Hainan to Vietnam. I'm one hundred percent certain that LeBoeuf trained for a time in Vietnam, which is a former French colony."

"Why are you so certain?"

"Because he made amazing crêpes."

"Crêpes. French food, like I said."

Neil sighed. "Unless they're made with *rice* flour, in which case they are called *bánh xèo* and are definitely Vietnamese. Honestly, don't you do any research?"

"That seems a bit far-fetched," Nakamura said skeptically, "but we'll check LeBoeuf's résumé. So the next place Polo stopped was Borneo, and the next dead chef was Gaston Ungava. Was he born in Borneo or something?"

"No, at least not that I know of. But the connection is the food again. When I went to confront him about that shipment of char he hijacked, I could smell that he was salting the fish in his sinks."

"And?"

"Polo was famous for traveling along what's called the Silk Road. But he also traveled the Salt Route. Borneo is the main stop on that journey, and one of its most difficult national dishes is salted terubok."

"They salt running shoes?"

"*Terubok!* It's a kind of fish. It's endangered, so most chefs wouldn't have used it, but arctic char tastes very similar. I think if you go check Ungava's menu plan from last year, you'll see he was making this dish."

"I see some big assumptions here."

"I see a pattern only a top-notch chef could uncover,"

Neil said firmly. "You said the pattern would be something hidden to the police. Well, it's crystal clear to me."

Nakamura rubbed his forehead with his free hand and listened to Neil's expectant breathing on the other end of the connection. Could he really trust this hunch? When it came to food, the Nose had a knack for being sure and bang-on—and Nakamura knew it. But this time it wasn't about counterfeit spices or fake hot dogs.

This time, lives were at stake.

"Okay," Nakamura said finally. "I'll go with it, but I hope you're right."

"Of course I am. Now, good luck catching the killer," Neil said.

"What? You don't want to come over and sit in the squad car with me?"

"I have to get dinner ready. Also, I have a date tomorrow, and I want to be well rested."

He hung up the phone.

Now, a few hours later, Nakamura was hoping his phone would ring soon, with news that the killer had indeed been apprehended. As he waited, he thought back to the conversation with the Nose. What was the last thing Neil had said? A date? The Nose on a date? Nakamura couldn't imagine Neil in love with anything he couldn't cook.

Maybe he's a cannibal, Nakamura thought with a smile. He glanced at his watch. Time to see how the sting was going.

He grabbed his coat and headed out the door. But before he was halfway to his car his cell phone rang. Nakamura felt his heart leap. Had they already caught the killer?

Nakamura quickly flipped open his phone.

"Nakamura here."

"Um, hello Inspector," Stromboli said. He didn't sound happy.

"Please tell me you caught the killer," Nakamura said, pulling out his keys.

"No, but I did have an amazing daal curry."

"Congratulations," Nakamura said acerbically.

"I'm afraid there's been another murder."

"It's not Daloo, is it." It wasn't really a question.

"Nope."

Nakamura ran a hand through his hair, knocking his hat off in the process. "Who is it, then?" he asked, stooping to pick back up his hat.

"Ginger Naan. Her waitstaff showed up to help her prep for some party and they found her with a blue face . . . and a note."

"I'll be right over," Nakamura said. "Translate the note when you get there, but I think you'll find it mentions a visit to Kavali, India."

"Are we calling in the Nose on this one?" Stromboli asked.

Nakamura thought for a second. Neil had blown it, and because Neil had blown it, Nakamura had blown it too. He was furious with himself for ignoring the gaps in Neil's story.

"No," Nakamura said firmly. "I think that part of the investigation is closed."

"In fact," Nakamura said to himself as he flipped his phone shut. "I'll close it personally first thing in the morning."

CHAPTER TWENTY-THREE

A VERY BAD MONDAY MORNING

Do you know how much that stakeout cost?" Nakamura yelled at Neil. "With budgets getting tighter and tighter and the brass breathing down my neck!" He paced the floor of the dining room in Chez Flambé.

Neil just sat in a chair, shaking his head.

"But I have to be right," Neil said, incredulous. Ginger Naan? Sure, she was from the same part of the world as Daloo, but Daloo was far and away the better chef. Naan was a wizard with flatbreads, but she was little more than a one-trick wonder.

Neil shook his head. "I just don't understand."

"I do," Nakamura said. "You're in over your head, Neil. And now I'm in over my budget, and over my patience. And I'm *still* nowhere close to catching the killer."

"What are you saying?" Neil was having trouble processing everything Nakamura was spouting at him. He'd been up

late and had crashed on a fold-out cot in the kitchen. He had exams to study for and a week of meals to prep. Nakamura's knock on the door just after dawn had been the start of a very bad morning.

"Let me put this to you in a way you can understand. Your ego is like garlic; it's a little overpowering sometimes."

Neil didn't reply. He didn't have anything to say. He just couldn't figure out how he'd made a mistake. He didn't make mistakes.

Nakamura paused for a second before continuing. He could see that Neil wasn't taking this well, but that was no reason to stop. He took a deep breath. "What I'm really saying, Neil, is that your services are no longer required on this case."

Neil didn't say a word.

Nakamura shook his head, then walked to the door and stopped. Something on the carpet caught his eye. He stooped, picked it up, and looked back. Neil was just staring into space.

"I'll call you if we need any help tracking counterfeit chocolate bar smugglers," Nakamura called as he opened the door and walked out.

When Larry arrived an hour later, Neil was still sitting in the same chair with a look of intense concentration on his face.

"Thinking about how to NOT blow your big date tonight?" Larry shouted jovially as he walked into the restaurant. Neil didn't answer. He had all the smells and clues and dead chefs swimming around in his brain.

There was a pattern here. He knew it. He just had to discover it.

Larry grabbed his smock from the coat rack and started to tie it around his waist.

"Or are you mentally mapping out a magnificent menu for the week ahead?"

Neil looked up slowly. "Did you say menu?"

"Um, yeah. Menu. M-E-N-U. That's what we do on Mondays in the restaurant business. We plan the menu for the week ahead. I even have a trick for remembering." Larry held up his fingers and began to proudly count off the different parts of the menu. "Appetizers, first course, second course, soup course, main course, bread . . . or has there been a change in the protocol you didn't tell me about?"

Suddenly, Neil stood up and grabbed Larry by the shoulders. "How much of Angel's notebook do you have left to translate?"

"About eight pages or so," Larry said, looking a little scared. Neil had a wild look in his eyes.

"Larry, I need you to lock yourself in that office and finish the translation today. Today!"

"Um, okay," Larry said, trying to wiggle out of his cousin's grasp. For a fourteen-year-old, Neil was surprisingly strong. "But are you sure you don't you need some help with the prep and the menu?"

"The menu! The *menu!*" Neil laughed manically, letting go of Larry's shoulders and clapping his hands. "I've been such an idiot."

"I'm all for self-awareness," Larry said, backing away, "but could you explain a little more about *how* you've been an idiot this time?"

"The killer isn't just targeting the best chefs from each place Polo stopped, or even the chefs who can cook the best foods from those places. That was a false trail! The killer is going after something bigger—something *much* bigger!"

"What?"

"It's obvious now! The killer is assembling possibly the best *pan-Asian menu in the world.*"

Larry stared at Neil blankly. He even blinked once or twice. "I don't follow."

"Of course you don't," Neil said. "Look. Hold up your fingers again."

Larry did as he was told.

"Finger number one," Neil said, grabbing Larry's pinkie. "Appetizer, right?"

Larry nodded.

"Well," Neil explained, "I've eaten at Emily Almond's dozens of times. One dish has always stood out—her Singapore spring rolls. That's the appetizer the killer was after."

"Okay. Got it. Appetizer."

"Finger number two," Neil said, grabbing Larry's ring finger. "First course. That's Lionel's whitefish skewers."

"All right, all right, enough with the finger tricks," Larry said, pulling his hand away. "Just give me the rest of the menu."

"Second course—LeBoeuf's paté chinois," Neil said, "although I think my salmon is actually better."

"Oh, I'm sure it is," Larry said with a sigh.

"Maybe the killer doesn't want to overdo it with the fish?" Neil muttered. "That must be why I haven't been targeted yet."

Larry groaned. "Next!"

"Gaston Ungava's butternut squash soup. Not his specialty per se, but the perfect Ungava dish for this menu."

"Why was the Dutch guy, Cruyff, killed?"

"Because his Sri Lankan coconut lamb—the main course—was to die for."

"Or kill for, apparently." Larry grabbed a stool and sat down, his forehead creased in concentratrion. "Now, Neil, I know I'm not a culinary genius like you, but these dishes are from all over the place. Wouldn't they clash if they were on the same menu?"

"That's the most amazing thing," Neil said. He closed his eyes and imagined the tastes of the different dishes mixing together. "You would think so, but the killer has chosen brilliantly. The spring rolls lead perfectly into the fish, then into the rustic charm of the pâté. The spices and textures are magical!"

Neil was standing in place, swaying back and forth as if he was being carried along by the flavors. "Then the diner cleanses the palate with the soup. That carries right into the glorious herbs and tender meat of the lamb. Then there's wonderful flatbread throughout the meal to lap up the juices. This killer knows how to cook and is stealing the recipes!"

"Okay, but you just mentioned flatbread. That was Naan's specialty, I take it?"

"Yes. But there's even more subtlety to the pattern."

"How, exactly?"

"Let's look at Ungava's butternut squash soup as an example," Neil said. "That soup was Ungava's real specialty, not the salted char. Although . . ." Neil's mind and mouth were racing. "Although the fish from Borneo was part of the reason the killer picked him!"

"So wait a minute," Larry said, scratching his head. "It's not only the dishes for this supermenu? I'm totally confused. My head usually hurts at this time of day, but now it's starting to throb."

"It's more complex than that. There are two patterns behind the killings. They intertwine . . . sort of like DNA. The killer is using two different keys to pick each victim. Place *and* taste. I had correctly guessed the first part, but not the second."

"So Ungava has connections to Borneo . . . through what exactly?"

"Through the salted fish he was known for," Neil said.

"But that's not the dish the killer wants for the menu?"

"Exactly! The killer wants the soup because that's next on the menu. So the fish from Borneo links Ungava to the pattern that is based on place, and then his soup links him to the pattern that's based on the menu."

"I think I get it," Larry said, although he still wasn't one hundred percent certain.

"*And* it explains why Ginger Naan was killed next, and not Daloo. We were only considering the place, not the taste combinations, when we told Nakamura to stake out Daloo's place."

"We?" Larry asked with an incredulous look on his face.

Neil ignored him. "Ginger was both from the place where Polo really stopped—"

"Kavali, in northeastern India."

"Yes. *And* she made the best flatbreads in the world."

"Which the killer is using for this menu."

"Yes."

Neil stopped and considered for a second. "Dessert is next. If we can figure out the next place Polo stopped, I'll tell you who has a connection to that place *and* who also makes the best dessert for this menu. And this is the end of the menu, so it must be the last murder. If we don't catch the killer now, we never will."

"I'll get to work," Larry said.

Neil watched Larry disappear into the office.

The killer was a genius, no question about that, Neil thought. Neil knew all about genius chefs. He was one. And he had trained under another one for years: Angel Jícama.

CHAPTER TWENTY-FOUR

DNA

Sean Nakamura sat at his desk, staring at the latest note from the mystery killer. "Who left you behind, you stupid little clue?" He looked at it from all sides and even held it up to the light.

His phone rang.

"Nakamura here," he said.

"It's Bunson down at the lab, Inspector. We've run those tests you asked for."

"And?"

"The fingerprints on the killer's notes match one of the set of prints on that Chinese notebook you gave us."

Nakamura exhaled slowly. This was not welcome news. The lab results led Nakamura to an inescapable conclusion: Whoever had left the notes on the dead chefs had also handled the notebook.

Nakamura had seen both Neil and Larry doing just that in his office. There were only four sets of prints on the notebook. One was his. One was Larry's. One, Neil's. One . . . a mystery—perhaps the prints of the person Neil got the notebook from in the first place.

Nakamura knew that even though he'd let Neil smell the killer's notes, he hadn't let him touch them. So if the prints *were* Neil's, how had they gotten on the notes? Nakamura didn't like where this was leading. Neil was becoming a prime suspect.

But that was impossible.

Nakamura hated to admit it, but he had a soft spot for the Nose. He felt protective of him, despite Neil's arrogance and many other faults. Nakamura might almost say he felt like Neil's surrogate dad. Neil's parents left Neil on his own too much, Nakamura thought. They bankrolled his business, but Nakamura wasn't sure he'd ever seen them hug him.

And there was also the fact that Neil had helped Nakamura a *lot* over the past few years. The cases they'd cracked together had helped Nakamura forge a career.

So he was going to give Neil a huge benefit of the doubt.

"And the hair from the Ungava crime scene?" Nakamura held his breath as he waited for Bunson to answer.

"It matches the hair from the crime scene *and* the hair you picked up from the floor of the restaurant."

Nakamura sighed deeply. Not good, not good at all. Still, just because the hairs all matched each other, it didn't mean they were Neil's. But it was an awful coincidence. All the hairs had been red. Larry was a dirty blond. To be really sure, Nakamura would need a hair taken directly from Neil's head.

"Anything else?"

"Nope."

"Thanks, Bunson."

Nakamura hung up the phone. He was going to pay yet another visit to Chez Flambé.

"Turkey," Larry yelled from inside the office. He'd been in there a couple of hours, working away on his translation.

"Turkey?" Neil yelled back. "Should I add baby back ribs and cheeseburgers to the menu as well? This isn't the Ozarks. I thought I told you to worry about the notebook."

"Not turkey the food, goofball," Larry yelled back. "Turkey *the place*. That's where Polo headed next."

Neil stopped chopping the vegetables. He carefully placed his knife down on the countertop. "Is that the end of the notebook?"

"No," Larry called. "There are still a few pages left. I'm going to grab a coffee and then finish them off."

Neil didn't hear him. He was lost in thought. "Turkey," Neil said softly. "Turkey, Turkey, Turkey . . . and dessert." Dessert. The grand finale to cleanse the palate before heading home. There were many great dessert makers from that part of the world here in Vancouver. Who was the best?

No—Neil caught himself. Not just the best, but the one whose dessert would perfectly complement the mix of spices and flavors in the other dishes.

There was Sami Revani's baklava. It was wonderful, but too sweet following the Ungava soup with its emphasis on subtle spices and root vegetables. Atom Havla's pumpkin tarts were great as well, but too understated for this menu.

Neil ran through all the chefs he could think of. Some used too much cinnamon, others used too little. Others too much honey, or not enough cream, or too many pistachios. Finally, after considering dozens of possible desserts, he had it. "Sumia Saffron," he yelled so loudly that the pots rattled.

It had to be Sumia! Neil could still taste the fig compote and ice cream she'd prepared for his thirteenth birthday party. That, and a cup of strong Turkish coffee, would guarantee any chef a hefty tip at the end of the evening.

Sumia was undoubtedly the next victim. Neil opened his phone to call Nakamura, then snapped it shut. Nakamura had told him he was out of the investigation. He was no longer wanted. Neil didn't like being wrong, and he really didn't like being embarrassed.

"Larry," Neil called. "I have to go visit Sumia Saffron."

Larry didn't answer. Neil opened the door to the office and peeked inside. The window was open and Larry was gone.

Sumia Saffron opened her recipe book and placed it on the kitchen counter. She looked at the recipe for one of her signature desserts: *incir tatlisi*—baked figs and cream. The figs were about to be perfectly prepared—stuffed with nuts, sugar, and spices—then baked and served with whipped cream. Or maybe it would go well with pistachio ice cream. Sumia mulled this over.

Today was Sumia's day off. It was a day to experiment with new mixtures and spices. She sprinkled some more cinnamon into the mixing bowl as she hummed along to a new CD. It was Kiran Ahluwalia, a modern master of *ghazal*—songs and poems from Sumia's homeland that were all about the painful side of love.

Sumia ran her fingers over the figs to choose only the plumpest and juiciest.

Kiran was singing about a man who would rather die than lose the woman he loved to another man. *Perfect music for a perfect dish*, Sumia thought.

The phone was ringing in the background, but she wasn't going to answer. She'd even turned the answering machine down, so she could listen to the music while she worked on her magic potions. Sumia could make fighting couples fall back in love by the end of one of her meals.

She dipped a spoon into the nut-and-spice mixture then raised it to her lips. Suddenly, she dropped the spoon with a clatter. There was a footstep behind her.

"Too much cardamom?" a scratchy voice asked. Sumia turned around quickly. A person was standing in her kitchen, wearing a bulky coat, gloves, and a ski mask. The intruder slowly pulled a tiny thermos, a handkerchief, and an ornate wooden box out of the coat's pockets.

"Who are you?" Sumia asked. "Is this the mysterious spice from the note?" She reached slowly toward the knife she'd put down on the counter next to the figs.

The intruder smiled. Sumia could see a shock of red hair peeking through one of the eyeholes in the mask.

"Neil? Neil Flambé, is that you?" She was relieved. Neil often dropped by to see what new dishes she was putting on the menu, but he'd never come over in costume before. Poor thing! His face must be breaking out. "You scared me," she said, turning back to her work. She closed the recipe book; she didn't want Neil looking over her shoulder.

"Now tell me what I can do for you. I'm working."

The intruder didn't respond, but came up behind Sumia and grabbed her wrist, twisting her arm into the small of her back.

"Ouch!" Sumia cried. "Neil, that hurts!"

With one hand, the figure placed the thermos on the counter and unscrewed the top. Steam rose from inside, and with it Sumia could smell the unmistakable aroma of masala chai.

"Tea? You're going to force-feed me tea?" Sumia said as she struggled. The more she moved, the more her arm hurt. She tried to use her free hand to punch or scratch at the intruder's face. She landed a couple of slaps, but could feel her shoulder starting to separate with each swing. She stopped, breathing hard.

The intruder was now dropping small seeds into the thermos. A brown froth formed at the top.

The intruder lifted the thermos to Sumia's lips. It smelled . . . wonderful!

Inexplicably, Sumia found herself craving a taste.

The intruder obliged, allowing the liquid to trickle into Sumia's open mouth.

Sumia could taste the chai and . . . and cumin. But what a cumin! It was so rich. Sumia was overwhelmed by intense warmth, an incredible sense of well-being. The

cumin and chai had mixed together to form a third intense flavor. It was utterly amazing. It was unlike anything she had ever experienced.

It tasted like sweet cinnamon as it hit the tip of her tongue, then like roasted almonds as it hit the middle. A rich, smoky aroma came in at the finish.

Chefs searched their whole lives for an experience like this. Sumia's arms went limp, and instead of spitting out the liquid, she greedily swallowed it all.

She smiled.

Then everything changed. As soon as she swallowed the mixture, her esophagus began to swell and constrict. She had trouble taking a breath. She reached for her throat. Part of her knew that she was choking to death, but she could concentrate only on the exotic taste. She continued to smile, even as she collapsed on the hard, cold tile of her kitchen floor. She gazed up at her red-haired attacker, who saluted her, grabbed her recipe book, and ran away.

Now the intense feeling started to ebb, and panic took its place. Sumia gasped in as much air as her closing throat would allow. She knew she had only a few breaths left. She crawled toward the phone as quickly as she could. Everything was starting to spin. Streaks of lightning seemed to flash in front of her eyes. The last thing she did before everything went black was dial 911.

CHAPTER TWENTY-FIVE

ALLEY CATS AND ALLEY CHATS

Sean Nakamura knocked at the door at Chez Flambé. There was no answer. He peered inside, but couldn't see any movement.

He had been here only a couple of hours before. Where the heck was Neil? Maybe he knew who was knocking and was refusing to answer. Nakamura had been pretty gruff during their last conversation.

He started to walk around to the back. A herd of enormous cats rubbed up against his legs as he looked for a way into the kitchen. No luck. Everything was locked.

Nakamura heard whistling and turned around. Larry was strolling down the alleyway and stopped in front of a window. He seemed perplexed that it was closed. He took a sip from an enormous cup of coffee and whistled some more.

"Larry," Nakamura said, walking over to him. "Do you have any idea where your cousin is?"

"Nope," Larry said. "I thought he'd be here."

"In the alleyway?"

Larry smiled. "I'm here, aren't I? So are you. It's a popular place." The cats purred in agreement.

"Why don't we start with *why* you are here?" Nakamura asked.

"Or with why *you* are here," Larry countered.

"I'm looking for Neil."

"He's not here."

"I KNOW THAT."

"I'm just here to sip my coffee and maybe chat with the felines."

"About what?"

"Neil, I guess. Apparently he's a good topic for alleyway chat."

Nakamura's phone rang and ended the ridiculous back and forth. It was Stromboli.

"Don't tell me," Nakamura said. "There's been another murder."

"Almost. We got a 911 call from Sumia Saffron's place."

"Sumia Saffron?" Nakamura repeated. "I know her. I've eaten at her restaurant."

"Well, maybe there's good news for your next reservation. When the ambulance arrived they found her on the floor of the kitchen. She had the brown residue on her lips, but she's not dead. She's unconscious, and the hospital is keeping her isolated, in case she comes to. We've got guards at the door to protect her, and Singh is ready to write down anything she might say . . . if she doesn't croak."

"Was there a note?"

"Yup. It mentions Polo making some stop in Turkey to drop off the princess."

Nakamura sighed. It would have been helpful to

know that ahead of time, he thought. The translator the police had hired to decipher the Polo journal had proven to be even slower than Larry. He was a tenured professor at the university, and he wasn't used to working all day. He was still locked in an interview room at the precinct translating the passages about Polo in Borneo.

"Head over to the hospital and call me the second Sumia wakes up."

"You got it, Inspector."

Nakamura clicked his phone shut and put it back in his pocket.

Larry was making weird faces at the cats, almost as if he were trying to wiggle his nose and whiskers like they did. He was saying, "Meow? Neil? Meow?"

"I'm done here. I'm off to look for your cousin," Nakamura said, rolling his eyes.

Larry looked up at closed window. "That Sumia you were just talking about wouldn't happen to be an expert in Turkish desserts, would she?"

"Yes." Nakamura said, clearly taken aback. "Why?"

"I think I know where Neil went."

CHAPTER TWENTY-SIX

SAFFRON RED

Nakamura pulled up outside Saffron's and parked his car. A team of officers was poring over the crime scene inside the kitchen, but he was looking for a different kind of evidence. He turned off his car and waited outside.

No more than five minutes later, he spied an exhausted looking Neil Flambé running up the street. Neil's chef's smock and jeans were ripped, and he had scrapes on his face and arms.

As soon as Neil saw the yellow police tape cordoning off the bistro, he fell to his knees. "I'm too late," he puffed.

Nakamura got out of the car and slowly walked over. He wished Larry had been wrong. He wished Neil had been miles away with a strong alibi.

"Fancy seeing you here," he said. "Why the rough and tumble look? Did you get into a struggle?"

"Someone sabotaged my bike. I was halfway here when the front wheel fell off. I ran the rest of the way. But I'm obviously too late."

"Why were you headed here in the first place?"

"I figured out the pattern," Neil said, huffing and puffing between words. "It's not just a travel route—it's a menu. I tried to call Sumia and warn her, but she didn't answer."

"Did you try to call me?"

"You made it clear the police were done with my services," Neil said. His breathing had slowed again and his voice had taken on an icy edge. "And besides, after the last . . . mistake"—even saying that word left a bitter taste in Neil's mouth—"I didn't think you'd believe me."

"You're probably right about that," Nakamura said. "I'd let you into the crime scene to sniff around, but I'm afraid we've already removed Saffron from the premises."

"Is she dead?" Neil asked.

"Why wouldn't she be? Do you know something we don't?"

Neil narrowed his gaze and stared hard at Nakamura. The inspector was being awfully evasive. "This is the second time this week I've felt like I'm being interrogated by you," Neil said.

"Maybe you are," Nakamura replied. "Why don't we take a ride down to the precinct and I'll ask you some questions." Nakamura reached down to help Neil up.

"Ouch!" Neil yelped. "You yanked my hair!"

"Sorry," Nakamura said. He put his hand under Neil's arm and lifted him firmly. "Now come along quietly, and we'll have a chat."

As Neil got to his feet, he felt a swell of anger. Earlier today, Nakamura had woken him up to yell at him. Now he'd just yanked a chunk of hair out of his head. This morning he'd insulted Neil's talent, and now he was attacking his honesty. Neil stood up and pulled his arm away.

"If you're telling me that I'm a suspect, then you can arrest me."

Nakamura made no move to grab his handcuffs.

"Fine," Neil said. He brushed the dirt off his pants and started to stomp away. "If you'll excuse me, I have to go get my bike out of a ditch, and then I have to clean up and get back to work. If you want to see me at the precinct, call my mother. She's my lawyer."

He stormed off.

Nakamura watched as Neil made his way down the street. Neil stopped at a corner and turned back toward where Nakamura stood watching him. "You can save your cell phone minutes, by the way. I'm innocent." A second later he was gone.

Nakamura carefully placed two red hairs into a plastic evidence bag. "I hope you're right about that, Neil," he said. "I really hope you're right."

Just then, his cell phone buzzed.

"It's Stromboli, sir."

"What's up?"

"You should come over to the hospital. Saffron's awake."

"Has she said anything yet?"

"Yes. . . ." Stromboli's voice trailed off.

"Well . . . WHAT did she say?"

"You won't like it, boss."

"Stromboli, I'm a cop. I see stuff every day that I don't like."

"Well, Saffron keeps saying one word over and over." Stromboli paused.

"What word?" Nakamura asked.

"She keeps saying, 'flambé, flambé, flambé.'"

CHAPTER TWENTY-SEVEN

STRONG-ARM TACTICS

"Traffic along Broadway is a total mess," said a voice from the car radio. "It's best to avoid that route this afternoon."

Just great, Nakamura thought. He hoped Singh and Stromboli had taken a shower that morning. It was getting stuffy.

Nakamura, Singh, and Stromboli sat squished together in the clammy backseat of a squad car. Nakamura tried again to roll down the window, but then he remembered that the windows in the back of a squad car don't roll down. A little trick to keep the suspects who usually sat there from trying to escape.

There was an empty seat in the front, but Police Chief Heather Strong was driving, and when the chief drove, there was no riding shotgun.

Traffic inched along. "This is crazy," Strong said, exasperated. She was holding the steering wheel so tightly that she looked like she might break it in half. "That's it! I've had enough waiting!" She flipped a switch

195

and turned on the siren. The cars ahead grudgingly moved to the right to let the police pass.

"Technically, you're not supposed to do that unless you're on an emergency call," Singh called from the back.

Chief Strong swung her head back and snarled. There was no more backseat driving advice after that.

Nakamura didn't say a word. He sat still, thinking. Things were starting to go terribly wrong, and he didn't like it a single bit. For one thing, Chief Strong was now in charge of the investigation . . . and Nakamura wasn't.

The chief had stormed into Saffron's hospital room just after Nakamura had arrived. "I've been getting a lot of heat from the mayor's office," she'd announced to the room, ignoring the nurses' pleas for quiet. "He's asking why we haven't cracked this case yet."

Nakamura had been a cop long enough to know what that meant.

"I'm taking over the case," the chief had said. "As of *right now*."

Yup, that's what it had meant. Nakamura was no longer in charge. Now his job was to take orders, not give them.

Then there was the gathering mountain of evidence against his protégé. The clues were starting to come together, and they were forming an arrow that pointed at one prime suspect—Neil Flambé.

There were the red hairs that Singh had found at the crime scene. There were the matching fingerprints on the journal and the notes. Then Sumia Saffron, in her lucid moments, kept saying Neil's last name, over and over again.

As soon as Chief Strong heard that, she had pulled Nakamura into the hallway outside Saffron's room and presented him with yet another piece of evidence.

"You may be interested in this note we found at the crime scene."

"I already know about the note that mentions a visit to Turkey."

"This is a different note," the chief said.

She handed Nakamura a stained piece of paper.

"Dearest Sumia,
I have just come into possession of a spice that is out of this world. I am offering you an exclusive chance to have it for your very own, for a very good price. Intrigued?

If so, leave your door unlocked between noon and one this Monday afternoon. I know you will be working then.

If the door is locked, I'll be offering the spice to Mr. Date at the Moroccan Menu across the street. Good-bye and I promise this is a good buy."

"It's not signed," Nakamura said. "It could be from any spice dealer in the city. Chefs are always looking for an edge on the competition."

"That's true," said the chief, "but take a look at this." She held up a second piece of paper. It was an English essay from Secord Secondary School, dated a few days ago. "I grabbed it from the garbage outside Chez Flambé."

"That's not very sporting," Nakamura said calmly.

"That's not the point," Chief Strong replied. "We're

trying to solve a serial murder case here, not play nice with our friends."

Ouch, Nakamura thought.

"Notice anything similar?" asked the chief.

"Yeah," Nakamura said, "it's the same handwriting."

The chief turned over the piece of paper. There at the bottom (after the phrase, "and that's why this book was so lame") was the signature of Neil Flambé.

Nakamura just stared at the paper. He didn't know what to say.

Chief Strong didn't have the same problem. "I think it's time we all took a closer look at—what do you call him?—the Nose?" she'd said.

And that's why Nakamura and his colleagues were now crammed into the squad car, on their way to Secord Secondary School. They were going to search Neil's locker.

Nakamura hoped they wouldn't find anything. He wasn't one to ignore evidence, but something about the whole situation was bugging him.

There was no doubt that the kid could be an ego-tistical jerk, but Nakamura still didn't—just *couldn't*—actually believe he was a killer. What was his motive? Revenge? Greed? He was just a kid, for crying out loud! He'd asked Chief Strong what she thought the motive might be, and she'd barked back, "I guess you can ask him that later. Over cookies and milk!"

Nakamura didn't offer the chief any advice after that.

He was tempted to call Neil and give him a chance to explain his side of the story, but that was the sort of thing that got cops fired. "Never get too close to an informant or a source" was even carved into the bathroom stall at the precinct, right over the line "For a good time call 911."

Still, the question nagged at him: Why was there so much evidence stacking up against Neil? It was all coming together way too easily.

Nakamura's thoughts were interrupted by the chief.

"We're here," she yelled as she flipped another switch and turned off the siren. "Grab the bolt cutters, Nakamura. Singh, bring the evidence bags. And Stromboli, get a hazardous materials kit."

They walked through the front doors, checked in with the office, and, after a bit of searching, located Neil's locker. Nakamura had a bad feeling as he stared at the drab gray metal door. For some reason, the ten lockers on either side were all unoccupied.

"Stand back," the chief said. She placed the bolt cutters over the lock and squeezed. It snapped right in half. Strong swung the locker open violently, jostling everything inside.

"Pee-ewwwww!" Nakamura said.

He had been prepared for the smell of shoes and stale gym shorts, but not for the severely pungent odor that hit him now. For some unknown reason, Neil had a cooler full of cheese in his locker. "What is *this*?" The chief pulled out a plate holding a runny blue slab of something or another. It looked like it had a green fungus on top.

"Maybe it's the murder weapon?" Singh asked. Stromboli quickly took out a mask from the hazmat kit and put it on.

"It's a block of *Vieux Boulogne*," Nakamura said. "It's the smelliest cheese in the world." He'd spent enough time with Flambé to know that one. Actually, he was surprised the cheese didn't kill someone with a nose as sensitive as Neil's. "Maybe he keeps it in there to keep everyone else out?"

They glanced down the hallway at the empty lockers. "I think you're onto something there," said the chief.

They stuffed the cheese into an airtight bag. The locker also contained three chef's hats, a couple of chef's coats, three aprons, a hot plate, a number of cookbooks, three spatulas, and a cast-iron frying pan.

Finally, under a box full of dried herbs, they found Neil's notebooks. Most of the stuff inside was boring: math equations, notes from English and science. Neil had come up with a recipe for "roasted fetal pig" in his biology class. "Don't think I'll try that one," Nakamura said.

A few minutes into their search a stubby guy with a short haircut came over to see what they were doing. He held a half-empty bag of Cheez Doodles and the orange residue from the snack food was smeared all over his mouth, sort of like the smile on a clown's face.

"Why you looking through Crumbé's locker?" he asked, stuffing more Doodles into his mouth.

He must have thirty of those things in there, thought Nakamura.

"Never you mind, sonny," said the chief. "This is police business. Now run along."

"Did Flambé finally off somebody?" asked the kid. "He was always talking about it, bragging how he had a master plan to take over the chef world. It was weird, 'cause I thought he couldn't cook for crap." As he spoke, bits of half-eaten Cheez Doodles fell out of his mouth and got trapped on his shirt.

"What did you say your name was?" asked Nakamura.

"I didn't," the boy said. And he turned and walked away.

Nakamura was just about to follow him when the chief let out a loud "Aha!" She'd opened Flambé's home-ec binder. Inside, neatly stacked, were the recipes for Emily Almond's Singapore spring rolls, Lionel Perch's whitefish, pâté crêpes a LeBoeuf, Sri Lankan coconut lamb, Ungava's butternut squash soup, and Ginger's Indian flatbread.

"Where's the Turkish recipe from Saffron's place?" Nakamura asked.

"He must still have that with him," said the chief. "Maybe if you'd searched him instead of chatting with him earlier, you'd have found it."

Nakamura counted to ten in his head.

"And lookie what we have here." The chief pulled out a small wooden box. She handed it to Stromboli who carefully opened the lid with a pair of tweezers.

Inside were dried leaves, spices, and seeds.

"Hey, Spice Squad guy. Any idea what all this is?" the chief asked Nakamura.

Nakamura did. He'd seen versions of these spices and herbs hundreds of times while doing work with Neil.

"Cumin," Nakamura said, pointing at the thin brown seeds. "And the spices for masala chai: cardamom, cloves, nutmeg, and some cinnamon sticks."

The chief smiled at Nakamura. "Good boy, Inspector. Now, I'm going to tell the mayor we've got our man—or boy—and you are going to pay your young friend a visit, with an arrest warrant."

Nakamura looked down the hallway. The Cheez Doodle–faced kid had vanished. Nakamura let out a long sigh. The chief was right—it had to be done. But this was going to be one unpleasant order to carry out.

CHAPTER TWENTY-EIGHT

DATES

Neil was supposed to clean out his locker at school on Monday, but after a morning spent getting yelled at by Nakamura, crashing his bike, and seeing another chef poisoned, he'd decided to skip it. He'd just show up on Tuesday with a mushroom risotto for Principal Ivy and all would be forgiven.

Anyway, Neil had more important things to worry about now. He had to shower and change, for one thing. He'd never been out on a real date before. He wanted to look good.

Most of his work clothes had food stains on them. Neil debated giving his dad a call to see if he had any clothes he could borrow, but his dad hated being bugged at work. "I need to concentrate to get paid, to keep you in ham and gourmet mustards," he'd said the last time Neil had called for some advice.

Neil walked into his parents' closet. There was a row of nice dark suits. Neil was almost as tall as his dad now. He grabbed a silver-gray suit from the back and read the label. "Armani. Italian, like Isabella. That'll certainly do."

He turned on the shower tap and checked himself in the mirror. No zits, thank goodness. And no facial hair, either. He was almost fifteen, for crying out loud. What was taking so long?

Well, at least he didn't have to risk cutting himself shaving. Imagine showing up for dinner with toilet paper stuck on his face! He shuddered at the thought, then jumped into the stream of warm water. Isabella wanted to meet around seven at the Indian restaurant. That was still about an hour away. *Time for a quick shower and then a hop onto the bus*, Neil thought as he tilted his head back and let the water splash him in the face.

The doorbell rang. Neil ignored it. Whoever was at the door kept ringing and ringing. *Buzzzzzzzzzzzzzzzzzzz*.

"Fine!" Neil said, exasperated. He stormed out of the shower with the shampoo stinging his eyes. He headed to the door, wiping off the suds and tears with a towel, and opened it with a jerk.

It was Larry. He was dressed in a suit, and he'd even tamed his hair into an almost orderly ponytail.

"What do you want?" Neil yelled through the tears.

"Hey, nice bathrobe." Larry laughed. "Where're your hairnet and curlers?"

Neil looked down. In his hurry to get the door, he'd grabbed his mother's pink robe.

"You should shut the door," Larry said as he walked past Neil and into the house. "You don't want to scare the neighbors. And you're lucky it wasn't Isabella coming to pick you up as a surprise. She'd have run away screaming."

"All right, I get it," Neil said, shutting the door quickly. "What are you doing here?"

"I'm your chaperone," Larry said, spreading out his arms. "Ta-da!"

"You're kidding me!"

"Nope." Larry smiled. "Apparently your mom doesn't want you going around by yourself at night anymore."

"She told you that?"

"When I called her earlier, looking for you. You really should answer your cell."

"Darn it! I turned it off this morning." Neil ran into his room and turned the phone back on. What if Isabella had called him and he'd missed it?

The screen blipped on. There were a bunch of missed calls from Nakamura and then another bunch from his mother.

"Actually, you're lucky I called Auntie Marge when I did," Larry yelled down the hallway. "She was going to cancel the date altogether, until I agreed to go along."

"You think my mom's a little freaked out that I'm going out on a date?"

"Yeah, that's part of it, but the dead chefs thing probably has her more freaked."

Neil scrolled through the last few missed calls.

Nothing from Isabella.

But there was a call from Angel, from just a few minutes ago. That was weird. Neil had been trying to work up the nerve to call Angel. Angel was certainly capable of devising the plot he'd discovered, but Neil just couldn't believe Angel was a killer. He'd figured it was time to confront Angel directly. But now Angel had called him. Neil wondered if he'd have time to call him back after his shower.

"Don't worry, cuz," Larry called. "I won't cramp your inimitable style tonight. But I do think you might want to try a different color scheme. That pink does nothing for your complexion."

Neil just scowled as he walked past Larry and back into the bathroom. "I'll be out in five minutes," he said, slamming the door behind him.

"I'll go warm up the Harley," Larry said.

Neil opened the door quickly. "We're taking the motorcycle?"

"Of course! And don't wear anything too nice. I only have one set of riding clothes, and there are a lot of bugs out tonight."

Angel Jícama settled back down onto the bamboo mat he'd laid out on his living room floor. Incense burned in a small bowl beside him. He needed to meditate. He needed to completely forget the last few minutes.

He'd just spoken to Neil.

The phone had rung just as Angel was getting ready to meditate on his menu. It was his own special ritual. He spent an hour each afternoon sitting still, reflecting on how to best prepare his Silk Road selections.

Some days he would spend the entire time just imagining the taste of the garlic. How should it be chopped? How should it be sautéed? Once he'd arrived at a sense of calm certainty, he would get up, head to the kitchen, and make dinner.

Neil's call had come just as Angel was about to light the incense. Their conversation had started with a bang and ended with a bang, like two unbearable dashes of cayenne pepper.

"I just want you to know that I don't think you're the killer," Neil had blurted out.

"Um, hello to you, too," Angel said. "I wasn't aware I was a suspect, but thanks for the vote of confidence."

"It's just that, well," Neil stammered, "I smelled this smell in your place the other day."

"Smell?"

"It smelled like the brown residue the cops have been finding on the lips of the dead chefs. I think it had something to do with the spices and dried leaves from your notebook."

"I thought you might have the notebook. That's why I called you. I was worried that I'd lost it."

"Um, well, the police have it, actually."

"What?"

"Well, we went to Nakamura's office to show him the notebook. I didn't tell him we got it from you. Angel, your notebook is Polo's secret diary—the one from your friend's family legend and the same one the killer has been using for the notes."

For a moment, Angel didn't speak. When he did, his voice was filled with awe. "I never even suspected! I guess I should have taken Chabui's story more seriously."

"Angel, I can't talk long, but I have an important question. Where did you get the leaves that are inside the notebook?"

"Everywhere, really. When Chabui and I traveled together we went to Borneo, India—"

"Northern India? Like Kavali?"

"Yes, and also Vietnam, Sri Lanka, Turkey. We collected all sorts of spices and herbs from those places, and I pressed them in the notebook as we went along."

"Angel. . . ."

"Yes, Neil."

"You traveled the same route as Polo! The same route he outlines in his private journal. The same route the killer has been using to choose each victim."

"It's a bizarre coincidence, that's all."

"And the whole Silk Road theme for your menu this year is a weird coincidence too?" Neil cringed at the uncertainty in his own voice. He had called Angel to tell him he *didn't* think he was the killer. Was he wrong?

"I have no desire to kill anyone or to steal anyone else's recipes."

"I didn't say anything about stealing recipes."

"Why else would someone target chefs, Neil? You might be a suspect as well. You're always looking for new recipes."

"Or you could be working with someone else to kill off the chefs. Letting them do the dirty work."

"Enough of this silliness! You've seen my garden, Neil," Angel said, defusing the tension in their back-and-forth. "I prefer to do my own dirty work."

Neil couldn't help but chuckle. "Touché. But, Angel, you must see why you'd make a great suspect."

"Yes. But you don't suspect me anymore?"

Neil considered for a moment. "The smell I mentioned? I smelled it at your place, but when I opened your notebook at my restaurant, the smell wasn't there."

"And?"

"Well, maybe I was wrong about the smell."

"So you're giving me the benefit of the doubt."

"I guess I am," Neil said. "But why did the smell happen only when I was at your place and not when I was looking at the notebook in my kitchen?"

"I don't know. Why don't you come over and we can try to recreate the situation?"

Angel could hear Larry's voice come through the phone, "C'mon, lover boy, we're going to be late."

"Angel," Neil said. "I've got to run." He felt there was more he wanted to say, but he didn't know what exactly. "I've got a date."

"A date?" Angel said with a clear smile in his voice. "With somebody special?"

Neil was surprised how pleased he was that Angel was pleased. "Yeah, at least I think so, maybe. She's that sixteen-year-old perfumier. Her name is Isabella— Isabella Tortellini."

Angel froze. His eyes grew wide with horror. His fingers went limp and the phone slipped from his hand and fell to the floor.

Clunk!

"Angel?" Neil said. "Angel?"

Angel didn't answer.

Neil thought he could hear Angel breathing.

"NEIL! Never be late for a first date!" Larry called from the doorway.

Neil turned his attention back to his phone. "Um, Angel, I guess you dropped your phone."

Angel didn't answer.

"I'LL TALK TO YOU LATER," Neil yelled down the line. Then he flipped his phone shut and ran outside.

After that conversation, Angel had left his phone off the hook.

He'd hoped he would never hear that name again. He had prayed, in fact, that he'd escaped that part of his life. Just thinking about it made his hands shake and a knot form in the pit of his stomach. He needed to get a grip. He needed to lose himself in his meditation.

Angel stumbled back to his mat.

He sat down, automatically struck a match, and lit the incense. He began to hum slowly. *Hum, hum, hum . . . ahhhhhhh.*

In a few minutes he was far away from reality. He was back in his dream kitchen. He was cutting garlic. He was mixing spices. He was making chai. He hummed again, utterly lost in his world of imaginary savory and spice.

Nothing could distract him when he was in this state. Angel didn't notice the beeping of the phone. And he didn't even flinch when the mail arrived and a letter faintly scented with cumin floated down to the carpet beneath his mail slot. He wouldn't open the letter until hours later, just before seven o'clock, and by then it was too late.

Sean Nakamura sat on a large oak bench outside Judge Brock's chambers. The judge was putting the finishing touches on the arrest warrant for Neil Flambé—on several counts of murder in the first degree. The evidence in the locker had been all the judge needed, but more was coming, anyway.

Nakamura's phone rang.

"Nakamura here."

"It's Bunson from the lab again, sir. The hairs you provided were a perfect match. Neil Flambé's for sure."

"Thanks, Bunson," Nakamura said. There was no happiness in his voice as he added, "Good work."

A few minutes later the judge called him in and handed over the signed warrant.

"I can't believe this young man had us fooled for so long," the judge said. "It's too bad. I ate at his place just last week. He makes a mean beef tenderloin."

"Yeah. It's also too bad about all those dead chefs."

"Well," the judge said with a cough, "good luck catching him before he kills anyone else."

Nakamura nodded. "Now all I have to do is figure out where he is."

CHAPTER TWENTY-NINE

ROMANO AND JULIENNE

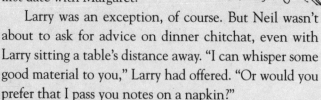

Neil felt a little uneasy in his chair. He was sitting in Yogi's restaurant on Commercial Drive. Isabella hadn't arrived yet, and he was trying to play out in his mind how he should act when she got there.

Romance, like cooking, wasn't a Flambé family tradition. Neil's father once admitted he'd hired a consultant to write a script for his first date with Margaret.

Larry was an exception, of course. But Neil wasn't about to ask for advice on dinner chitchat, even with Larry sitting a table's distance away. "I can whisper some good material to you," Larry had offered. "Or would you prefer that I pass you notes on a napkin?"

"I'd prefer that you leave."

"All right, here's the deal. I'll stay for a bit. I brought the last few pages of the notebook along, so I'll translate those while you two get all lovey-dovey. If you haven't scared her off after five minutes, I'll go grab a coffee up the street and you can call me when you want a ride home. Deal?"

"Deal."

Not that Neil saw this as a *big* romantic rendezvous, he told himself quickly. He just liked the way Isabella looked and smelled and talked. He was confused. Was he romantic after all?

Neil thought back to all the meals he'd cooked for couples in his restaurant, the looks on their faces as they gazed at each other over the dishes. He'd never thought of that as romance before. For him, it was simply a sign of their happiness at being in the presence of his glorious food.

Sometimes, though, the couples stared more intently at each other after eating his salmon and his potatoes. Sometimes they held hands or kissed, and that was all the dessert they'd need. Then they'd talk long into the night. Maybe his *food* was romantic. He thought of how his simple dish of prawns had touched more than just Isabella's taste buds.

Neil had never really considered this part of his cooking life before. It made him feel kind of warm inside. That was a new feeling for him as well. He worried for a minute that he was getting sick.

"Maybe there's hope for you yet," Angel's voice said inside his head. For a moment, Neil considered calling Angel again, just to see if everything was all right.

But then Isabella walked in. Her hair was down, falling in ringlets around her face. She wore no makeup; she didn't need to, Neil thought. Her skin was the color of a fine olive oil. She was wearing a cashmere shawl, the color of cinnamon. She gazed at him and smiled as she waited beside her chair. Neil stayed in his seat and fumbled out, "Um, hello, and um, thanks for, um, coming and um . . . good evening."

"*Buona sera,*" she interrupted. "And what does a lady have to do to get some help with her chair?" Neil was up like a shot, cursing his own rudeness and lack of manners. But Isabella just laughed again and said that she didn't expect a fourteen-year-old to know about the ways of the world.

Neil's face turned bright red. "I'll be fifteen in a couple of months," he said.

Now it was Isabella's turn to feel bad. "No, no! I was only joking. I am very glad to be here and very impressed by your suit and your cleanliness." Neil had worn one of his old chef's jackets on top of the Armani suit for the ride over. Neil suspected that Larry had tried to hit every swarm of insects he could. When they'd finally arrived, Neil had tossed the bug-stained jacket into the alleyway outside the restaurant.

Isabella's hulking bodyguard Jones had walked into the restaurant as well. He had taken the chair across from Larry. Neil saw Larry take a nervous gulp and excuse himself.

"Call me," he mouthed to Neil as he walked outside. "And don't blow it!"

Isabella gave Larry a little wave as he backed out the front door.

"Now," Isabella said, turning her attention back to Neil and leaning across the table, "what shall we talk about?"

They talked about a lot, or at least Neil did. As they

ordered their dinner, he told her how much he loved cooking and how hard it was to get anyone to believe he could do it when he was younger. His parents had shown no interest. They knew he loved food, but thought he was way too young to be near a stove or oven.

Then they'd hired a French nanny who had humored him by letting him play in the kitchen. He'd cooked her coq au vin. It was nothing more than chicken with some onions, garlic, and a simple wine sauce, but he had made it to perfection on his first try.

His nanny had gained thirty pounds before his parents starting asking questions—and discovered their son's incredible skill. After that, they'd let him cook and cook and cook. They didn't have much personal appreciation, sadly, but they noticed how often their clients kept inviting themselves over for dinner.

Isabella nodded and laughed and asked all sorts of questions. She also answered some of Neil's.

She had moved to Vancouver a few months before, on her own. Her mother had hired Jones to keep an eye on her when she went out of her apartment. He was more of an old family friend than a professional bodyguard.

"Do you miss Italy?" Neil asked.

"Sometimes," she said. "Mother visits me often, but there are some special things for sure that I miss."

Isabella described growing up in northern Italy's Piedmont region, close to the mountains. She described how beautiful the Alps are in spring and how that's where she fell in love with nature and flowers and the earth's wonderful smells.

"I used to visit my grandmother. She lived in a villa right on the side of a mountain. My father grew up there and learned to cook from her and the other villagers. He knew every edible root and flower and plant."

"It was Angel who taught me the true skills for cooking," Neil said as their meals arrived.

Suddenly, Isabella sat rigidly straight in her chair.

"Did you say Angel?"

"Angel Jícama. He's the most amazing chef! I guess he's even a kind of philosopher . . . now that I think of it." Neil was suddenly struck by how little he really noticed about other people.

"Anyway, he lives not far from here, just up on Fifth Street. You can't miss his place. He's got a rooftop garden and a backyard that's like a miniature farm. Maybe we can go visit him later."

Isabella dabbed at her mouth with her napkin. Her smile had vanished, replaced by what looked like an angry glare.

"I am sorry," she said, placing the napkin on the table and smoothing it roughly with her hand. "If you will please excuse me for a minute."

She stood up and walked away.

Neil sat at the table in a state of shock. Isabella had gone from charmed to cold in a split second. What had he said? *I talked about myself too much,* he thought. *I talked about Angel being a great chef. Maybe that reminded her of her dad.*

How could he have been so insensitive? Who was he kidding? Insensitive was his middle name! A short time ago, Neil had sat in Angel's apartment and made a quick list of all the people he might call his enemies. He was suddenly struck by the thought that perhaps he wasn't totally innocent himself.

He thought of all the times he'd been cold and unfeeling to his parents, Larry, Angel, Nakamura . . . even to Berger. Now he'd been that way to Isabella as well.

Where *was* Isabella?

He'd assumed that she had gone to the washroom, but she had been gone a while. Was she still in there? Was she crying? Was she cooling off? Neil took a quick look around the restaurant. There was no sign of her. He'd blown this date big-time.

Neil half expected Jones to walk over and smack him on the head. Neil knew that if Larry were still here, he'd do it for him. Neil looked for Jones. He was gone too.

That's when Neil also noticed that Isabella had taken her shawl when she'd walked away. Had she gone altogether? Had Jones helped her slip away unnoticed?

Neil stood up. His phone rang. Batman again.

"What's up, Nakamura?" Neil said. "I thought you and I were done?"

Neil heard the tone in his voice. Cocky, rude. He thought again about how insensitive he'd just been to Isabella. Maybe it was time to try being more considerate, or at least more polite, to the people in his life.

"I mean, how can I help you, Nakamura?"

"What the . . . ?" Nakamura said, clearly confused by the sudden politeness. "Well, since you asked so nicely, Neil, I need you to come outside."

Neil looked out the large front window of the restaurant and saw Nakamura standing next to a squad car.

"Has there been another murder?"

"Just come out here and I'll tell you everything."

"Okay, just give me a second," Neil said.

He took one more look around, hoping Isabella would show up. There was still no sign of her. He placed his napkin down on the table and buttoned his jacket.

He sighed. Isabella was gone.

He stood up, smoothed his jacket, and walked out the door.

Neil was outside only for a second when Officer Stromboli came out of the shadows and grabbed him. He spun Neil around and pushed him up against the squad car. "Hey, easy on the kid," Nakamura said.

"What the heck is going on?" Neil yelled.

"Neil Flambé," Stromboli said, "you are under arrest for the murders of Lionel Perch, Emily Almond, Paul LeBoeuf and Gaston Ungava, and for the attempted murder of Sumia Saffron."

From a darkened alleyway across the street, a silent figure watched the arrest. When Neil Flambé was finally pushed into the squad car, the figure chuckled, then took out a GPS.

"Your selected destination is four blocks away," said the device. "First, turn left. Then go straight forwa—"

"Oh, never mind. I know where he lives," the figure hissed, shutting off the GPS. "And everything is working out perfectly."

CHAPTER THIRTY

GUNPOWDER AND EXPLOSIONS

Isabella marched up the street toward Angel's apartment. Her right knee was a little scuffed, thanks to the fall she'd taken in the alleyway outside the restaurant. Some idiot had thrown a dirty chef's jacket away, and she'd slipped on it as she climbed out of the bathroom window. She ignored the pain.

It was starting to get chilly. Isabella wrapped her shawl around her shoulders and walked more quickly. She was glad she'd brought it with her. She'd figured she might need to use it as a rope to lower herself out of the restaurant. This was one trip on which she didn't want Jones, or Neil Flambé, tagging along. Luckily, the window had been large and on the ground floor, so she was able to jump out quickly, before being followed.

Neil had said she'd easily recognize Angel Jícama's apartment. As she crossed Fourth Street she heard the faint bleating of a goat and caught the unmistakable smell of purple hyacinth carried on the breeze. She smiled. Just about there.

The building almost looked abandoned. The brick

was dirty and old, and a few of the windows on the main floor were covered in plywood. There was only one light on, and it shone from a window on the top floor.

"Angel," Isabella whispered to the shadows.

It was fate that had brought her to Vancouver, it had to be. She was finally going to come face-to-face with the man who had killed her father.

Larry sat down with his third coffee. He'd snagged a private booth at the café and had his Han'er dictionary and the photocopied pages of Polo's notebook spread out in front of him. He had scribbled notes and corrections on every available bit of white space.

He took a big slurp. "Ahhhh," he said with a smile. "Caffeine and the great Kublai Khan, what a combo!"

Larry had made a bet with himself that Neil would screw up the date with Isabella by the time he'd finished his second cup. Miraculously, Neil hadn't phoned yet. In fact, Larry had had enough time to finish translating the notebook.

The last chapter was weird and frightening. Marco Polo wrote it as a letter, or maybe, Larry thought, as a kind of written confession to God of his great sins. Polo had only hinted at his great disaster earlier in the notebook. Now he spelled it out.

Polo said that he had brought a great weapon onboard his ships—a weapon he didn't know was a weapon at first.

Larry examined his notes.

"We had gathered spices from everywhere we weighed anchor. We hoped to sell them in Persia for a great price. Then a calm stopped us at sea for weeks. Food ran out. There was nothing left but the barrels. The crew, in desperation, locked us up—the Polos, the captain, and the princess. Then they broke into the stores. They mixed what they could to make a kind of soup. We heard the shouts of singing and joy from below the deck. Then the shouts grew quiet, one by one. We heard gasping and clawing, and then we heard nothing."

The Polos and the princess spent an uneasy, sleepless night, wondering what had happened. In the morning Polo broke the lock on the door. He emerged to see scores of dead men, their faces blue and twisted into hideous smiles.

Neil had described the faces of the dead chefs to Larry. It sounded the same.

Larry figured that this explained why so many of the crew died on the trip and why the Polos and the princess survived. They'd been locked up during a starvation-induced mutiny.

"The princess, in her hunger, snuck a sip of mixture. We stopped her before she could consume more. She began to choke. We held her head so that her throat could not completely close and she lived. The princess appeared drugged and could not have done this for herself. After a few minutes she was able to take a deep breath. This seemed to please the seas, as a breeze immediately filled the sails of our ship."

At first, Polo had looked on this discovery as an amazing opportunity. His unfortunate crew had concocted a horrible but effective weapon. Polo had scooped the remaining spices and gunpowder back into their barrels. He no longer planned to trade the cargo. Now he hoped to use it to help Venice rule the world.

Then disaster struck closer to home. The confession continued.

> *"My relatives broke into the gunpowder and spices last week. The mixture has now found its way into Venice. It has killed dozens. Many were my friends. They have all died with the same horrible smiles on their blue faces. The Doge and his officials believe it is a plague, brought to Venice by the remains of our crew. I will not correct them. There is no way to trace the poison once it has done its horrible work."*

Larry read the last paragraph of the notebook.

> *"I had hoped to use this weapon in war, but it is too dreadful. The only hope I have now, the only consolation, is that the deadly mixture has all been used up. There is no more, and the spices can be mixed again only by traveling my exact route home. I swear to God Almighty that I will never tell where I have truly been."*

Larry put down his coffee. "Wow," he whispered to himself. That explained it. That was why Polo hadn't included his real route home in the official version of his journey home that he wrote with Rustichello. Larry knew that he had found the key to the whole mystery . . . sort of.

The murder weapon was a mixture of spices—spices that Polo had assembled on his journey home. And the spices had to come from the exact places Polo had visited. But the spices didn't kill on their own. Apparently, they had to be mixed with gunpowder.

And that was where Larry got stuck. He took another sip of his coffee and reread the passage again.

"Gunpowder . . ." Larry let the word play across his lips as he sat back to think about what he'd just read. Gunpowder was a weapon on its own, for sure, but Polo didn't mention anyone getting shot.

Larry sipped again, and thought some more. Who the heck would ever eat gunpowder? The crew had been starving and desperate, but Polo's relatives in Venice weren't. Even still, gunpowder? It must taste awful.

Larry took a final long drink of his coffee, lifting his chin to get the last drop.

As he did, his eyes fell on the cans and packages that lined the wall behind the front counter of the café.

"What the—?!" he said, spitting the coffee over the top of his papers. His eyes locked onto a small green can with the word "GUNPOWDER" in red letters on the label.

Larry was up like a shot. He bumped and pushed his way to the front of the line, ignoring the angry shouts of the patrons behind him.

"What is that?" he shouted at the woman behind the counter, pointing at the can.

"What?" she said, glancing over her shoulder.

"That!" Larry pointed again.

"That?" The woman squinted at the shelf and seemed to focus on the green can.

"Yes, THAT." Larry was practically yelling now.

"That's tea," she said with a shrug.

"Gunpowder is *tea?*" Larry said, incredulous.

"Yeah," she said. "It's one of the oldest kinds. It's from China. It's rolled up in little balls that look like gunpowder. You add hot water and the tea leaves—poof—expand."

"Tea!" Larry shouted. "Polo didn't mean *gunpowder* gunpowder!" He reached across the counter and landed a huge kiss on the server's cheek. "He meant gunpowder *tea!*"

"That's great," the woman said, backing away. "Now, please, there are fifteen caffeine junkies behind you who are going to kill you if you don't move, like, right now."

Gunpowder tea. *That* was the key. First the killer had to find all those specific spices. Then the killer had to mix them together with not just any tea, but *gunpowder* tea. Then add the cumin and voilá, an all-natural untraceable poison. *That's* why Polo never mentioned tea when he and Rustichello wrote their account. It was part of what had killed his crew and friends, part of the life he wanted buried forever.

Larry grabbed his notes and sprinted down to the restaurant to tell Neil what he'd found. He arrived just as a police cruiser was pulling away from the curb.

"Nice place," Larry said, chuckling. "I hope it wasn't the chef they were arresting."

Larry walked inside. Neil wasn't at the table. Neither was Isabella. Jones the human boulder was gone too.

"Uh-oh," Larry said. "This doesn't look good." Neil must have *really* messed up the date. He walked up to the front desk.

"Excuse me, *gorgeous*," he said to the waitress, "but have you seen a kind of geeky redheaded guy or a really cute Mediterranean-looking young woman? Or maybe this huge guy, probably ate with his fingers, grunted?"

"They all left," she said, frowning. "The young woman went to the bathroom and never came out. The big guy went looking for her about a minute later. Then he walked out the front door and turned right."

Larry loved waitresses. They noticed everything.

"The redheaded kid took a phone call and ran out. Then he left in that police cruiser. He may have been in cuffs."

"*What?*"

"Cuffs. You know, as in arrested?"

"Oh no," Larry said. Why would the police arrest Neil? And if Neil *had* been arrested, his mom and dad were going to kill Larry.

"And they stiffed me on the bill, *handsome*," the waitress said. "Since you obviously know them, you can cover it." She handed Larry the bill for Neil, Isabella, and apparently Jones's dinner as well.

"A hundred dollars!" Larry shrieked.

Now *he* was going to kill Neil. He paid the bill, then ran into to the alleyway to grab his motorcycle.

Larry stopped.

Jones was sitting on the seat, staring right at Larry.

Larry saw his eyes. He didn't look happy.

"You and this machine aren't going anywhere until you tell me where I can find Isabella."

Neil had never been arrested before. He'd been in prisons, sniffing for contraband spices and smuggled food, but he'd never been behind bars for anything *he'd* done wrong.

Now he was stuck in the back of a clammy squad car with Nakamura, on his way to jail. Neil tried his best to convince Nakamura that he was innocent. Nakamura sat next to him and said, "I'd like to believe you, Neil, but there's a lot of evidence, and the chief gave me no choice. She's watching me like a hawk."

"What evidence?" Neil asked.

"I'm not allowed to say," Nakamura said.

"Hey, Nakamura," Neil said, his recent vow to be kinder suddenly forgotten. "Remember how you got promoted to inspector in the first place? That was thanks to *my* nose and a little thing called intentional salmonella poisoning."

"Yeah, at the Ritz Hotel. I remember. Insurance scam."

"Well, a little payback here, okay?" Neil said.

Nakamura sighed a long sigh. He knew the evidence was substantial, but something was still nagging at him. It was all fitting together too easily, and there was still no clear motive. He owed Neil a chance to explain himself.

He whispered to Neil, "Pretend to be hurt, like you have a concussion."

"What?"

"Flop your head onto my shoulder. Act like you're deeply asleep."

Neil did his best imitation of Larry at eight in the morning. "I don't feel so good. My head hurts. I need a coffee," Neil said, and then dropped his head onto Nakamura's shoulder. Stromboli turned around and Nakamura just shrugged. "I guess he hit his head when you were putting the cuffs on," he said.

"I was really careful this time. I didn't hurt him a bit."

"Well, maybe he hit his head when we put him inside. He's got a huge lump on the top here."

"Oh, sorry, kid," Stromboli said.

Neil just moaned.

"Hey, can you turn on some music or something?" Nakamura asked. "The traffic is a mess and I want something to distract me from this kid's breathing."

"Sure thing, Inspector," Stromboli said. He turned on a classic rock station.

"Thanks," Nakamura said. Then he whispered low so only Neil could hear. "Saffron is more lucid now. She'll recover, but she says it was you who jumped her."

"What?" Neil said, a little too loud. Stromboli turned around quickly.

"Talking in his sleep." Nakamura shrugged again, lifting Neil's head in the air, then cringing a little as it came back down on his shoulder blade. "See, I can't even wake the kid up when I do that. He's out cold."

On cue, Neil shouted sleepily again, "Ouch, my head."

"All right, all right," Nakamura whispered, "don't overdo it. Anyway, Saffron says she heard a young guy's voice and saw red hair underneath a ski mask. Neil, we've found your hair at two of the crime scenes. And your prints are on the Polo notes. Can you explain that?"

"No," Neil said.

"Then there's the handwriting."

"What handwriting?"

"The chief found a note at Saffron's, saying that there was a new superspice you'd found and that you'd give her a chance to sample and buy it if she would meet you alone in her kitchen. It was in your handwriting and it had traces of the spices all over it."

"But there were no notes like that at the other crime scenes. I would have smelled them!"

"Unless you're the killer and didn't want them found."

"That's ridiculous," Neil said.

"That's circumstantial evidence," Nakamura said. "And the worst is your locker at school."

"What about it? I'm surprised you got past the cheese."

"Well, we did. And we found a box inside with some cumin seeds and the spices for a chai. The lab is looking it over right now. Then there's the clincher—your collection of the original recipes from each murdered chef tucked inside your home-economics binder."

"Home-economics binder? I never even open that stupid thing," Neil said as loudly as he safely could. The folder had lain in his locker, completely untouched, since that last day in the library.

The library! Neil sat up like a bolt. He'd had his folder with him that day! Berger had come to ask him for an assignment he'd missed. Neil had handed him the folder and turned back to reading *Mastering the Art of French Cooking*.

Like a clumsy Italian salad dressing, everything was starting to congeal horribly in his brain.

Young voice.

Pathological hatred of Neil.

Anybody could get a red wig and a ski mask.

It made dreadful sense.

"Bergerrrrrrrrrr!!!" Neil yelled.

The driver turned around. "Hey, Inspector," he said, "do you want me to put a gag on him as well?"

"No," Nakamura said, "but get the chief on the horn, pronto."

CHAPTER THIRTY-ONE

VENDETTA

Angel Jícama had been meditating for more than an hour. It had started well, and he'd quickly lost himself in his dream kitchen. But now his body and mind were struggling for movement. He tried to concentrate on his cooking, but it was like trying to hold water in a sieve. No matter how he tried, the unhappy memories began to flood back.

He remembered all too clearly that horrible night—his final battle with his archrival, Signor Fabio Tortellini.

It had been more than a decade ago. They had been the two most accomplished chefs in Italy. Critics could never decide which of the two was the best chef, and they both found this gastronomically galling.

Angel had suggested a head-to-head duel to settle the question once and for all. The cook-off would take place in the catacombs, directly underneath Angel's world-famous Vesuvius Trattoria.

Word quickly went out to the world's wealthiest food-crazed patrons. Dozens of people paid plenty to witness this battle of the titans. Neither Angel nor Tortellini had ever lost a cooking duel before.

The night of the duel arrived, and the cramped, damp cave was packed with onlookers, all taking bets on who would finally win. Thousands of euros had changed hands, and the catacombs reeked with sweat and anticipation by the time the two chefs arrived and took their places.

Since the duel was technically on Angel's home turf, Tortellini was allowed to pick the dish. Angel showed no surprise as his adversary unveiled two deep fryers and the ingredients for pesce scorfano fritta, his delicate fried Adriatic Red Scorpion fish. It was his specialty, and it was dangerous. The Scorpion fish has venomous stingers that protect a wonderful flaky flesh. A chef has to filet the fish without getting stabbed. Then the fillet is dipped in egg batter and fried quickly at an extremely high heat.

It was at that moment that Angel tragically upped the ante. Angel was sure he would win, but he wanted there to be no question as to who was the greatest chef.

Angel handed Tortellini a silk napkin. "Put it on," he said. "Tonight, Signor Tortellini, we cook blindfolded."

Angel remembered the look of panic in Tortellini's eyes. It was the one moment in his life he desperately wished he could take back. He should have stopped there and called off the duel, or backed off the bravura of the blindfold . . . but his pride pushed him on.

He didn't just want to win. He wanted to humiliate Tortellini.

He did much more than that.

Thanks to the blindfold, Angel didn't see the accident.

He only heard the horrible scream as Tortellini pricked his hand on a stinger, stumbled, and then fell, tipping over his vat of boiling oil. He screamed again.

The crowd gasped, then cheered.

Angel had won.

Angel had expected to feel joy at defeating Tortellini, but instead he felt an incredible aching emptiness. He tore off his blindfold. Tortellini lay on the ground, severely burned and moaning in pain.

Angel rushed over to help him. The oil on the catacomb floor was so hot, it singed the soles of his shoes.

There was nothing he could do. The burns were too severe.

Tortellini used his last bit of energy to pull a picture of his daughter from his coat pocket. He died holding it to his chest.

As his arm went limp, his hand fell and the picture slipped into the oil and caught fire. Angel stared at the image of a serious-looking young girl. Her eyes remained until the last, and, as the photograph turned to ash, they seemed to burn into his soul. Angel could even hear her voice saying, "Murderer."

He *was* a murderer. His pride had killed a great chef, a husband, a young father.

The head of the local police had come up and put his hand on Angel's shoulder. "Don't worry about this mess," he said. "An accident, clearly. I will take care of everything. All I ask is a table for me and a lovely companion tomorrow evening. And congratulations on your victory."

Angel had said nothing. He had just stood and watched as Tortellini's lifeless body was carried away.

Angel never set foot in his restaurant again. It meant nothing to him anymore. He sold it and secretly sent the money to Tortellini's widow. She'd used the money to support her daughter's love for flowers and perfume. At least something beautiful had been added to the world through their pain.

These days, Angel gave the bulk of his earnings to charity. Hundreds of people benefited from the money he raised from his annual meal.

In some way, maybe that helped make up for his great sin. He needed to not give in to his grief-filled memories now. He needed to get his Silk Road meal ready. He needed to remember the people who relied on him. He needed to go on.

He needed to concentrate on his meal.

One more clove of garlic, Angel thought at last. He got up from the floor and made his way to the kitchen. He prepared everything—the knives, the herbs, the meat, the pans, the cutting boards—like a priest getting ready for a religious ceremony. Then he turned his attention to the spices. He hummed to himself as he measured and prepared. But something was wrong. He stopped humming and stood perfectly still. Then, slowly, he passed his nose over the array of bottles and leaves in front of him.

There was the faint trace of a different smell, a different spice. He sniffed closer. The smell wasn't coming from his spice collection. It was wafting in from the living room. Angel made his way toward his front door, still sniffing. He looked down at the stack of letters that had accumulated underneath his mail slot. Every day Angel received at least forty new pleas for a dinner invitation. He lifted the envelopes and read the return addresses of the wannabe diners.

"Sultan of Brunei? Nope." He threw it in the recycling bin.

"Bill Gates?" Angel peered over at his computer. It was flashing "Windows update, loading." It had been flashing the exact same message for two weeks. He threw that request letter into the bin as well.

Then he came across an envelope with no return address. It was written in what looked like Neil's handwriting. *Odd*, Angel thought. He sniffed it carefully. This was where the smell was coming from. It was cumin, for sure, but mixed with other spices, too.

Angel took another sniff. There was cardamom from (*sniff*) Borneo. He could smell some dried ginger (*sniff*), possibly from Sri Lanka, and (*sniff*) a hint of cinnamon from India . . . and the cumin was from Mongolia.

It was a sophisticated blend.

Was *this* the combination of spices that Neil had smelled at the murder scenes? Had he finally discovered the source? Then why write to him about it, with the spices inside a letter? Why not just drop by or call?

Angel opened the letter.

Angel,
I have found an incredible spice mixture and am
enclosing a sample in this envelope. Tell me if the
cumin isn't the greatest that you have ever tasted.
Try it on some lamb with a nice side dish of dates,
or—even better—sprinkle a little of the cumin in
with these other spices in a masala chai.

   I would love to bring you more. Please leave
your door unlocked between seven and eight tonight.
I know you will be at home working.
Neil

It was a setup. Angel absolutely knew it was a setup.
There was no way Neil would suggest using these spices
to make a chai, not after the phone call they'd had earlier. The clock struck seven. Angel rushed to the door.
He'd never locked it before, but he was going to lock it
now. But just as he reached the door, the handle turned
and the door swung open.

   A voice said "Hello, Angel. Long time no see."

   But all Angel could see was the gun pointing straight
at his chest.

Billy Berger sat at his desk counting out crisp new
hundred-dollar bills. He had thirty of them. They'd
arrived in unmarked envelopes starting a couple of
months back. Inside had been bags of Cheez Doodles,
the money, and instructions.

   As he counted Billy got so excited that he accidentally
knocked over a giant stack of video games. They fell onto
the ground, tipping over the bowl of salt-and-vinegar

potato chips he'd just brought upstairs for dinner. The chips added to the pile that grew daily on his carpet. How was he supposed to tell tonight's fresh dinner apart from the chips he'd spilled last night?

Billy smiled. He didn't have to. He had enough money now to buy fresh chips whenever he felt like it, and he felt like it a lot. He looked at the pile of bills again. The guy behind the counter at the local Munchie Market was going to be awfully glad to see him over the next few months.

As for the mess? His mom would eventually clean his room. She usually waited until the smell started to waft down the hallway. It wouldn't be long now. The remains of last week's hot dog breakfast were already turning green underneath his bed.

Three thousand bucks! And it had been the easiest money he'd ever made. His first mission, the initial letter said, was to figure out Flambé's locker combination. His second mission? To grab a couple of the jerk's hairs.

Simple, he remembered. All he'd had to do for the first mission was to jam himself into the locker across the hallway with a set of binoculars. He'd had to whale on the kid who owned the locker a couple of times, but he eventually agreed to sneak Billy in before class let out. Then he'd just watched as Flambé spun the combination lock.

The hair thing was a little more trouble. The last thing he wanted to do was to touch Flambé's head, money or no money. Luckily, the guy was always getting haircuts for some photo shoot or TV interview, so Billy had just trailed him for a day or so and then combed through the barber's trash can. He'd used his dad's old raincoat and hat to keep from being recognized.

The second letter came a few weeks later, with ten more hundred-dollar bills inside. This one asked Billy to lift a couple of Flambé's essays from English class. That was a little trickier. It meant he had to get close to the geek without him running away. But he was able to do that by being quieter than usual.

By the time Flambé noticed Berger standing behind him in the hallway, he'd already lifted three pages from his backpack. Berger had just smiled and walked away. He'd even grabbed some unused sheets as well. He'd left everything, as instructed, in an envelope behind Gunter Lund's fish shop.

Just for fun, he'd even pinched a massively ugly fish that morning. He didn't like fish much, but he *loved* the way the fish had shattered the window at Flambé's precious restaurant.

"That was priceless," Berger chuckled to himself. "I told the jerk I'd get back at him."

The most recent letter had come right before school ended. It was actually a package with the words "Open with gloves on" written on the front. Inside there had been a bunch of recipes, a small wooden box, fifteen more bills, and a note. The note told him to hide the pages in one of Flambé's binders, specifically a binder he wouldn't open again before school ended.

Easy, Berger had thought. Neil spent all of his time in home ec making fun of the teacher. Berger wasn't sure he'd ever even seen him take notes. It was about the only thing they had in common. The toughest part of the whole assignment had been swallowing his pride and being nice to the hammerhead that day in the library.

Luckily Flambé didn't seem too suspicious. His parents were probably the types who told him to "always try to make friends, even with people you don't like." Crap like that.

Billy stared at the envelope again. Along with the notes and money, it had also contained a packet of leaves and some little seeds that looked like mouse poop. There had even been a note saying to try them together in a nice warm cup of tea, maybe with his next plate of Cheez Doodles. The note said it would be a taste experience he wouldn't believe. Maybe the note had also said what the stuff was. He couldn't remember now. He'd burned all the notes in his parent's fireplace, also as instructed.

His stomach rumbled.

Billy turned the packet over in his hands. It looked and smelled like those weird spices Flambé was always using when he cooked for the teachers. He shuddered. It didn't really matter what it was. He'd have to be half dead from starvation before he'd go near anything that looked or smelled like *that*.

His stomach rumbled again. With all this cash, starvation was not an imminent threat.

"Time to pay a visit to the Munchie Mart," he said.

He grabbed the top bill and made his way down the stairs and out the front door.

Inspector Sean Nakamura was standing at the end of the Berger's driveway, in front of a squad car. The lights flashed in Billy's eyes.

"What the heck is going on?" he said, lifting his hands to his face.

"Well, if it isn't Mr. Cheez Doodle," Nakamura said, recognizing Billy from their brief encounter at Neil's locker. "So we meet again. I have a few questions for you, and I need them answered right away."

Neil Flambé sat on the stained collection of old planks that passed for a bench in the Vancouver Detention Center.

Nakamura had called the chief with his suspicions about Berger, but the chief wasn't about to let Suspect Number One go without some hard evidence that he was innocent. So Neil was stuck on the plank while Nakamura was off on a mission to get some. "If you're right about Berger," Nakamura had said to Neil, "I'll come back for you as soon as possible. In the meantime, get a hold of someone who can help you."

Neil had been taken to a desk and given a phone. It was big and black and plastic—one of those phones that you see in old movies. It seemed to be covered in a thin layer of grease.

"You get three chances to reach someone," Stromboli said, handing the heavy receiver to Neil, "then it's back in the cell."

"Thanks," Neil said sarcastically.

He tried to call his mom. No answer. He hung up without leaving a message. If she was nervous before, she'd have a heart attack now. Any conversation with her would have to take place in person.

"Strike one," Stromboli said.

Neil tried his dad, but all he got there was a busy signal. He put the receiver back on its cradle with a *clunk*.

"Strike two," Stromboli said.

He thought about trying Angel, but he didn't want to risk not getting an answer. Their last phone call had ended with Angel's line going silent. There was only one other person Neil could call. He sighed and dialed Larry.

The phone rang . . . and rang . . . and rang.

Neil's eyes darted toward Stromboli. His finger was poised above the phone, ready to press the cradle down and hang it up.

"Strike th—"

"Hello?" Larry finally picked up on the tenth ring.

"LARRY!" Neil had never been so excited to hear his cousin's voice.

"Neil? Where are you?"

Stromboli pulled back his finger with a frown. "You have one minute."

"I'm in jail! They arrested me for murder! You've got to come and get me out!"

"Um, that's probably not a good idea, Neil."

"What? Why not?"

"Well, first of all—and trust me on this—they are not going to let me 'get you out' when you're in on a murder charge."

240

Neil hadn't thought about that. Larry was right. Nakamura was his only hope on that front.

"And second, I have a five-hundred-pound, very angry gorilla riding on the back of my bike, and you don't want to see him right now."

"Jones?" Neil said.

"Yeah. He thinks you and I did something with Isabella, and he's making me drive him all over town looking for her, or *you*. If I can ditch him, I'll head over, but it might take me a while. He's handcuffed me to the bike while he searches some warehouse near the restaurant. I had to do some major gymnastics just to get the cell phone out of my back pocket. Luckily I used to date a really cute contortionist from Cirque du Soleil. . . ."

"Thirty seconds," Stromboli said.

"Larry!"

"Neil, I have something important to tell you."

"Do it fast!"

"I finished Angel's Polo notebook. Gunpowder is tea, Neil. It's *tea*. And when it's mixed with spices from some specific places Polo visited, it becomes poisonous, or toxic, or something. Anyway, it apparently smells and tastes amazing, so you want to drink it, but if you do, you die. *That's* why Polo didn't want anyone to know where he went. The killer discovered the mixture somehow, and is using it as the murder weapon."

Neil thought for a moment. He remembered the traces of tea and cumin on the lips of the dead chefs. It was a horrible and cruel way to kill, using the chefs' own love of food to trick them into swallowing poison.

That also explained the mystery smell. How could Neil have been so stupid? It wasn't a single spice or herb, it was something entirely new, created by the mixture of *all* the spices with the tea. He was a chef, after all. He should have realized that great ingredients, when mixed together properly, equal more than the sum of their parts. It was part chemistry, part magic.

"Larry, keep trying to shake Jones. I'll tell Nakamura about the gunpowder and the mixture when he gets back from Berger's."

"Berger's?"

"I'll explain later."

"Oh crap! Here comes Jones. He doesn't look happy."

"Time's up," Stromboli said, reaching for the receiver.

"Wait, Neil, one last thing," Larry called out.

"What?"

"You owe me a hundred bucks."

Stromboli grabbed the phone and hung it up. "Back in the cell, Nose."

So Neil found himself pacing around the tiny cell, waiting for Nakamura and trying to figure out how he'd gotten into this mess.

Neil didn't like to second-guess himself, but now that he'd had time to think, he saw the loopholes in his Berger-as-a-serial-killer theory.

"Berger isn't bright enough to pull this off," he said out loud as he paced from wall to wall. "He does less homework than *I* do, so why would he know so much about Marco Polo? He wouldn't."

Neil paced some more, stroking his chin.

"And there's no way he could work out such a complicated menu. He eats Cheez Doodles, for crying out loud! These murders are being carried out by someone with an expert knowledge of the world's foods and how best to prepare and present them."

How would Berger possibly be able to figure out the cumin-and-chai combo?

Neil also wasn't sure Berger hated him *that* much.

There was no question that Berger was involved, but he had to be working with someone else. Was it Angel? He knew more about great food than anyone else Neil knew. Was it Olive Green? Or Carlotta Calamari? Or Isabella? She knew food too. It was in her blood.

Neil had seen how dangerous she looked when she was mad, that night at his restaurant when she told him about her father's death. And then there had been the way she'd reacted when he'd mentioned Angel at dinner. Almost as if she knew him, and hated him.

All at once, a lightbulb went on in Neil's head. "Oh my gosh," he realized with a flash. "Angel killed Isabella's dad!"

It explained everything! Angel's hatred of duels. Isabella's behavior when Neil had mentioned Angel's name. And he'd told her where Angel lived! What if Isabella was the killer?

She knew smells, and she knew cuisine. Maybe she had been nice to Neil so that she could frame him for the murders. Maybe she wanted to start a world-class restaurant to honor her father's memory. Maybe she was going to finish it all off by killing Angel. She'd have revenge for her father's death, and the added satisfaction of using Angel's recipes as her own. Neil didn't want to believe it, but he could see that it made sense.

Maybe she had assembled the spices for one of her

perfumes and discovered that she'd concocted a cumin-scented poison instead.

Neil could almost imagine the cumin smell right now, it was so vivid.

"Actually"—he sniffed the air—"it *is* vivid."

Neil looked around. The smell was coming from *inside* the jail.

Two police officers had just brought another prisoner into the cell across the way. He seemed a little disoriented, like he'd had a bit too much to drink. He was wearing a baseball cap with "Go Sabres" written on top, and his clothes looked like they hadn't been cleaned in about a year.

He stank, but not just of urine and old smokes. He stank of . . . "Mongolian cumin!" Neil yelled.

Neil ran to the bars. "Hey . . . hey!" he yelled to the police officers. "Where did you pick up this guy?"

"What?" said one of the officers. "Why?"

"He smells funny," Neil said.

"Duh," said the cop. "When we found him he was sitting in an alleyway on Commercial Drive, sifting through a garbage bin."

"The Drive and what?" Neil asked.

"Uh," the officer said, thinking. "I think it was at First."

"First and Commercial Drive?" Neil was thinking out loud. "That's right across from Yogi's, the restaurant where I was having dinner with Isabella."

244

"Isabella?" the officer asked. "Isabella who? What are you babbling about?"

"Never mind," Neil said. "This is important. Did you find anything on him that might look like spices or maybe tea leaves?"

"Yeah." The officer seemed surprised. "Yeah, we did. He had this powder all over his jeans. We thought it might be drugs, so we looked around the alleyway. There was a little pile of it right next to the bin. How did you know that?"

"It *is* a drug," Neil said. "A lethal drug. I need you to get Nakamura on the phone right away. We've got to get to Angel Jícama's apartment!"

CHAPTER THIRTY-TWO

SPICES, SAVORY, AND SECRETS

"This squad car runs as slowly as your brain, Nakamura," Neil Flambé said.

"What happened to 'How can I help you?'" Nakamura asked.

"Politeness is overrated," Neil said, sitting next to Nakamura in the backseat of the squad car. "C'mon!" Neil yelled to Stromboli. "Drive faster! There are lives at stake."

Sean Nakamura looked closely at Neil. The Nose was scared and confused. He was worried that his mentor, Angel, was either the final victim of the Marco Polo murderer or possibly *the* murderer. That was a lot to deal with for anybody, let alone a fourteen-year-old boy.

Nakamura put his hand on Neil's shoulder. "Neil," he said, "We're going as fast as we can. I won't say it will all be okay, but we'll do everything as quickly and carefully as we can."

Neil just gave a loud sniff. Nakamura wasn't sure, but he thought he saw a tear in Neil's eye, glistening in the glare of the flashing lights.

Nakamura continued. "I've been a cop for a long time. Rushing in never works; it just screws things up."

Neil turned and stared out the window and said nothing.

Angel sat still in his chair—not that he had a choice.

"That butcher's twine is a bit tight," Angel said. "You're not tying up a rib roast, you know."

"Oh, poor baby," said the woman. Her dyed red hair bounced around as she tugged and pulled on the rope, making sure it was secure. "You do look like a nice big fatty one, though. I always said you put too much butter in your bouillabaisse."

"You certainly haven't changed much, Carlotta," Angel said sadly. "You're still wrong about how to make good food—such wasted talent."

"I'll ignore that," she said, standing up and rubbing her hands. "Don't worry. I'll take the rope off soon. I need these to hold you only long enough for you to have a little *aperitivo*."

"Ah, the *aperitivo*—a small something to drink before dinner," Angel said. "Unlike you, it's a wonderful Italian creation."

"I disagree."

"I'm assuming I won't enjoy this *aperitivo* very much."

"You'll enjoy it *too* much," she said. "That's the secret. It's a combination of tastes so intense, it kills you. You love it *so* much, you don't notice you're choking to death."

The lid of a pot clanged in the kitchen.

"Ahh," she said, "music to my ears. The water and

milk—the base for any really good chai—are boiling. Well, Angel, what do you think about a little tea?"

"I'd prefer a Sri Lankan, maybe a really good mountain-grown blend such as a Watawala Royal Ceylon," he said.

"Ha-ha," Carlotta replied as she made her way toward the kitchen. She stopped. She had reached into her pocket to grab the bag of lethal spices. It was gone. She cursed. The bag must have fallen out in the alleyway when she'd pulled out that stupid GPS.

"Looking for something?" Angel asked.

"Shut up," Carlotta said. "I had a packet of spices, if you must know. I was going to use it to kill you." She patted the pockets of her jeans and shirt. Nothing.

"Well, I'll guess you'll just have to release me and try again tomorrow."

"No, I don't think I will," Carlotta said suddenly. "In fact, I am so clever that I amaze myself!"

"Do tell."

"I mailed a package of the spices to you. The only reason I dropped by was to make sure you'd actually drunk it. You clearly hadn't, but now you will!"

She walked over and grabbed the envelope and the package that Angel had dropped when she'd burst through the door. She made her way back to the kitchen.

"I think you'll enjoy my own special chai-and-cumin blend better than those snooty brand names," she called back as she reached the stove. She dropped some leaves and a few specks of cumin into the pot and stirred them into the hot water and milk. "It's to die for."

"Very clever," Angel said. He wasn't laughing. "By the way, I love what you've done with your hair."

Carlotta made her way back to the living room. "It's the same red as Flambé's. Easier for the witnesses to identify. At least the one witness I let live. You won't be the second, by the way."

All at once, it occurred to Angel why Neil had noticed the mystery smell in his apartment that day. He'd been cooking with Mongolian cumin and making tea at the same time. It was some very old tea he'd picked up in Beijing years before. When the smell of the leaves in the notebook had hit the smells hovering in the air, it had all combined into Neil's mystery smell. Later on, when Neil opened the notebook without those background smells, he smelled only the leaves in the notebook. Angel felt an overwhelming sadness that he would never get to tell Neil about his discovery.

"Aren't you going to give me the tea right away?" Angel asked. "And get rid of me quickly?"

"Tsk, tsk, tsk," she said, wagging her finger at him. "A proper tea is always allowed to steep. And it takes at least five minutes to blend the flavors for a really good chai." Carlotta sat down across from Angel and laid an egg timer on the floor between them. She turned the dial to five minutes.

"You always struck me more as a 'frozen dinner and microwave' kind of cook," Angel said. "Neil certainly found that out. That's why you're doing this, isn't it?"

"Revenge is a dish best served with chai, I always say." Carlotta smiled.

"What was the name of that restaurant again? Chez Mediocre, wasn't it?"

"Chez Miscellaneous," Carlotta said, and then scowled.

"No-name tuna—*tsk, tsk, tsk* yourself. You needed to accept that setback and move on."

"Because of that comment," she said, "I think I'll let the tea steep a few minutes longer. It's more painful that way." She reset the egg timer to six minutes.

Angel just sat back and sighed. "Here it comes. I've seen enough James Bond movies to know that you'll now spend this extra time revealing the details of your evil plan."

"And I've seen enough James Bond movies to know that I should do that quickly." She checked the timer. "The mixture will be perfect in about four and a half minutes. So, here's the short version."

She cleared her throat and began.

"To start with, I never forgave you for kicking me out of your kitchen."

"That was a hard decision for me, and you know it. It was for your own good. You needed to find your inner chef—"

"Stuff it, Yoda," Carlotta said. "Then that Flambé brat visited my restaurant and ruined my new life. We both know how that happened. But a funny thing happened in jail. I was in a cell with an Asian spice smuggler who told me an interesting story. It concerned Marco Polo and this old legend about a deadly cargo of spices. It was a blend of spices from places he'd stopped on his journey home. Mix the spices with a certain tea—gunpowder tea or, *gāng paò de* tea, as it's known in China—and it's a lethal and undetectable poison. Organized criminals had tried for centuries to discover the mixture, with no luck."

"But you've obviously discovered it," Angel said.

"This is where it gets interesting. I get out of jail, and I decide to travel a bit, maybe look at this whole Polo thing. . . ."

"And plot your revenge on Neil?"

"And on you. I was starting to hatch a plan that involved killing you, framing Flambé, and setting myself up with the best Asian-inspired restaurant in the world."

"Where you would serve canned tuna?"

Carlotta didn't reply, but she reached down and added another minute to the timer.

"I went everywhere Polo told people he went. I studied every map I could find, every book I could read on Polo's journey home. I got good food and learned a lot of new skills . . . but *no* poison. I decided to visit Venice, to see if there were any clues there. I dropped by the map room in the Doge's palace. There was Marco Polo's journey to Asia and back painted right on the wall for all to see. So, how did four hundred years of criminals—"

"Including you," Angel interrupted.

"Yes, fine. How did *we* keep missing the correct locations of the spices? I was wondering that and looking at the map closely when I heard someone come up behind me." She checked the timer again. "Three minutes."

Angel tried to wiggle his fingers loose, but it was no use.

"It was this pompous windbag named Antonio Fusilli," Carlotta continued. "He kind of reminded me of you, actually. He clearly thought I was cute, and he was trying to impress me. He told me that he was a descendant of Polo. He told me that Polo traveled a different route from the one shown on the map. 'Oh really,' I said in my most girlish, cutesy voice, 'how fascinating. Tell me more, handsome.'"

"Ah, Carlotta." Angel sighed. "So beautiful, yet so deadly."

"Did you know," Carlotta said, leaning close to Angel's ear and whispering, "that they repainted the map room after a mysterious disease tore through Venice in the 1300s?"

"No."

"It's true. The connection? It was no disease. It was these killer spices. The Venetians got into Polo's stores somehow and started making tea. Imagine their excitement at the exotic spices they discovered in the barrels in Polo's warehouse! But instead of a great big tea party, it was more like a great big bunch of funerals."

"It sounds awful," Angel said.

"It was great business for the undertakers," Carlotta said dryly. "Polo felt all guilty and told everyone that it was some disease his crew had picked up on the way home. He made sure to destroy any trace of his real route. He thought he had."

Carlotta looked at the timer. "Two minutes. It turned out that Antonio knew of a secret diary that described the real journey. I asked him if he should be telling me this and he said, 'The diary is perfectly safe, especially from a harmless little pixie like you.' So I batted my eyes a few times, bought him dinner, and used my feminine wiles to get some more tidbits of information."

"And then you killed him and took the notebook?" Angel asked.

"After spying on him for a few weeks, of course, to figure out where he had the book hidden. He was a sweet guy, just not so bright in the end. Like I said, he reminded me of you."

"So what's the secret?"

Carlotta just checked the timer again.

"One minute left. The secret? It's the ultimate fusion cooking. The spices come from places Polo really traveled, not the places he and Rustichello cooked up for their book launch. The right spices from very specific places in Borneo, eastern India, Sri Lanka, and elsewhere, mixed together properly with the tea, give you the most amazing taste experience of your life. But the downside? It kills you. You'll have a nice healthy swig in just a few seconds, and I'll have my revenge on that little brat."

"Revenge on him by killing me?" Angel said. "You overestimate the depths of our relationship. Neil is better with ingredients than people."

"Oh, I don't think so," Carlotta said. "I think he will find that he misses you desperately. Especially as he's rotting in jail."

She got up and walked back to the stove. "It's all worked out. The police needed to 'uncover' a complicated murder mystery that only a master chef could devise. I left them a few false trails at first—just to buy time—like pouring rancid puttanesca sauce on Flambé's vegetables and sabotaging his bike. I figured that would get them looking at other suspects. That idiot Berger almost ruined things when he threw a tuna through the window of the restaurant."

"You get what you pay for," Angel called at her. "Cheap tuna and cheap henchmen."

Carlotta growled.

"No matter. In the end, all roads lead to Neil Flambé.

The police will have found the stolen recipes in his locker by now, along with a box of spices. They have notes with his fingerprints and in his handwriting, or as close as I could duplicate it. And I gave that pathetic Sumia Saffron only enough poison to knock her unconscious. She'll have fingered the redheaded wonder as well. In fact, she must have. I saw them arrest him just a little while ago."

Carlotta walked back into the living room, holding a funnel and a teapot. She set them down on the floor next to Angel's chair.

"Why not just kill Neil?" Angel asked. "Why this elaborate plan?"

Carlotta looked intently at Angel. "I don't want Flambé dead—I want him alive and suffering. Revenge is sweetest when it's total and complete."

"You are a twisted person," Angel said sadly.

"Neil Flambé *humiliated* me! He destroyed my reputation. He took everything from me. Well, now it's my turn to humiliate *him*. While he's rotting in a filthy jail for murder, I'll be serving the greatest menu ever assembled to the biggest spenders in the world. Look me up in Dubai at the new Chez Mediterranean. The grand opening is in three months!"

She laughed an evil laugh, and smiled.

"Oh, wait—you won't be able to make it to the opening, because you'll be dead."

"And how do you plan to escape after you kill me?"

The egg timer buzzed loudly.

"Oh, no more discussion, Mr. Bond. Tea's ready!" Carlotta grabbed Angel's hair and yanked his neck straight back. He gasped. She was stronger than he'd expected.

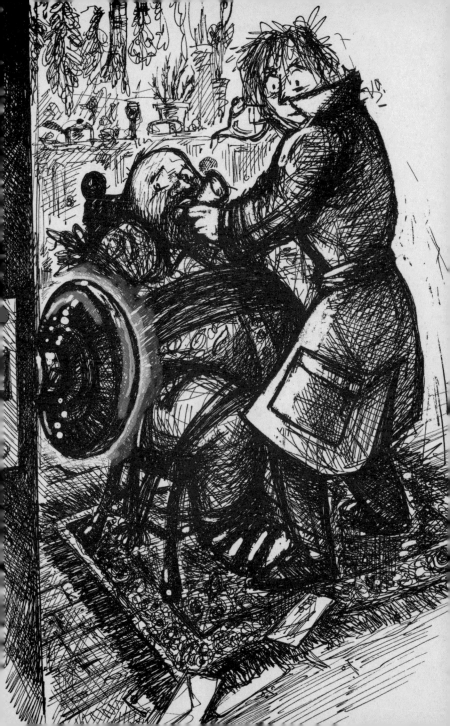

She quickly wound more butcher's twine around his fore-head and the back of the chair, to hold him firmly in place. Then she picked up the teapot and funnel and forced the funnel between his lips. The amber liquid, with its overpowering scent of cumin and chai, and the poison created by their mixture, stood ready to pour.

It smelled wonderful. Despite his dread, Angel found himself eager to taste the concoction.

It was at that moment, however, that Angel noticed a new aroma in the air—fresh lavender. Neil hadn't described *that* when he'd told Angel about the poison. He wondered what it could be. It didn't seem to be coming from the teapot or the funnel or Carlotta's clothes. But it didn't matter. It was quite possibly the last thing he'd ever smell. He closed his eyes and prepared for whatever happened next.

Just as the first drop made its way into Angel's mouth, Carlotta heard a faint click and realized her plan had just hit a hitch. She'd forgotten to lock the door behind her.

Isabella was surprised by how easy it was to get into Angel's building. The lock on the front door was miss-ing, and the hinges were hanging by only the thinnest strips of metal.

How strange, she thought, *to find Angel living in a place such as this*. Isabella had assumed Angel would be living the high life of a rich chef. She'd assumed that he'd profited from the misery of people such as her father.

She walked through the front door of the dilapidated building, and stopped. Now that she was so close, Isabella wasn't exactly sure what she was going to say or do. She had spent years imagining what a confrontation with Angel Jícama might be like.

Angel would be evil, unfeeling. He would threaten to kill her as he had killed her father. He needed to keep his secret safe. She would have no choice but to defend herself, and would very likely have to kill Angel in the act.

But now that she was actually here, Isabella realized this had been a fantasy. She deplored violence. And there was something else that gave Isabella pause. Neil revered Angel. She was attracted to Neil, she realized. Could Neil know a different man than the one she'd imagined?

Tears rolled down her cheeks as she stood motionless in the building's grungy front hallway. Bitterness had consumed her for so long that it was bewildering to admit other emotions into her heart.

"Don't cry, *figlia mia*."

Isabella shuddered. It was almost as if her father were standing next to her now. Had she imagined it?

"My death was my fault as well. Vengeance solves nothing."

Still, she wrestled with her anger. "No, father! You were innocent."

"How do you know? You were just a child, at home with your mother."

Isabella wiped her tears away and peered into the gloomy stairwell ahead. She was sure her father's voice was coming from somewhere in there. And he was right. What did she really know about his death?

"Angel was the last person to see you alive, Papa."

"*Sí, sí.*" The voice seemed to be moving up the stairs. Isabella followed.

"Perhaps I need to see him not for revenge, but for the truth?" she called.

"Yes, daughter."

She took another step.

"Papa, what do I do?"

There was no answer from her father, but Isabella was definitely hearing voices ahead—real voices. An animated conversation was taking place in the apartment at the top of the stairs. Isabella tiptoed up the steps and listened as carefully as she could. She heard only scattered words, "Neil . . . murder . . . Marco Polo."

Then there was no sound.

Isabella's heart raced. Something was happening inside.

She reached for the door and carefully turned the handle. Then she peeked into the apartment. The first thing she saw was a head of red hair. "Neil?" she said.

But the face that turned to greet her was not Neil's. It was a woman she had never seen before, and she was leaning over a large man with a funnel in his mouth, holding a steaming pot of liquid and looking really ticked off.

"I don't believe it," the woman said. "The brat's girlfriend! Want some tea?" And with that, she lunged at Isabella. Unfortunately for Carlotta, she misjudged the distance she needed to travel. She flew past Isabella and into the side of the door, smashing her face. Her arm sprang back, still holding the toxic teapot full of masala chai and cumin. The lid flew off and the warm liquid splashed all over Isabella, drenching her beautiful shawl.

Isabella was too shocked and disoriented to move.

Carlotta felt blood flowing from her lip, and she used her sleeve to wipe it off. She shoved the door closed and locked it. Then she took the key out and put it in her pocket.

"*Piccolo bestia*. You little beast!" she said, wiping the blood on her sleeve.

"You don't need to translate," Isabella said. "*Conosco molto bene l'italiano*."

"Really?" Carlotta said. "Then how about '*Ho una pistola*'?" Carlotta pulled a gun from inside her coat as she spat out the words.

Over in the chair, Angel was starting to gag. Isabella let out a shriek as she saw his eyes start to roll in his head. His face was turning blue. He stared at Isabella. "I'm sorry," he said in a rasp, with tears in his eyes.

Suddenly, Isabella felt a pang in her heart. That simple apology was like a magic spell. Angel was her last connection to her father's old life as a chef. She knew right away she did not want this man to die. She moved toward him just as Carlotta pulled the trigger.

Isabella fell to the floor. Blood trickled from her head, staining the carpet.

Carlotta smiled and prepared to fire again, just to make sure the little witch was dead.

BANG!

The front door shook as if it had been hit by a truck. Carlotta flinched and misfired, sending the bullet into the floor inches from Isabella's motionless body.

"The police!" Carlotta cried in a panic.

BANG!

The police smashed at the door again.

Carlotta took cover behind Angel. She glanced at Isabella. Despite the banging, Isabella didn't move.

BANG!

A few more blows from the ram, and the police would be inside. Carlotta had to think—and think fast. How could she save her beautiful plan from disintegrating? She took a quick look around the room.

There was the note in Neil's handwriting lying on the floor. In the kitchen were the spices that matched the spices in Neil's locker. Isabella was dying or dead, so she wouldn't be able to finger anyone. Berger would have drunk the deadly tea she'd sent to him by now, and he'd be dead too. No witnesses. Neil would still be Suspect Number One.

Or maybe . . . maybe Isabella was in on the murders too?

"I *am* brilliant." Carlotta smiled a twisted smile.

Angel was turning bluer by the second. His eyelids fluttered. She reached down to his hand and cut it loose. Then she placed the gun in his fingers, making sure his prints were all over the trigger. She could afford to leave it behind. A good chef is always prepared, and she had another gun in her coat, in case she met any opposition during her getaway.

When the police walked in, it would look just like a good old-fashioned double murder. The boy chef sends his girlfriend to kill his mentor and steal his recipes. The mentor defends himself and kills the girlfriend. Perfect!

Carlotta practically danced her way to the rear window of the apartment. It overlooked the alleyway behind the building. There was a low fence on the other side, and then a dimly lit park.

She opened the window and took a quick look around. There were no cops on the fire escape. They were all trying to break in through Angel's door.

There was another loud *bang* and the door began to buckle.

Carlotta gave a wave to the room, then slipped through the window and was gone.

On the floor of the living room, Isabella stirred. She could hear loud noises, and she felt a searing pain in her temple. She reached for her head. The bullet had just grazed her, but it hurt. She felt woozy as she opened her eyes. Her vision was a little blurry, but she could make out the figure of a woman climbing out the window.

Now she could hear the police trying to crash through the front door. Every nerve in her body told her to just lie down, give up and wait for the police to break in and help her. But her brain told her that by the time the police broke down the door, the woman who'd shot her and poisoned Angel would be blocks away. Isabella couldn't wait.

She struggled to her knees, and as soon the room stopped spinning, she forced herself to stand. She went to the door to unlock it, but the key was gone. Isabella clenched her fists. She'd have to go after the woman herself.

"Father, I need your help," she whispered as she crept out the open window and down the fire escape.

That witch, that *strega*, wasn't going to get away. Not if she could help it.

Neil crouched down beside the squad car. He could see the light from Angel's apartment. The police had walked slowly into the building. Then they'd heard a gunshot and had rushed up the stairs.

Neil wanted to rush inside as well. But Nakamura had ordered him to stand back. Neil had obeyed, but reluctantly. Why couldn't he be in there helping?

Now he could hear the police upstairs battering against the door. "What the heck is going on up there?" Singh and Stromboli had stayed behind as well. Their guns were out and trained on the front door.

A slight breeze came up and tousled Neil's hair and tickled his sense of smell. Neil sniffed. On the breeze, he could detect the unmistakable smell of . . . fresh lavender perfume. "Isabella!" he said.

He sniffed more deeply this time. The breeze was coming from the north. Neil bolted from behind the squad car and ran toward the north side of the building.

Thankfully, Stromboli and Singh paid no attention to him, and Neil rounded the building in seconds. The scent of lavender was getting stronger. He ran faster.

He heard a gunshot and a scream, followed by an evil laugh.

CHAPTER THIRTY-THREE

I SCREAM, YOU SCREAM

Neil's heart pounded as he sprinted down the alleyway behind the building. Angel's goat bleated softly
as he passed. The rundown park was just a few feet away,
and that was where the lavender smell was coming from.

The old streetlights flickered and hummed.

Neil could barely make out two shapes in the gloom.
Isabella was running after someone. Another shot rang
out. Isabella ducked, then straightened up and ran on.
"Isabella isn't the killer," Neil realized with a sudden and
unexpected feeling of relief. "She's *chasing* the killer."

Then the farthest figure tripped over something.
Neil heard a shriek, a woman's voice. He saw a flicker
of red hair in the light and then Isabella was on the
woman, struggling for control of the gun.

Neil ran as fast as he could.

"Isabella! It's me, Neil!"

"Neil," Isabella called.
"Help me!"

But the woman was older,
bigger, and stronger, and just
as Neil lunged to grab her

arm, she wrested the gun away. In one fluid motion she grabbed Isabella around the throat and pointed the gun at her head.

It was then that Neil saw the murderer's face: Carlotta Calamari! It hit him like a punch in the stomach. "So it's you," Neil said.

"Yes, you little worm, it's me."

"Look, Carlotta, please put the gun down. Isabella has nothing to do with this. It's me you hate. And . . ." he paused and took a deep breath. "And I'm sorry about the tuna, and the Michelin stars."

Carlotta laughed a hollow laugh. "An apology?" she said. "It's too late for that, Flambé." Isabella started to fidget, until Carlotta pushed the gun muzzle tighter against her temple.

"Well, well, this is quite a pickle," Carlotta said, sneering. "Where shall we all go from here?"

Carlotta had to admit she wasn't entirely sure herself. Her plan had been almost perfect. Frame Flambé, check. Poison Angel, check. Confound the cops with the false trails and the Polo notes, check. Steal the greatest recipes from the greatest chefs, check again. Then relocate to Dubai and start a new restaurant with the greatest menu that the world had ever tasted. It would be a restaurant that even the wretched critic Jean-Claude Chili would have to recommend. That was supposed to be checkmate.

The problem was the useless pawn right here in her arms. Why hadn't Isabella cooperated by dying back at the apartment?

Think, think, Carlotta said to herself. Was there a clear way out of this?

She could shoot Isabella and Neil on the spot. That would certainly cheer her up, but it would also get the cops on her tail . . . and she'd had enough of jail for one lifetime. What else? What else?

Just then Flambé offered her an escape hatch. He raised his hands in a sign of surrender. "Take me," he said. "I'm the one who made you do this. Take me with you."

"Why not just kill you both right now?" Carlotta said.

"Because then you'll never know the source of my potatoes."

Carlotta flinched. Pommes de Terre à la Flambé? She imagined Jean-Claude Chili sitting in her restaurant, wiping the last delicious morsel from his lips, pulling a hammer drill from inside his charcoal-gray suit and personally bolting a three—no, an unprecedented *four*-star Michelin plaque on the front door.

"I just need to write down the directions," Neil said. "It's a secret location up in the Pemberton Valley."

Carlotta was suspicious, but as long as she kept the gun on Isabella, she was certain Neil wouldn't try anything stupid.

"I need a pen and some paper," he said.

Carlotta's mind raced. She was improvising, like all great chefs do. This time, she wouldn't let Flambé ruin anything. In fact, he was unwittingly going to help her get away scot-free.

"Don't move, either of you, or I'll shoot," she said as she quickly released Isabella and reached into her pocket. She grabbed a pen and a scrap of paper and threw them to Neil. "Write out the recipe for the potatoes as well," Carlotta said as she grabbed Isabella again.

Neil sat down on the ground next to Isabella and started writing in the faint light.

This was perfect, Carlotta thought. She could get the spuds *and* the recipe. Then . . . then she would shoot the girl. Yes, it was making sense! Flambé would be so shocked, she could easily grab him, dump some poison in his mouth . . . then wrap the gun in his lifeless hand. Yes! She could even use a scrap of the paper he was writing on for the suicide note.

"While you're at it," Carlotta said, impressed with her own cleverness. "Write the lines, 'I am so, so sorry' and sign it. I want to have it framed as a memento for my new kitchen."

Isabella stayed absolutely still, looking sideways at the woman who had a gun pointed at her head. Neil was giving in too easily. Why didn't he do something? Why was he doing everything this madwoman asked? Even Isabella knew they weren't going to escape by cooperating.

"Neil, it's some kind of trick," she said.

"Shut up!" Carlotta said, pressing the gun barrel so tightly against Isabella's head that it left an impression in her skin. "Now do as I say, Flambé, or I pull the trigger."

Carlotta watched as Neil carefully drew a map. The line went up the valley, followed a path alongside the Lilloet River, and ended at a farm that was tucked into the woods. Neil marked it with a star. Then he carefully wrote 'I am so, so sorry' and signed his name.

Neil stood up to hand the note to Carlotta. He reached out his hand and stopped. He started shaking, his whole body beginning to tremble. His nose crinkled and his forehead creased. Then, all at once, Neil Flambé started to sob and sob. His chest heaved with great sighs, and he buried his face in his palms.

Carlotta couldn't believe it. The kid was blubbering like a baby! This cocky kid who had ruined her life without a blink of remorse was just a sniveling coward? For a long second she stood and stared, hardly believing what she was seeing. It was like icing on the cake watching Flambé fall apart. But enough was enough. It was time to end this.

Neil buried his head in Isabella's shawl and blew his nose.

Carlotta shoved them both away from her. She quickly reached for the packet of cumin before she remembered that it wasn't there. Then she also remembered she didn't have any tea either. Stupid! Now what?

Neil had had the same thought three minutes earlier. But unlike Carlotta, he'd already made a plan, thanks to his nose. As he'd followed Isabella and Carlotta into the park, he'd noticed that mixed in with the smell of Isabella's lavender extract had been the unmistakable smell of the Marco Polo chai mixture. As soon as he'd caught up with them, he knew where it was coming from—and it wasn't Carlotta. His recent "breakdown" had confirmed Isabella's shawl was still wet. Now it was time to act.

A foot away from Neil, Carlotta cursed. She was out of options now. She'd have to shoot them both and deal with the consequences later.

Just as she was about to pull the trigger, Neil grabbed Isabella's shawl and jumped. The movement didn't stop Carlotta from firing, but it threw off her aim. The bullet hit Neil on the right shoulder. He screamed out in pain, but his momentum carried him toward her.

Together, they smashed into the asphalt—Neil on top and Carlotta underneath. The blow knocked the gun out of her hand, and it skidded away. Neil acted quickly. He held Isabella's shawl over Carlotta's face and wrung the fabric. There was just enough of the deadly liquid soaked into the fabric to do the trick. A stream of amber liquid drizzled out and trickled into Carlotta's mouth. She gagged and swallowed. Before she realized what was happening, the deadly mixture of cumin and chai started to work. Neil could make out the smell of the poison, growing fainter as it was absorbed.

Immediately, Carlotta's breath became shorter. She reached her fingers out for her gun, but it was nowhere near. Neil stood up. He stared at Carlotta in disgust. She had murdered so many of his friends. . . .

Friends? Yes, friends, he thought at last. He hadn't thought of them all that way before now, he realized, but that's what they were: his friends.

Carlotta gagged.

Neil met her panicked gaze. Suddenly, his anger was gone. He was looking at a dying woman. As Carlotta desperately gasped for breath, Neil realized he couldn't be like her. He wasn't a murderer.

Isabella came up behind him then, and they both stared at Carlotta. Her face was quickly turning blue. She reached for her throat.

"Have you killed her?" Isabella asked.

Neil didn't answer. He closed his eyes and prayed that the poison wouldn't kill Carlotta, that she would just be knocked out, like Sumia Saffron. Carlotta hadn't shown the same compassion to Lionel Perch, Paul LeBoeuf, or Angel, but Neil realized that that

didn't matter. There had been enough death. He wouldn't cause anymore.

He turned to Isabella. "Run back and get Nakamura. Make sure he gets an ambulance here ASAP."

"Yes, of course, Neil," she said. She ran off in the direction of Angel's apartment.

Neil watched Isabella go, then turned back toward Carlotta. He kneeled down and lifted her head onto his lap. He supported her shoulders and cradled her head in his arms craning her chin backward. It opened her throat just enough for her to gasp in air. Not a lot, but enough, perhaps, to keep her alive until the ambulance arrived. Carlotta's eyes rolled back in her head. She was unconscious, but not dead. At least not yet.

Neil looked at his right shoulder. It hurt like heck and was bleeding a lot. He felt faint, gripped by a sudden desire to sleep, but he had to keep Carlotta's head up or he knew she would die.

Then the park started to spin. Just before everything turned to red and then black, one final question began to bang against Neil's skull.

Was Angel dying too?

Sean Nakamura was standing by the window in Angel's living room when he heard a gunshot coming from the small park across the alleyway. He peered into the darkness, but couldn't make out anything at all.

One of his officers was pumping up and down on Angel's chest. He'd stopped breathing a moment after they'd broken through the door. They'd cleaned his mouth out with water and had run a tube down his throat. There was an ambulance on the way, and Naka-mura hoped it would come fast.

Nakamura wanted to make sure there weren't any more deaths tonight, inside the apartment or in the park.

"Stay here until the ambulance arrives," he called back as he leaped out the window and ran down the fire escape.

A second shot rang out as he made his way into the park. He pulled out his own gun and advanced slowly. Running into a gunfight only got you killed. He slipped from lamppost to lamppost and even snuck behind the playground slide as he got nearer to the commotion.

Suddenly, he made out the figure of a woman run-ning toward him, fast.

Nakamura slid behind an old oak tree and waited.

As soon as she ran past the tree he jumped out.

"Freeze!"

The woman stopped cold. Her body was tense. Nakamura could tell she wanted to bolt.

"Turn around," Nakamura said.

The woman turned around slowly, and the streetlamp illuminated her panicked face. It was the girl they'd seen with Flambé in the Indian place, just before they'd arrested him. Isabella something or other. A famous perfume maker. Was she the culprit? Berger had said he had no idea who sent him the letters.

"Where's Neil Flambé?" he asked, inching closer, not lowering his gun.

"Please," Isabella said, "he's back there." She ges-tured with her eyes toward the back of the park. "He's hurt. He needs help. Please call an ambulance."

"There's already one on the way for the guy you left behind in the apartment," he said.

"Angel?" she gasped. "Is he . . . is he still alive?"

"I don't know," Nakamura said. "Would you prefer him dead?"

It suddenly occurred to Isabella that this policeman was talking to her like a suspect. When he had ordered her to freeze, she had been scared. Now she got angry.

"You listen to me," she seethed. "Neil is back there"—she pointed into the gloom—"by the wading pool with some maniac. She's been poisoning all the chefs and now she's dying herself. If it was up to me, I'd let her!" Isabella wiped a trickle of blood from her forehead.

"And if there's an ambulance coming for Angel, you'd better get another one for her. I don't want them helping anybody before Angel, least of all the woman who poisoned him and shot Neil.

"Neil needs an ambulance too," she added. All at once, Isabella felt drained and angry and worried. Her head ached and the dizzy feeling had returned. "Neil's been shot in the shoulder. He needs help, NOW!"

Nakamura clicked his walkie-talkie. "Stromboli, get another ambulance over here right away. Send it straight to the park."

"Now"—Nakamura turned back to face Isabella—"where's Neil?"

"Follow me," she said. And they ran back into the shadows.

They could hear the wail of an ambulance in the distance as they reached the middle of the park. Neil and Carlotta lay next to each other on the asphalt—a puddle of blood spreading beneath them.

CHAPTER THIRTY-FOUR

JUST DESSERT

Gunter Lund sat down in his chair and let out a deep sigh.

It was a hot day, even for summer. He took out a handkerchief and wiped the sweat from his brow. He could see Renée hauling in the last catch of the day and carefully placing the beautiful salmon, hake, and flounder onto beds of crushed ice. Soon the chefs would be calling in their orders.

As if on cue, the phone rang. Lund picked it up. He was shocked at the voice he heard on the other end. It was a voice Gunter Lund hadn't heard in weeks. Instinctively he held the receiver away from his head, but the voice was surprisingly quiet. Gunter had to bring the receiver back to his ear.

"Gunter, I'd like the two best salmon you have," said the voice of Neil Flambé, "as soon as you can get them here. And some really fresh perch, please."

Lund actually had to strain to hear the order. "*Two* salmon?" he repeated reluctantly. The last time he'd asked Neil Flambé to repeat an order, he'd practically lost an eardrum.

"Yes, Gunter. Two. Can you count that high?"

Well, it wasn't an imposter, Gunter thought.

"Look Gunter, I'll pay top dollar. I'm having a special reopening party tonight for a special friend."

"Friend? *Freund?*" Gunter thought. Neil Flambé has friends?

"And Gunter," said this strangely quiet Neil, "I just want to say that you always have the best fish in town." Gunter could hear Neil pause for a second and take a deep breath. "Gunter . . . I also want to say thanks," and he hung up.

Gunter Lund stared incredulously at the phone. He was finally shaken out of his stupor by the annoying beep-beep-beep of the off-the-hook line. "Renée," he called out to his partner, "give me some perch and two of your . . ." Lund paused. "*Three* of your best salmon. We have a special order tonight."

Neil Flambé allowed himself a small smile as he flipped his cell phone shut. The fish would be here soon. It was time to start prepping the potatoes. "Larry," Neil said, "I'm going to show you how to prep these spuds properly. I need a little expert help."

"My, my! I am honored." Larry smiled, marching across the kitchen. "As long as I don't have to smell any salmon."

"No problem," Neil said. He handed Larry a brand-new chef knife. "Now get to work."

Larry stared at the knife, refusing to reach out and

take it from Neil's hand. "Isn't this that expensive French one you're always using?"

Neil smiled and nodded. "Look at the blade." He held it out to Larry.

It was an exact replica of Neil's special knife, but it had the name "Larry Flambé" engraved on the shiny metal.

For once, Larry had nothing to say. He just hugged Neil, his eyes watering.

"Ouch, careful there, cousin," Neil said. "My right shoulder is still a bit tender." The doctor said the muscle damage from the gunshot wound might never fully heal. Neil was getting pretty adept at chopping and prepping with his left hand these days, but he was not up to his own exacting standards—not yet.

"Stupid onions," Larry said, sniffing. Larry had mostly recovered from the black eye Jones had given him when he'd caught him on the phone with Neil. Larry hadn't been able to shake Jones that night or to convince him that he and Neil had not kidnapped Isabella. Nakamura had finally tracked them down and explained everything. Larry had said there were no hard feelings and had even give Jones a lift to the hospital.

Since then, they'd become friends—of a sort. Jones had even started giving Larry boxing lessons. Of course, Larry also let it slip to Neil that Jones had a good-looking sister who helped him teach.

"Neil," Amber called, poking her head in the kitchen. "Here's the menu Zoë and I decorated."

"Cool," Neil said. "Let's have a look."

After his ordeal, Neil had vowed to find out more about the people in his life. He'd discovered that the twins were graduate students at art school. They were also really gifted. He'd even let them show their artwork in the restaurant.

"But I get ten percent of any sales," he'd said. He wasn't running a charity, after all, but a world-class restaurant.

Amber showed him the menu. She'd done the handwriting in a rich blue ink. Neil took it in his hands.

A special dinner in honor of my friends
Some living and some gone

Appetizer
Singapore spring rolls à l'Almond
First Course
Whitefish Lionel
Second Course
LeBoeuf's pâté crêpes
Soup
Squash and thyme bisque d'Ungava
Meat
Sri Lankan coconut lamb de Cruyff
Sides
Ginger's flatbread
Pommes de terre à la Flambé
Dessert
Turkish figs—specially made and delivered today
by Sumia Saffron
Chai (sans cumin)
To Cleanse the Palate After Dinner
Fruits
Aged goat cheeses d'Angel

"It looks great," he said. Zoë had even decorated the border with watercolors of all the amazing dishes. "Go ahead and show it to the guests."

Amber smiled and held out her hand to take it back. "On second thought," Neil said, still holding the menu, "let me do it. Tonight's a private party, but tomorrow we reopen and it will be busy. You two, take a break."

"Cool!" the twins said.

Larry was doing fine in the kitchen—not great, but fine. Neil decided he could spare some time to chat with his friends until it was time to get back and help.

He swung the kitchen doors open and stood face to chest with a wall wearing a silk suit. Neil flinched by habit, then coughed politely and said, "Jones, I was wondering if Ms. Tortellini was up to entertaining a lowly chef at her table tonight."

Jones gave a lighthearted smile as he turned aside. "Certainly, Mr. Lowly Chef."

As Jones's impressive bulk cleared the horizon, Neil spied Isabella sitting underneath the Emily Carr painting. Her eyes met his, and she smiled. Jones moved a little more, and Neil saw Sean Nakamura busily chatting about how Carlotta was expected to get at least fifty years without parole. "The notebooks are going to a special secret vault. We don't want anyone making that killer tea again."

Jones finally moved enough for Neil to make out his guest of honor, sitting at the receiving end of Nakamura's story. He caught Neil's eye as well and smiled as big a smile as Neil Flambé had ever seen.

"Your mom and dad called," Angel said in a hoarse voice. "They had to work late, but they'll be here before the salmon is all gone." He laughed. "And your dad was wondering if you could make his favorite side dish."

"Macaroni and cheese?" Neil chuckled again. "No problem. But it's off the menu after tonight."

He walked over and gave Angel the biggest one-armed hug that he could.

Then Neil Flambé stood up and smiled. "Now, everyone. Let's eat!"

ACKNOWLEDGMENTS

It's said that too many cooks ruin the dish. In this case that's simply not true and I have many people to thank.

Jason Proctor, Joan Webber, and Cathy Simon were there at Neil's birth (over a wonderful meal of Belgian fries and Belgian beer). They also gave him his first home on CBC Radio One, as a ten-part series on the dearly departed *Sounds Like Canada with Shelagh Rogers*. Heather Brown and Rosemary Allenbach helped nurture him along that path and Anna Cummer gave voice to Neil and the entire gang—amazing!

My always-welcoming cousin Shauna; coconspirator Ross; and their own little sous-chefs, Rowan and Neil, deserve special thanks. The first draft and the first drawing of Neil happened right in their kitchen, my home away from home. Rowan, the red hair was a great idea. Neil, thanks for the name.

To Buddy and Marge, for the incredibly kind, and fortuitous, gift of *The Travels of Marco Polo* two summers ago.

And of course, I must honor and thank the people who helped Neil make the transition from radio drama to printed page—Charis Wahl, Linda Pruessen, Alison Carr, and thanks to John Wilson who helped put us all together.

To my brother Doug, and his wife, Anna, and daughter, Darcy, who know how to entertain, cook, and write a contract! And to my brother Tim, who knows how to cook a mean corned beef and cabbage.

And to my family (and toughest editors), Laura, Erin, and Emily. What should we have for dinner tonight?

Still not full?

Read Neil Flambé's next adventure

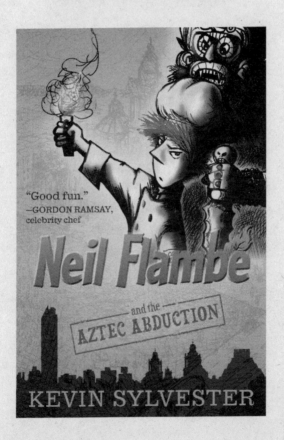

"Good fun."
—GORDON RAMSAY,
celebrity chef

Neil Flambé

and the
AZTEC ABDUCTION

KEVIN SYLVESTER

HIGH ALTITUDE AND HAUTE CUISINE

Neil Flambé looked down at his spotless, gleaming workstation. It was perfect. Of course it was—he'd prepped it himself.

Neil's cooking knives spread out from the right side of his giant maple chopping block in an obsessively neat row. There were ten knives in all, each with a specific task: paring, fish deboning, delicate slicing, chopping through huge joints of meat. All had been handcrafted and weighted for his hands, and his hands alone.

In just a few moments he was going to be reaching for them, unconsciously and quickly—and he did not

want to be "feeling around" for the right razor-sharp blade. That's how former three-star chef Reiner Saumagen had earned the nickname "Stubby." Stubby was currently working as a busboy at a burger-and-chicken-wing joint in Buffalo. Neil shuddered. He would be more careful.

With the knives securely in place, Neil had time for one last check of the rest of his station. He looked to his left. The stove and oven, all gleaming stainless steel and seething blue flame, were sparkling clean, within an arm's reach and preheated to 350 degrees.

He looked back at the countertop. His seasonings— salt, pepper, and containers filled with fresh herbs and savory of every size and color—sat at attention along the top edge of the cutting board. He felt like a magician with the ingredients for a magic potion. In a way he was. At fourteen (almost fifteen), Neil was one of the greatest chefs in the world. His food was often described as magical—and not just by Neil.

Neil allowed himself a self-satisfied smile. Soon he would be well on his way to winning the biggest cooking competition of his life. This wasn't some seedy one-off contest like the underground duels he had won in the past. This was the *Azteca Cocina*, a culinary cook-off featuring North America's top chefs.

He had absolutely no idea what he was going to be asked to cook.

He would only have one hour to cook it.

He was thrilled.

The *Azteca Cocina* was being held in the thin air and amidst the gorgeous architecture of Mexico City. A chef-to-chef battle would take place every other day for nearly two weeks, with every moment shown on TV. The winners of each battle would advance until only two remained, ready to face each other in a final thrilling cook-off on the Zócalo—the stone plaza that sat at the historic center of the city. Rumor had it that the square would be jam-packed with more than one hundred thousand hungry, food-crazed fans. The winner would be the chef supremo of North American cooking, and would also claim the $250,000 top prize.

But first things first. Today was Round One and Neil's opponent was Pablo Pimento. Neil smirked as he looked over and spied Pablo nervously wiping beads of sweat off his forehead. "Even Stubby Saumagen could beat this hack," Neil thought, "with his one good hand tied behind his back."

Neil didn't waste any more time sizing up the so-called competition. Instead, he took a few seconds to examine the scene of the battle. He and Pablo were facing off in the atrium of the wonderfully ornate national opera house, the Palacio des Bellas Artes. Two kitchens had been set up in a semicircle on a stage in the middle of the marble atrium. Neil's kitchen was on one arc and Pablo's on the other. Bleachers filled the remaining space and the crowd was heady with anticipation. Neil smiled as he saw spectators taking their seats, pointing at him and whispering hushed comments.

He was used to being on display, used to attention, but he knew he was still just a curiosity. Winning this competition was going to change that. He would be taken seriously not just as a boy chef, but as a *great* chef. And that would bring more customers—higher-paying customers—to Chez Flambé.

Even now, back in Vancouver, Chez Flambé was undergoing a transformation. Two weeks was a long time to close a restaurant, so Neil had decided to kill two birds with one stone (his personal preference? Free-range quail with a good pizza-oven brick). Chez Flambé was closed for renovations, expensive renovations. Amber and Zoë Soba, the twins who waitressed at the restaurant, were busy decorating and painting the dining room, and a brand-new fridge was scheduled for delivery any minute.

"Don't count your chickens before they're hatched," his mother had told him when he'd revealed his renovation plans and asked her to cosign for a temporary loan.

"I always count my chickens before they're hatched," Neil had told her. "They're called eggs. In fact, there are three unhatched chickens in each and every one of my world-famous omelettes."

Neil knew he'd be able to pay back the loan when (not if) he won the *Cocina*. "If" was not a word Neil used, or even thought, when it came to his cooking (unless "if" was included in sentences such as "Larry, if you don't dice those onions into smaller bits I'm going to dice you into smaller bits.").

Larry was Neil's older cousin and assistant—his sous-chef. Larry could cook pretty well, and he could follow orders—Neil loved to give orders—but Larry was also a bit of a flake.

Neil glanced over at his cousin, standing a few feet away at the far end of the steel counter. Larry met his gaze and smiled, the grin rustling the whiskers on his face. It was hard to tell, because Larry's perpetually disheveled hair was covering his eyes, but Neil thought he also gave him a wink.

"Larry, if you don't tuck that hair under your hat I'm going to personally give you a buzz cut"—Neil paused for effect—"with a rusty lemon zester!" Hair was not an ingredient Neil planned on including in any dish coming from his kitchen . . . especially not Larry's hair.

Larry didn't stop smiling for a second. He'd been working with Neil for a couple of years now and was used to the bluster. He carefully pulled a hair net out of his pocket, tucked his hair into it, and then slopped the whole mess up into his black sous-chef cap.

"Ready, spiffy and able to aid you, señor chef," he said with a salute. Neil looked Larry up and down. He worked hard to make Larry at least appear at home in the kitchen. Now that his hair was tucked up and away, he looked clean and ready. Except, Neil thought with a double take, for one thing.

"What is that?" Neil said irritably, pointing at Larry's stomach.

Larry looked down at the front of his chef's jacket. "What? I don't see any more stains."

"Look lower," Neil said. "What's that red thing tied around your waist?"

"You're right," Larry smiled. "It's a sash, not a belt! I have it on wrong. Hey, thanks for pointing that out, Neil."

As Neil stared incredulously, Larry untied the red fabric and lifted it up and over his head. One side came to rest on his left shoulder and the rest draped down across his torso. Now Neil could see that the sash had the words "Viva Zapata" stitched down the front, with a picture of the legendary Mexican revolutionary printed alongside.

"Viva Zapata?" Neil said.

"I looked for one that said 'Viva Frittata,' but they didn't have any."

"Ha ha," Neil said dryly. Larry had bought the sash at a tacky tourist stall the day before. Neil assumed it was a present for some girl back in Vancouver. Apparently, he had been wrong. "Why are you wearing that in my kitchen?"

"It's for good luck," Larry said, running his fingers down the soft red material. "Zapata was a big part of the revolution here—and don't you and I want to revolutionize the restaurant industry? Plus, I like his big mustache. I'm considering growing one just like it."

"Didn't Zapata die in an ambush?" Neil wasn't sure how he knew this, but Larry quickly reminded him.

"Hey! You've been paying attention to my guided tour!" Larry said happily.

"Sadly, yes. It's hard to avoid," Neil said, rubbing his temples. Larry had what Neil politely called an obsessive personality. He would throw himself into a subject with every fiber of his being—surfing the Net, reading every book he could—and then do his best to keep Neil in the loop, whether he wanted to be in that loop or not. Their trip to Mexico City had filled Larry with an incredible curiosity for all things Mexican, and he had given Neil a nonstop history lesson as they walked through the streets and markets.

They'd been in the city for two days. To Neil, it felt like a month.

"And besides, we're on high-def TV, and I look so good in a sash." Larry smiled.

"Do you have to wear it?" Neil asked, sensing he was not going to win this latest argument.

"Viva Zapata! Viva Team Flambé!" was Larry's response.

Neil was about to continue the argument when he heard the squeaking of wheels. The *Cocina* crew, dressed in white, was wheeling in huge carved wooden boxes. Inside were the ingredients for the opening

match, including the all-important secret ingredient upon which the entire meal would be based. Neil would have to live with the sash, for today.

"We'll discuss this later," Neil hissed.

"Aye, aye, *commandante!*" Larry saluted again.

There was one last thing Neil needed to do before he gave his full attention to his cooking. He looked at the crowd, scanning for one particular person. Their eyes locked. He smiled. She smiled. She was Isabella Tortellini, Neil's friend (quite possibly his maybe, sort of, he wasn't one hundred percent sure, girlfriend) and a world-famous perfume maker. Neil could faintly make out the smell of her latest lavender-scented concoction. She had taken a break from her own business—researching scents for a new line of Aztec-inspired perfumes—to show Neil some support. He appreciated the gesture, especially since it wasn't easy for her to be here. Her father had died in a head-to-head cooking duel with Neil's mentor Angel Jícama, but that had been an underground battle, not an organized and legal spectacle like the *Azteca Cocina.*

"*Buona fortuna,*" she yelled to Neil. Then, with a flash, the TV lights switched on, the house lights went off, and the kitchen set was bathed in bright light, leaving everything else in darkness. Neil was temporarily blinded.

A tall man in a shiny blue tuxedo stepped into a spotlight at the front of the makeshift kitchens and turned on his microphone. He was Rodrigo Hernandez, owner of the Cortez Corn Oil Company, the tournament's sponsor.

"Señors and señoras," Rodrigo spoke. "I want to thank you all for coming to this first battle of *Azteca Cocina.*"

Applause filled the room, but Neil paid no attention. He was concentrating on something else—the fresh bouquet of uncooked food.

"But what kind of battle WILL IT BE?" Rodrigo asked with a theatrical flourish. He gestured to the carved boxes, which were suddenly bathed in light.

Neil sniffed and waited for his secret weapon to kick in. Neil Flambé was blessed with a love for cooking, but also with an incredibly keen sense of smell. He used it to discern perfect blends of spices and ingredients, the exact mixture to make any dish perfect. Unbeknownst to any but his closest friends and family, he sometimes used his nose to help the Vancouver Police Force solve crimes. Now he was going to use it to get a head start on planning his menu. That head start, he thought, would be the difference between winning and winning easily. Neil caught a glimpse of Pablo in the lights of the cameras. He was still sweating.

"In just a moment, we will present these two great chefs with their secret ingredient! Will it be chicken thighs? Pinto beans? Rice?" Rodrigo was warming into his role, teasing the crowd and building suspense.

Neil smiled. He had caught the scent and the secret

ingredient wasn't chicken or pinto beans. Imperceptibly, he pushed his largest knife closer to the cutting board. The secret ingredient was lamb shanks.

"Psst, Larry," Neil whispered, covering his mouth with the back of his hand. He signaled for Larry to lean in closer. "We're going to make Oaxacan Mole sauce and lamb shanks."

"Whack-a-mole sauce?" Larry said. "On pancakes? I dunno. Sounds gross to me."

Neil tried to articulate the menu again, slowly, while still whispering, "I said 'whoa-hock-an mole-eh' sauce."

"Mohican bowling socks?"

"Never mind," Neil sighed, rubbing his temples so hard that he left an indentation. He gave up trying to whisper and turned to face Larry. "Look, as soon as we get the signal, just heat some oil and grate some chocolate as quickly as you can."

"You got it, Neil," Larry said. "You can count on me." He walked back to his place at the counter, still wondering what bowling Mohicans had to do with grated chocolate and cooking oil.

"The contestants do not know what ingredients are in these boxes." Rodrigo was now speaking dramatically in a low voice. The audience leaned in to catch his words. He practically scared them out of their seats when he yelled, "But now it is time to reveal all!"

The waiters pulled ornate metal keys out of their coat pockets and inserted them into the golden locks that held the lids on tight.

Neil was already running through the steps of the meal preparation in his head. The chocolate-and-chili-based mole sauce was pretty simple. But lamb shanks were packed with tough chewy meat, with a huge bone in the middle. Ideally, a chef would be able to stew the shank for more than three hours to get the meat really tender. Neil would have to speed up that process considerably. He pondered for a second before deciding on his plan. He would quick-fry the shanks to sear the flavor inside. Next, he would cut off the meat to make big stewing chunks. Then he'd throw it in the oven and leave it there until right before the final bell.

The bubbling mole sauce would do the job of slow-roasting the meat, and the resulting dish would be sublime. Poor Pablo, Neil thought. He was probably going to make a thin soup full of lamb meat chunks with the consistency and flavor of golf balls.

The men in white stepped aside and lifted the lids of their boxes.

"The secret ingredient is"—Rodrigo paused for full effect—"LAMB SHANKS." The crowd oohed and ahhed. Then the starting gun fired with a loud *boom*.

Neil rushed to grab his shank. He could see Larry starting the oil. Pablo was shaking from head to toe, and sweating so much he looked like he was marinating himself.

This was going to be a cinch.

Neil reached his box and looked inside. There, on top of the pink fatty joint of meat, was something Neil's super sense of smell hadn't detected: a handwritten note. A series of weird symbols had been drawn around the edges and in the middle, in a deep red, blood-like ink, were the words . . .

Neil Flambé,

You have ignored our first warning.

We are afraid that you are now going to lose this competition . . . on purpose, in the final. You may scoff, but consider this: We have your perfumed friend the flower bringer. If you win this competition, she will die. If you make losing too obvious, she will die. If you lose before the final, she will die. You must lose in the final. You will follow these instructions to the letter if you want to see her alive.

Do not attempt to contact the police or we will know and she will die.

We are watching.

XT

Neil glanced quickly over the open lid of the box. Isabella had been sitting in the third row from the back, right on the aisle. He squinted through the glare of the bright lights.

Her seat was empty.

Isabella was gone.

TWO WEEKS
EARLIER

It's not a duel!" Neil Flambé yelled, rattling the pots and pans that hung over his head. People who heard Neil yell were often impressed by how well the fourteen-year-old chef could imitate a bullhorn.

Angel Jícama, however, was unfazed. He just crossed his arms tighter and narrowed his eyes.

"Neil's right, Angel," Larry said. "It's actually more like six duels, spread out over two weeks."

Neil glared at his cousin. "You're not helping!" he fumed. He turned back to Angel. "It's just a TV show!"

Neil, Larry and Angel were in the kitchen of Chez Flambé. Larry and Angel were sitting on stools, watching Neil pace up and down between the stainless-steel counters. Neil was hoping to convince Angel to come to Mexico City as part of his team for the *Azteca Cocina*.

"I'm just saying that Angel may have a point," Larry said. "You know what they say 'If it quacks like a duck, it's quite often a duck.'"

"If it quacks like

a duck and I get my hands on it," Neil blared, "then it's duck à l'orange!"

Larry crossed his legs and lifted his hands into some kind of yoga position. "If the words are not correct, then what is said is not what is meant; if what is said is not what is meant, then what must be done will not be done."

Neil stood in open-mouthed silence for a moment. "What the heck does that mean?" he eventually asked.

"It's Confucius saying if it quacks like a duck it's a duck, no matter what you say it is," Larry said with a sombre slow nod, uncrossing his legs.

"It's confus-*ing*," Neil shouted. Then it hit him. "Wait. Let me guess. You're dating a Confucius scholar?"

"She has a name, you know. It's Rosetta," Larry said. As far as Neil could tell, Larry always seemed to have a different girlfriend, with a different area of expertise, and he went to great lengths to impress them. Neil knew that it was one of the main reasons Larry's head contained so many obscure bits of information.

Neil gave up trying to figure out what this particular bit had to do with whether the *Cocina* was a duel or not. "I think you need a coffee," he said. "You're brain is starting to hiccup through your vocal chords."

"I always need a coffee," Larry smiled. "Maybe if you drank some, you'd be able to follow my brilliant train of thought."

"That train derailed a few stations back."

"Ouch." Larry smiled. "I've said it before and I'll say it again: Please leave the jokes to me. I'm a professional."

"A professional idiot!" Neil yelled even louder.

"Yelling! Now that's something you're good at."

Neil grabbed for a paring knife and waved it menacingly at Larry. "Remember what else I'm good at? Preparing and cooking things that quack like ducks."

"Quack," Larry said, and then he started to shake with laughter. "Are you seriously threatening me with a whisk?"

Neil looked at his hand. He was sure he'd grabbed the paring knife, but he was indeed holding a wire whisk. He'd have to be more careful, more in control. Why did Larry drive him nuts so easily? He threw the whisk across the room in disgust, and it crashed through the back window. The cats that hung out below meowed their disapproval. Usually Neil threw out food he was unhappy with, not kitchen utensils. The cats hovered in anticipation whenever they heard him raise his voice. They were quite fat.

"Great," Neil said. "There's another repair I can't afford."

Chez Flambé was not in the best part of town. It had been a rundown fish-'n'-chips shop, slated for demolition when Larry won it in a poker game. It had cost thousands to clean up the layers of grease and calcified fish batter, and there were still plenty of other repairs needed.

Neil shook his head in disbelief, then rubbed his temples and looked at Angel.

"It's fine if you don't want to come, but you're not going to talk me out of going," Neil said.

"Talk?" Larry said, waving his hand in front of Angel's scowling face. "I don't think Angel has said a word in ages, although I think I heard him growl a few minutes ago."

Angel said nothing.

"Maybe that was his stomach growling," Larry smiled. "Angel, would you like a snack?"

Angel said nothing, even louder.

Larry chuckled. "I'll take that as a no."

Neil stopped in the middle of the floor, his back turned to Larry and Angel. "Look, Angel, I've already hired contractors to come renovate the kitchen and the dining room. Amber and Zoë have bought fabric and paint and new chairs. If I close the restaurant for two weeks without making any money, I'll lose everything. Anyway, this isn't some grungy little cook-off. This is the big time, a made-for-TV event with real sponsors. I won't be in any danger and I won't be putting anybody else in danger."  Neil avoided Angel's face, but he could easily imagine the look of disapproval that was etched there.

Neil and Angel had had their first real fight over a duel. A little more than a year ago,

Neil had accepted an invitation from a mafia boss in Venice to a chef-versus-chef battle. Neil had asked Angel to be his sous-chef on that adventure, but his mentor had said no. Neil stormed off and took Larry instead. Neil won, but after having a gun waved in his face, he'd been forced to accept only half of the promised cash.

Angel had first-hand experience with the dangers of the seedy side of international cuisine. Years before, he'd taken part in a deadly duel that had left another chef dead—chef Tortellini, Isabella's father. Angel had immediately quit the high life of haute cuisine, losing himself in back alleys and country markets around the world. He was in search of the real meaning of food, not culinary glory, not anymore.

"I was hoping you might come along this time," Neil added in an almost whisper. "You know Mexican cuisine almost as well as I do."

"Almost?" Larry choked. Angel's family, on his father's side, was from Southern Mexico—at least according to legend—so Neil was being cockier than usual, if that were even possible.

Angel uncrossed his arms and let out a deep sigh. "Neil," he said softly. "This isn't about my past and it isn't about putting other people in danger. You've already shown your willingness to do that to yourself and to Larry." Neil's shoulders tensed at the rebuke. "This is about how you continue to waste your gifts on these ego-boosting adventures."

"What do you mean?" Neil asked.

"Yeah," Larry added. "Neil's ego doesn't need any

boosting. Trust me." He spread his arms wide. "It's huuuuuuuuuuge."

Angel waved him off. "I mean this, Neil: Is your cooking great because someone else says it is? Or because it is?"

"I already get plenty of praise. I need the money."

"There are other ways to get money," Angel continued.

"Oh, really? From you maybe? You give all yours away!"

This was true. When Angel had returned from his self-proclaimed exile, he hadn't opened a restaurant. He had a different plan. He now cooked just one dish a year. He practiced and practiced until he felt it was perfect, or as near to perfect as he could achieve. Then he invited a handful of wealthy guests to come to his home and dine with him. They paid handsomely, but Angel gave almost all the money away to the city's food banks.

"Have you tried hard work and patience?" Angel said.

"Have you tried keeping food fresh in a refrigerator that's held together by duct tape?"

As if on cue, the compressor on the ancient walk-in fridge spattered and coughed.

Larry walked over and kicked it, and it came back to life. "I did the duct tape," he said jovially. "Kind of adds a homey touch to the place."

"I already work hard," Neil said.

"But you hunger for glory—"

Neil cut him off, speaking quickly. "If I'm hungry, it's for what I deserve. Someday I'll be the most famous chef in the world." He seemed to be talking to himself as much as to Larry and Angel. "I won't just have one dumpy restaurant, but a whole chain of Michelin-starred Chez Flambés. I'll be cooking with the best ingredients and not worrying about how much it costs. I'll have the best of the best." He turned to face Angel. "I want it fast. I don't want to be stuck here the rest of my life watching Larry fix things with his feet."

Angel walked over to Neil and placed his hand on his shoulder. "I didn't say patience was easy. But in the end, it is more rewarding. Believe me. You need to look inside yourself to see what it is you want. Fame and riches are easy goals. Can you search for something deeper?"

"The only deep thing I care about is my deep fryer," Neil said, shaking off Angel's hand.

"No matter how successful and rich you become, you will not be happy," Angel said, walking toward the back door, "unless you have happiness and peace inside you."

"That's crazy," Neil said. "I'm already great, and unhappy. I'll be happy and peaceful enough when I'm great and rich and famous."

The sound of sudden drizzle and wet cats wafted in through the broken window. Angel stopped and put on his raincoat. As he began to unfurl his umbrella he said, "I have lived this life that you want so desperately and have lived it to the end. It leads to misery and death. It took one life, and almost took my soul. I do not want it to take yours."

He walked out the door and disappeared into the late-summer mist.

Neil stomped over and slammed the door shut. The fridge sputtered and coughed again. He was so frustrated he almost wanted to cry. He respected Angel. Angel had always been there for him, even more than his own parents. But what he was asking of Neil, what he was always asking, wasn't fair. He wanted Neil to be content with this dump, with making great food for small crowds, with squirreling away small change when he could be charging top dollar at a ritzy downtown location.

Just because Angel had screwed up his own life didn't mean Neil would. He was Neil Flambé, after all. He wouldn't make the same mistakes as Angel. He'd learn from them, but he wouldn't repeat them. He was great, and he was going to become even greater.

He stood up straight. "Larry, kick that fridge again and grab some scallions and garlic. Dinner service starts in four hours. Let's prep."

"You got it, Neil. Anything else I can do?"

"If you really want to be useful, why don't you start dating a chef who's an expert in Mexican cuisine?"

"Her name is Juanita. I'm meeting her for dinner next week."

MAKING SCENTS

This weather is horrible," Isabella Tortellini said to the gloom. She drew the hood of her cloak tightly around her face. August was often the most beautiful month in Vancouver, but it was her luck to arrive just before one of the rainiest and coolest on record. She had moved here from Northern Italy a few months before, and this was not the weather she'd hoped to find in her new home. Thank goodness she would be in Mexico City soon, enjoying the warm, dry weather and the wonderful fragrances of the surrounding countryside.

She had been invited to visit by the head of the Xochipilli Tallo flower farmer's collective—a fair-trade

organization that hired poor people from the city slums and took them to farms to grow organic flowers. It wasn't a profitable business, yet. But if the flowers and their scents were up to her exacting standards, Isabella was going to pay top dollar to secure them as a supplier.

"Don't count the cents when you make great scents," read the banner on her website. Isabella Tortellini had made a name for herself in the perfume industry by using only natural, fair-trade ingredients. Others might make bigger profits, but Isabella wasn't worried about that.

She had booked her tickets immediately. And Jones, her sort of bodyguard (he was more of a big, scary-looking family friend), had insisted that she book him a flight as well.

They had met this morning to go over the details.

"I called some contacts I have down there," Jones said. "The farm seems to check out."

"Xochipilli—what a strange name," Isabella said.

"Apparently Xochipilli is the name of the Aztec flower god."

"Flower god?" Isabella perked up immediately.

"Oh no," Jones said. "I've seen that look before."

Isabella ignored him and pulled out her phone. She typed in Xochipilli and searched the Net. Her eyes grew wider and wider as she read. "I never knew flowers were so important to the Aztecs." Isabella clicked from site to site. "They traded them as currency. Sometimes they even ripped out food crops to make room for more flowers."

She looked up at Jones with an enormous smile. "A culture that values flowers and perfumes more than gold!

This is fascinating. Perhaps I will develop a whole line of Aztec-inspired fragrances!"

Jones sipped his herbal tea. "I'm sure it will be a success. Most of your crazy ideas work out . . . eventually."

"Yes," she said, "you're right. This is a great plan."

"Um, that's not exactly what I said."

"I will need to spend extra time there." She'd started tapping her phone again, and before Jones realized what she was up to, she'd changed her flights.

"There," Isabella said with a sigh. "Two more weeks in Mexico."

Jones spat out his tea. "WHAT?!" He was not happy. To begin with, he wasn't a big fan of spontaneity, and Isabella consistently was. Then there was a problem with timing.

Isabella raced on. "I'll mostly stay in Mexico City, but now I have time for plenty of side trips to the country and the farms."

"But I'm supposed to be back in Canada before that flight home you just booked."

Isabella patted Jones' hand. "Don't worry so much," she said. "I didn't change your flights, just mine. You go to your little camp and have a good time playing with your friends."

Jones growled. "It's not a little camp, and we are not playing."

Jones had enrolled in an elite nature survival course in the Arctic. He and his guide would be dropped on top of a glacier with nothing but their clothes, a flashlight, a fingernail clipper and a pack of bubble gum. Cell phones were prohibited. He would be completely unreachable for at least a week. Three other pairs of thrill-seekers would be dropped miles away. The first pair to make it to Tuktoyaktuk got a trophy, bragging rights and first place in line to be treated for the inevitable frostbite.

"I'll drop out of the course," he said firmly.

"No, you will not," Isabella said, just as firmly. "You've been on the waiting list for two years."

"I don't like the smell of this."

"My perfume?" Isabella smiled.

Jones didn't. "I don't like the smell of you walking around a foreign country alone. You were only supposed to be there a few days, not two weeks."

"Don't worry so much," Isabella said. "Neil and Larry will be there to help protect me after you leave. Larry can even help me with my research."

Jones had scowled so fiercely Isabella worried he was going to break a tooth. "Those dolts couldn't protect themselves in a tank with a bazooka."

"I'll be fine," Isabella laughed. "I'm from a foreign country, you know. They're not so scary."

Jones did smile at this, sort of. It was more of a very slight tremor along his upper lip. "I guess I treat you as too much of a kid sometimes. I forget you are sixteen."

"Almost seventeen. And I promise I'll stay close to crowds. There are more than 20 million people in Mexico

City, so that should be easy."

"It also makes it easy to get lost," Jones said.

Isabella patted him on the back of the hand one more time and smiled.

What a wonderful coincidence that she would be in Mexico at the same time as Neil, although she still wasn't comfortable with his reasons for visiting. He'd told her "it's not a duel" a few too many times. What was it her mother had said about "people who protest too much"? Still, even she felt there was something special about this trip, something that could put Neil in the top echelon of chefs. She knew first-hand how hard it could be to make it in business when everyone around you saw only a child. Neil was a great chef. She would offer her support, and keep her worries to herself. Besides, if he won, he would never have to do this type of competition again, or so she hoped.

She was almost at Chez Flambé now. There were benefits to having a relationship with Neil Flambé, and a standing reservation at his restaurant was one of them. Of course, Neil didn't cut her any slack on the bill, which actually made her respect him more. The last thing a strong young woman wants is a fawning suitor.

The drizzle turned to rain. "This weather is perfect for *Pommes de Terre à la Flambé* and pan-seared salmon," she thought as the wind helped the damp chill find its way past the warm wool of her shawl.

She heard the crash of shattering glass and stopped. Was someone breaking into the restaurant? She hurried her pace and turned the corner just in time to see a large figure moving under the dim glow of the light over the back door of Chez Flambé. Even though it was early afternoon, it was as dark as night. She slipped into the shadows and held her breath. The alleyway in this part of town was not a place to be caught alone with a stranger.

The figure stopped a few steps away from her and turned to look back at the restaurant. The street light illuminated the profile of a middle-aged, bearded man.

It was Angel. Isabella slowly let out her breath. She still found herself fighting against the years of bitterness she had harbored for this man. But as she grew to know him, she found none of the evil she had expected to find; instead, she had seen only sadness and remorse.

"Angel," she said, stepping out of the shadow and touching him on the shoulder.

He gave a surprised shudder, but quickly recognized the voice of the young woman. He turned to face her with a kindly smile.

"Isabella! What are you doing out in this mess, especially with such a nice shawl?"

"It is a very warm shawl and can stand plenty of punishment—a gift from Jones."

"A man who knows about punishment," Angel chuckled.

"Let me guess what brings you out, with your rather shabby *impermeabile*." She looked askance at Angel's worn and frayed trench coat. It was missing at least three buttons and seemed to be absorbing as much rain as it shed. "You ought to at least keep enough money to dress yourself properly!" She tried in vain to prop up his collar around his neck, but each time it fell sloppily back.

She gave up. "So, Neil is trying to get you to go with him. Correct?"

"Yes."

"And you refused." It wasn't really a question.

"Yes."

"And you will not help him prepare for this competition, even though he stubbornly insists he will go no matter what."

"Yes." Angel couldn't help but smile. Isabella had a way of making an interrogation seems like a pleasant chat. "You know him very well, don't you?"

"Yes," she said, smiling. "And like you, I know that he has an ego the size of a *balenottera azzurra.*"

"A blue whale," Angel translated.

"*Sí.* But he is a great chef, there's no doubt, and inside there is a nice, caring young man."

"I know. And I know that Neil is in danger."

Isabella started. "How do you mean? Has someone threatened him . . . again?"

"I mean he is in danger of ending up like me," Angel said with a frown. "Burning out and taking others down with him."

They let their history pass between them. Isabella spoke first.

"Angel, have you considered that he might need

your help, and not just your advice, to discover those truths himself?"

"I have tried. He does not want to listen. He only cares for what I can teach him about food."

Isabella paused for a second to think. "When I was a *bambina*, my mother would often tell me about the mistakes she had made when she was a businesswoman. She was a designer, you know."

"Yes. She made beautiful clothes. I remember her shows in Milan."

"But she did not have a *testa*, a 'head,' for numbers. She had to sell everything to her partner to stay out of *prigione*, 'prison.'"

"And she wanted you to avoid that life."

Isabella nodded. "But it wasn't until I started making mistakes myself that I learned anything useful. She stopped telling me what to do; instead, she started to help me understand what had happened to me. She would catch me when I fell, like a . . . how do you say . . . *saltimbanco?*"

"Acrobat."

"*Sí.* I fell from the high wire many times. She was always there to catch me, and she always sent me back up to try again." She looked at Angel. "Do you see what I am trying to say?"

Angel thought for a minute before responding. "It's too hard for me to go back to that life, to cook with him in anything resembling a duel or a competition. And, Isabella, it's not just about what happened. If truth be told, there is still a part inside me that I cannot stamp out; that still wants fame and glory. I must not fan that flame—in him or in me."

"You say it would be hard for you. Doesn't that often mean something is worth the effort?"

"Possibly."

"Come to Mexico City," she said.

"Why?"

An idea had suddenly occurred to Isabella. Jones was still threatening to cancel his trip. What if Angel agreed to be her chaperone? That would be perfect for everyone, she thought confidently. And once Isabella Tortellini had a thought, it usually became reality.

"Because Jones wants you to come."

"What? Why?"

"I need a chaperone, someone to keep an eye on me after he leaves. And you could also keep an eye on Neil. There would be no need to cook with him, but you would be there in case he falls from that high wire. Be there to help him go back up again."

Angel thought for a long moment. "I will consider it," he said at last. He gave Isabella a warm smile then turned to go. After a few steps he looked back. "Are you sure you're only sixteen?"

"My mother says I have an old soul," she laughed. "And usually a new shawl."

Angel smiled and walked away. Isabella watched him slowly make his way through the gathering storm, toward his apartment building. It would take him about fifteen minutes to walk there. Plenty of time, Isabella thought, for him to come around to her way of thinking.

She turned back to Chez Flambé, where she could make out Neil and Larry through a newly cracked window. They were busily chopping vegetables in anticipation of the evening rush. She watched Neil for a few minutes as his hand flashed through the air. Then she tapped on the kitchen door and walked inside.

Kevin Sylvester

is an award-winning writer, illustrator, and broadcaster. *Neil Flambé and the Marco Polo Murders* won the 2011 Silver Birch Award for Fiction. Kevin was particularly pleased by this because the kids vote! His other books include *Gold Medal for Weird* (Silver Birch winner in 2009!), *Sports Hall of Weird*, *Splinters*, and *Game Day*. He spends most of his time sitting in his attic studio, drawing and writing and listening to Neil and Larry arguing over, well, everything. He also loves to cook.